Honour the Dead

John Anthony Miller

Table of Contents

Prologue

Corriere della Sera
Milan, Italy Evening Edition
May 3, 1921

BODY FOUND IN LAKE COMO

A body was found by a fisherman just after dawn, lying face down in shallow water. Fully clothed, a single bullet wound in the back, it had been in the water for several hours.

Police found no obvious clues during the initial stages of the investigation. Authorities have discovered no clear motive, although they believe money may have been involved. Many have theorised that since the body was found a few hundred metres from the asylum, the murder may have been the work of a madman. Authorities vow not to rest until the perpetrator of the crime has been brought to justice.

The corpse was identified as …

Chapter 1

Lakeside Sanitarium
Lake Como, Italy
Two months before the murder

Dr Joseph Barnett looked through the French doors of his office and studied the last stubborn remnants of snow clinging to the mountaintops. Flowers had begun to sprout, offering the promise of spring, and weak rays of sunlight bathed the lake that sprawled beyond the grounds of the sanitarium, reflecting off the water so it shimmered like glass. He often admired the breathtaking view, collecting his thoughts, immersed in tranquility, absorbed in the peace that nature provided. And then, for reasons unknown, other than fate, other than the random seconds in our lives that place two people in the same place and time, that serenity was shattered.

Penelope Jones came to the sanitarium shortly after her first suicide attempt. Her husband had found her sprawled on the floor of a Monte Carlo hotel room with her eyes closed and face grey, an empty bottle of barbitone on the bureau beside her bed. Doctors saved her life – initial reports claimed a miracle – and she was released from the hospital a few days later. Authorities cabled the sanitarium shortly thereafter, providing notification of her impending arrival.

She came from a long line of wealthy socialites, her name and face recognised easily by most of the civilised world – as the privileged so often are. From England's little princess, a precious child with a smile that lit the heavens, she had become a desperate, haunted shadow, her eyes showing muted pain hidden in her soul. After the Great War ended, she moved continually – Paris, London and Monte Carlo – as if constant change would keep the demons from finding her.

She avoided publicity, but a world starved for stories after the most hellish conflict in human history proved that celebrities sold newspapers and magazines. They provided readers with an escape, insight into a fairytale existence, a world imagined and longed for, envied but misunderstood. When splashed against the backdrop of the Jazz Age, famous people often became infamous, whether they deserved it or not.

Penelope, or Miss Penelope as she was called even after her marriage, was admired by many because she had everything they wanted: a huge estate staffed with devoted servants; an education only the finest schools could offer; the love of the world's most desirable man. And even though she had every reason to love life, she despised it.

Her ancestors had been at the forefront of British affairs for several centuries, revered by most of the Empire's subjects, but the current generation was cursed by tragedy. Penelope's mother was killed in a train accident when she was a child and her brother died in the closing days of the war. He was a pilot, known for his aggressive attacks, accomplished, with many kills. He would have become an executive of the family's global business empire, had his life not ended before it had begun. He was their future, the best they could offer a healing world, stolen just as he stepped upon the world's stage. Penelope never dealt with his death and it may have spawned the steep decline that led her to the asylum.

Her husband, Alexander Cavendish, was also blessed with a long line of titled ancestors. The world's most eligible bachelor, he was blond with blue eyes, an impish grin, and seemed to have all the qualities women wanted: handsome, intelligent, articulate, charitable. He proposed to Penelope after a year-long courtship and then rushed off to France to fight, their love story plastered on many front pages. He survived the Great War when so many more had not, a captain in the British Expeditionary Force, a celebrated war hero for his bravery in the Battle of the Somme.

The door to Barnett's office opened and his receptionist led Penelope in. She wore a dark green dress, sleek, with a narrow lime sash around her waist, and high heels. She displayed an air of confidence, slender, almost too thin, with a trace of a frown curling her lips. The features of her face were hard and hollow, hinting of a harsher life than status implied. Her black hair was thick and long, wild and a bit tangled, as if several unsuccessful attempts had been made to tame it. Her olive complexion was accented by dark eyes that gazed upon him curiously, showing both amusement and mistrust.

"Hello, Mrs Cavendish, I'm Doctor Barnett."

She sat on the edge of the chair in front of his desk, looking uncomfortable, gazing about the room and not making eye contact. She didn't speak and seemed to absorb the surroundings, as if she wanted to be part of them, but couldn't. After a few awkward moments, she sighed and looked at Barnett. "I suppose you know why I'm here," she said softly.

He knew only what he had read in the newspapers which, whether factual or not, had provided some background information. But he didn't want his initial impressions to be based on a reporter's notebook. "I'm not sure that I do," he admitted. "Why don't you tell me?"

Her eyes left his and she glanced at the horrible scars on his left cheek, then noticed the gnarled left hand, frozen in place like an eagle's talons. "The war?" she asked, her eyes showing sympathy.

For a brief instant, his mind fogged − ... *a mortar shell, the explosion, hot shrapnel burrowing into his face and arm and leg. He could smell the sulphur, feel smoke stinging his eyes as his body fell to the ground, blood staining his uniform and then the soil, turning the mud crimson ...* He willed it away.

"Yes, the war," he said, forcing a weak smile. "But I'm better off than many others." He paused, glanced out the French doors to the lake and mountains beyond, the serenity dampening the hellish screams his mind remembered. He turned towards her and continued. "Let's get acquainted, shall we, and tell me why you came here."

She paused, looking anxious and afraid, and leaned forward. "Someone is trying to kill me," she whispered.

Although surprised, he tried not to show it. "Who would want to kill you?" he asked. His face was a mask of concern.

She shrugged. "I have suspicions. But nothing certain."

"Are you willing to share your conclusions?"

"No, not yet," she said. "But I have to figure it out quickly. Before they try again."

"Did you discuss this with the police?"

"Yes, but they didn't believe me." She looked away nervously, glancing at the door to his office. "Am I safe here?"

"Yes, of course," he said, watching her closely. "The sanitarium is private and has its own security personnel. You can rest assured."

"There were reporters at the entrance when I arrived," she said.

"They'll tire of waiting and they'll leave. As time passes and their stories are read and forgotten, the world will leave you alone."

"What if the killer is a reporter?" she asked.

"I'm sure the authorities are watching them closely."

"I can't even sleep, knowing another attempt will come."

"I understand," he said, edging closer, pretending to believe her. "Anyone would be worried under the circumstances. But why is your life in danger? What is the killer's motive?"

She was quiet, as if wondering whether to trust him. She glanced around the room, apparently ensuring no-one could overhear them, and then spoke quietly, barely above a whisper. "Why does anyone get murdered?" she asked "You know the reasons as well as I do."

He trained his eyes on hers, showing compassion and sincerity. "I'll help you find the answers," he promised. "And we'll make sure the perpetrator is brought to justice."

She studied him for a moment, apparently not convinced. Her eyes left his and she looked around the room again, perhaps searching for hints of the owner's personality. "Why Shakespeare?" she asked, pointing to a bust that sat on an antique cabinet in the corner of the office.

"It was a gift from a patient," he said.

"It's an unusual choice," she muttered, her mind apparently wandering. "I would have expected a famous psychiatrist or Plato or Socrates or someone like that."

"I'm very fond of Shakespeare," he explained. He decided to let the conversation wander, discussing whatever made her feel comfortable. He realised that the most important component of her treatment would be their relationship. She had to trust him.

"Shakespeare was an actor," she said, turning to face him. "He had less than three years of schooling and never left England. He isn't the author of the plays and sonnets."

"Why would someone use his name?" he asked, wondering what her point was.

"Because the true author, Edward de Vere, was involved in legal disputes with the Crown," she replied. "He was the Earl of Oxford, a man known for his intellect. And he travelled extensively to Venice and Verona."

"Locales prevalent in Shakespearean literature," he said. His curiosity was piqued, both by the content of the conversation and how intelligent Penelope was. He had never heard the theory and, even though they had strayed from his original question, any dialogue was good.

"Exactly," she confirmed.

"How do you know all of this?"

She glanced around the room yet again, furtively, as if to ensure they were alone. Then she leaned forward, closer to him. "Because I was there."

He was startled but didn't show it. He composed himself, thinking of all the possible explanations: a belief in reincarnation; a dissociative identity disorder impacted by different generations; delusional thought patterns; schizophrenia. He decided to pretend her comment was normal and that anyone could have made it.

"Then I suppose you would know more than anyone else, having lived in that time," he said. "Did you know Shakespeare personally, or should I say, did you know Mr de Vere personally?"

She studied him closely, her face taut. "You don't believe me," she said. "Nobody does."

"It's certainly something we'll discuss," he assured her. "I'm anxious to know more."

"I have a professional doctorate in English literature," she said. "I did a research paper on who Shakespeare may have been, assuming it wasn't who we think it was. That's when I realised I lived during that period."

He tried to relate to her. "Many cultures believe in reincarnation," he said. "If that's what you're implying."

She didn't answer. "I have a minor degree in history also," she continued. "One from Oxford, the other from Cambridge."

"I'm impressed," he admitted. "Prestigious schools and difficult subjects to master."

"I suppose," she said, yawning. "I'm a bit rusty, though. I've been pursuing other activities." She winked and then laughed.

He smiled, but wasn't sure what the wink or laugh suggested. "Would you like to talk about your education?" he asked.

"No, not really," she said and looked away. After a moment, her eyes again focused on him. "I need to stop the nightmares. The doctors gave me pills to help me sleep, but they only make it worse."

"Tell me about the dreams," he said, leaning back in the chair and giving her space.

She ignored him. "Do you know my father?"

"No, I don't know your father, but I do know of him."

"Do you know my husband?"

"Yes, I do," he said softly, battling the memories. "I served with him in France." He tried to maintain his composure, even though it was difficult. He didn't know the British war hero; he knew a different Alexander Cavendish.

"I'm not what you expected, am I?" she asked.

"No, you're not," he admitted, rattled by the changing conversation. Either she couldn't focus or the wandering discussion was intentional, a well-devised diversionary tool.

"I like to keep people off balance. Every time you see me you'll see a different part, but you'll never see the whole."

"Why is that?"

"I've never done anything with my education except search for who I am."

"And who are you, Penelope?" he asked. He studied her for a moment. Her behaviour was so erratic it was starting to seem like an act, staged to keep him off guard, and not consistent with who she truly was.

She stared at him, not blinking, not looking away. "You need to find that out," she said.

"It took a lot of courage for you to come here," he said. "The first step in your recovery is recognising that you need help."

She again looked away and was quiet for a moment. "I like Como," she said. "My family came here many times on holiday."

"Is that why you chose our facility?" he asked. "Because of the location? Or because I served in the war with your husband."

"My husband chose the sanitarium. He speaks very highly of you."

Barnett was confused by Cavendish's recommendation. They weren't friends and never would be. "I'm sure we can help you," he said, fumbling with a reply.

"I don't see how," she said with a hint of annoyance. "I've been to the best psychiatrists in the world and they couldn't help me. Why would I think you can?"

He leaned back in the chair. It was a fair question. "Why do you think I can't?" he asked.

She stood abruptly, looking at her watch. "My husband is waiting for me," she said. "I have to go."

"We haven't completed our session," Barnett protested, surprised the discussion had ended so soon.

"My father is coming tomorrow," she said as she rose and walked to the door. "If he approves, I'll be your patient."

Chapter 2

Penelope left Barnett's office wondering if he really wanted to help her. He didn't seem to believe that someone was trying to kill her, but neither did the police. And his approach was strange; he acted more like a distant observer, examining her like a biological specimen, his reactions guarded. He seemed uncomfortable with her Shakespeare dissertation, unless he didn't understand it. People were intimidated by intellect; she had learned that a long time ago. But there was something about him that she liked, although she couldn't identify what it was, and her instincts told her she could trust him, even though they had talked for only a few minutes.

The hallway was tiled with a rustic ceramic, the smooth plaster walls painted beige and accented with crisp white moulding. Doctors' offices occupied most of the second floor, the doors all closed, a brass nameplate attached to each. There were leather chairs and small tables with magazines placed upon them sporadically spaced along the corridor. Penelope paused to look at a magazine that had her image on the cover, the headline describing the attempt on her life in Monte Carlo. She flipped the pages to the article and, although it was written in Italian and difficult to understand, it described her supposed suicide attempt, not an attempted murder. Even the reporters had got it wrong.

Halfway down the hallway was a large marble fireplace, polished and perfect, and she stopped to study a rifle hanging above the mantle, its bolt open. A brass plate with etched lettering was fixed beneath it. 'Mai più', it read. *Never again.* She thought of the war to end all wars, the dead and the living, and after studying the unloaded rifle a moment more, she turned and left.

She strode down the hallway to a sweeping stairway that ended in the lobby. It was grand, the steps growing wider as they descended, Italian marble with hand-crafted balusters. The lobby was painted a snowy white, sunlight splashed into the room through arched windows, and a crystal chandelier dangled from the ceiling, casting a muted glow on the room below. It was furnished in Art Nouveau – buffets, tables and lamps – tastefully accented with Impressionist paintings and Murano glass. Leafy potted plants sat beside sofas and chairs, providing privacy for visitors. A registration desk was located by the entrance, hand-carved with lion's paw feet, an attendant reading a magazine. He glanced at her as she entered and smiled politely.

Penelope liked the building. It was a beautiful Italian mansion, warm and inviting, uniquely designed and built by the best craftsman of native marble and stone. It was originally constructed for an American railroad tycoon, became a hotel shortly thereafter, and was made into a sanitarium a decade before. It served as a hospital during the war, a place where patients with severe injuries spent months convalescing.

She left the building and walked across a cobblestone drive tucked under a balcony accessed from the second-floor dining room. She looked back at the building. The exterior was pale yellow with white trim, accented by large windows, the moulding fluted with a broad crown. It was a massive structure, standing proudly over Lake Como, tucked into a slope that led to the mountain behind it.

She took a stone path across the manicured lawn, shaded by juniper trees, sprawling branches reaching to heaven like tentacles of an octopus, bent and crooked. They were planted in different parts of the property, shading the site and providing privacy welcomed by patients. Wooden benches placed at the trunks offered respite to those who sought it, and on a bench near the shore of the lake Alexander Cavendish watched a boat pass by slowly. A man stood in the bow, casting a fishing line.

Alexander Cavendish had studied world history at Cambridge and was allegedly poised to fill an important foreign post in His Majesty's government before the war began and changed the hopes and dreams of millions of men and women. His engagement to Penelope, encouraged by both families, was hastily announced two years after the war began, and was followed by long absences while Alexander fought in France. The couple married just after the Armistice, but both had changed dramatically in the interim. The charming bachelor had vanished, the twinkle in his eye replaced by a vacant stare, while Penelope's steep decline seemed to start when the ceremony ended, or perhaps sooner, when her brother died. The world watched the pair anxiously – the wealthy, incredibly handsome bachelor and the haunted heiress – unable to find happiness no matter where they looked.

"That wasn't a very long meeting," Alexander said as Penelope gave him a quick kiss and sat beside him.

"I couldn't stand much more," she complained. "Psychiatrists are all the same. A concerned, compassionate stare with probing questions a child would ask, then the promise to make you well. I've heard it so many times before."

"Aren't you being tough on Dr Barnett, darling?"

"I did like him," she replied, "but he didn't seem to realise that my life is in danger."

"He was in my regiment during the war," he said, dismissing her last statement. He looked away, his mind apparently wandering, and muttered, "He was in the Medical Corps, badly wounded."

"I think he still suffers. His face is scarred; he limps and his left hand is paralysed."

"I intend to visit him to discuss your treatment. Maybe after you're settled. Did you see your accommodations?"

"Yes, I did," she replied. "It's a large suite, bedroom and parlour, with a balcony. I should be comfortable there. It's only for a short while."

"You need to stay until you're well," he said. "However long that takes." He hugged her, pulling her close. "Is your father still coming tomorrow?"

"Yes, he has an appointment with Dr Barnett and then I'm meeting him for lunch. He'll be staying at a villa a few kilometres down the lake. We stayed there on holiday before the war."

"I hope he wasn't offended that I didn't stay with him," he said. "But I didn't want to impose. We'll each be more comfortable in our own residence."

"Is the cottage I leased acceptable?"

"Yes, it's a great location."

"I know it's cramped. But it was so serene, tucked in that grove of trees by the lake."

"No, it'll be fine, although it is very tiny. But I'll manage. And it's not far from town should I choose to take my meals there."

"I'm hoping they'll let me leave the sanitarium overnight," she said.

"I think you should focus on getting better," he advised. "Maybe later, after Dr Barnett is comfortable with your progress, we can discuss time away from the hospital."

"I don't remember you mentioning Dr Barnett during the war," she mused, thinking aloud. "Were you close to him?"

"We did our duty," he replied curtly. "That's what men do during a war. There was no time for friendship."

After a short pause, she asked tentatively, "Are you sure he's a good doctor?"

"No need to worry, darling," he said cheerfully. "Everything will be fine. And I realise you're the patient, but this ordeal isn't easy for me, either."

"No, I suppose it isn't," she said, her mind wandering. "But I'm glad you're here with me." She tried to remember the last few years, but somehow the days blended together, passing quickly but meaning nothing. She had endured them, but she hadn't lived them.

He paused, clearing his throat. "I'm so sorry, darling," he said, "but unfortunately, I have to go to London. That's why I wanted to make sure your father would be here."

"London?" she asked, surprised. "Why? You've just arrived."

"It's horrible timing, I know," he admitted. "But my father needs help, something about one of his companies. There's also a charity event for war widows; they so depend on my support. But I shan't be too long. Ten days at most."

Penelope pouted. "Alexander, how inconsiderate."

"Inconsiderate?" he asked, incredulous. "Darling, I found you a good doctor, someone I know personally, just to ensure you get the best care possible."

"I know I'm being selfish, and I do appreciate all you've done for me," she said. "I really do."

"And you're in a good location where your privacy will be protected," he added. "I don't want reporters bothering you. I just want you to get well."

She hesitated. "It's just that I need you. Someone is trying to kill me."

"You'll be safe here," he assured her. "And darling, no-one is trying to kill you. That's why you're here. You need help."

"I'm sorry, really I am," she said. "And I hate to be such a burden. But I do think my life is in danger. I just wish you didn't have to leave."

"I don't want to go," he said, "but I have to. There's a difference. I have commitments – volunteer work, business to attend to. It's important and it can't be helped. Please try to understand that."

She sighed. "I do, but I suddenly feel very alone."

"I'll speak to security at the sanitarium to ensure you're protected. And I'll leave London as soon as I can."

She was pensive for a moment, struck with an idea. "Maybe you can tell King George that someone is trying to kill me."

"I can certainly do that," he said with a hint of sarcasm. "I'm sure he'll be anxious to help."

"I don't know why I didn't think of it before," she said optimistically. "He can call Scotland Yard."

"He probably doesn't have any jurisdiction in Italy, darling, but I will certainly ask him."

"Please do. I'm sure he can do something. I am a British citizen."

"There's one problem," he said, grinning. "We don't know the king well enough to ask for his help."

"I know the king, don't I? Wasn't he at our wedding?"

"No, darling, he wasn't at the wedding."

"I'm confused. Maybe I don't know King George. Maybe I only think I did. But it still isn't a bad idea. If he can't help me, no-one can."

"Your father will look after you while I'm gone," he said. "And after I return, I won't be leaving again. I'll stay here in Como until you're well."

Penelope looked at the lake and then the massive mountains behind it. She was a strong woman, much stronger than they all thought. "I can defend myself," she said. "I'll catch whoever is trying to kill me. Then everyone will finally believe me."

Chapter 3

Another cottage sat on the edge of the lake, surrounded by beds of roses and edelweiss, nestled in the mountains' shadow. It was located on the opposite side of the hospital grounds from the dwelling rented by Penelope Jones, a half kilometre from the sanitarium and convenient to the road that led to Como and the smaller villages around it.

Joseph Barnett had lived there since the Great War, a psychiatrist suffering as severely as his patients. The war in France, with splattered blood and trenches tunnelled to hell, had yielded to peace in Italy, with placid lakes and peaks perched in heaven. The memories were starting to fade, not as sharp as when they occurred, the bombs not as loud, the cries not as anguished. But they still interrupted sleep and destroyed the daily activities that, when added up, equal our lives.

The sanitarium welcomed him and he initially treated those who had served, the survivors, for many came to the Italian Lakes seeking sanctuary just as he did. It was strange to see German and French, Austrian and English, Italian and Irish, gathered in the same hospital when all had been combatants only months or years before. Gradually the population of tormented soldiers diminished and he began to accept patients with more varied ailments.

As each day ended, he confronted the past and faced the future, revelling in the tranquility that the location provided. He gained much success in the circles of academia, treated patients ranging from destitute to starlet, and gained a reputation that travelled the world, even if he did not.

He had met his wife Rose in a French hospital in Amiens after the Battle of the Somme. She was a British volunteer from Devon, a sweet, compassionate young lady, strong and independent, with a penchant for protecting the weak and disadvantaged. She had auburn hair and a splattering of freckles, her name describing her perfectly: beautiful but fragile and welcoming but guarded, like the thorns that travelled the vine.

She trained as a nurse when the war began, temporarily postponing her true passion which was the love of words. She had mastered the English language as few could ever hope to, assumed she would become a journalist or maybe a writer, but a world war intervened. Nurses were needed, so that's what she became.

She captured images while the war raged: murdered and maimed, defeated and defiant, tortured families, devastated civilians, spending hours after her shift scribbling in notebooks tucked in a box under her cot. When the conflict ended and Europe was only a shadow, a ravaged civilisation, she published an anthology: *Poems of the Great War.* Her writing was emotional, moving and memorable, and she deftly captured the pain and suffering of those that passed and the emptiness left in those that lived. The anthology was popular, selling across the continent, translated into a dozen different languages.

Barnett had spent almost two years in the hospital, released just as the war ended. A few days later, he and Rose were married. She was a devoted wife, and she was able to quiet his cries in the hours before dawn and ease the depression that sometimes consumed him. She stood by him, a rock on which to lean, holding and moulding, making not breaking, the man to whom she had committed her life.

"I accepted two new patients today," he said as he and Rose sat on a stone patio, enjoying a glass of Chianti and admiring the sun as it set behind the mountains.

"You have too many patients already," she said, always protective. "Can you care for two more?"

He assured her it was no burden as he watched her warily, wondering how to tell her that Cavendish's wife was among them.

"Tell me about them," she said, knowing she was his trusted confidant, an alter ego, a sceptic when one was needed, an ally when one was not.

"The first is a French artist," he explained. "His name is Lafite."

"And what brings him to the sanitarium?"

"He's a painter who thinks he's as good as Van Gogh."

"Is he?"

"I don't know," he admitted, "but he's just as unstable. He cut off part of his left ear to be like the master."

"Why would he ever do that?"

He thought for a moment, framing his original assessment of the patient. "I think subconsciously he realises he's a mediocre painter, never to rival renowned artists. But he wanted to identify with them."

"So he cut off his ear?"

"It seems," he said. "At least from our initial discussion."

She smiled. "I think he may be difficult. Who is your second patient?"

"It's an interesting young woman."

She sipped her wine. "Interesting because of her instabilities?"

Barnett thought for a moment. "Perhaps, but more for the life she's led."

"Moral, immoral, rich, poor?" Rose guessed, apparently trying to imagine the patient.

"Very rich, morality unknown."

"What makes her so interesting?"

"I learned something from her," he said. "She's lived a life we all would envy. Very wealthy, a doting and supportive father, and she apparently has a devoted husband. She has anything and everything she could ever want."

"Then what brings her to you, I wonder. What else did you learn about her?"

"She has advanced degrees in literature and history."

"What did she do during the war?"

He paused, watching the horizon as it swallowed the sun. "I had Olivia, my receptionist, research the family," he said. "And apparently, she was a professor at Cambridge during the war."

"Why isn't she still a professor?"

"She married a few weeks after the war ended. I was told her husband didn't want her to teach so she vacated the post."

"She seems capable of functioning at a high capacity, even given her condition," Rose said.

"Yes, that's true," Barnett agreed. "But her instabilities began as the war ended. It's been a rather steep decline."

"Maybe she needs the stimulation she had at Cambridge, or something comparable."

"I hadn't thought of that," he mused aloud. "Maybe intellectual activity would improve her condition."

"Maybe she needs challenges, whether it's teaching or something else," Rose said, as if trying to imagine what drove the patient. "Does she spend time with her husband?"

"I think he travels often, usually alone."

"That doesn't seem like much of a marriage."

Barnett looked at his wife. "No, you're right," he agreed. "It doesn't."

"What are your thoughts?"

"She's so unhappy it made me wonder if happiness stems from the struggle to survive, the battle to better your life and that of your family, ambition and drive, goals that are great and maybe not attainable, so you always have something to strive for."

"She has no goals because she has everything anyone could ever want?" Rose asked. "That's a philosophical premise, but maybe she has what you think most people want. But maybe it's not what she wants at all."

Barnett smiled, reached over and kissed her on the cheek. "I've always believed you're the best psychiatrist in this family."

She laughed. "I'm not sure I agree," she said. "I listen and try to learn, but only say what I think. It has no basis in anything."

"There's something else," he said, knowing the information would disturb her.

"What is it?"

"Her name is Penelope Jones."

Rose Barnett thought for a moment, the name apparently familiar. Then her face paled. "Cavendish," she muttered.

Chapter 4

"Help!" Penelope screamed. She looked frantically around the room, dimly lit by moonlight funneling through her open window. "Someone tried to kill me!"

The door to her suite opened, the hinges creaking. "Signorina Penelope," a voice called from the hallway. "Miss Penelope."

"Stay away!" Penelope shouted. "It was you, wasn't it?" She scrambled out of bed and went to her bureau, searching for a weapon, anything she could use to defend herself. She opened a drawer, grabbed a slender nail file and held it behind her back

"Miss Penelope," a voice said in accented English. "It's Adele, the nurse. Are you all right?"

Penelope leaned against the wall, hiding near the door, and peered into the sitting room. Light from the hallway spilled in, pointing a path to the bedroom, and she saw a shadow cross the threshold. She grasped the file firmly.

Adele approached tentatively. "Miss Penelope?" she asked softly. "Are you awake?"

As Adele entered the bedroom, Penelope lunged forward, thrusting the nail file toward her, sticking and stabbing, fighting to save her life.

Adele screamed and raised her hands to fend off the attack. "Miss Penelope!" she yelled. "Stop!"

Penelope choked, as if suffocating, and attacked more viciously. She waved her right arm back and forth, the nail file clenched in her hand. She probed, searching for a weakness, warily waiting for Adele to retaliate.

"Miss Penelope, I'm not going to hurt you."

Penelope kept fighting, tears streaming down her cheeks. "You tried to smother me!" she screamed.

"Help!" Adele shouted. "Emilio, help me! It's Miss Penelope!"

Several moments passed, the battle waging with neither gaining an advantage. Penelope began to weaken but refused to surrender. Adele held her arm, unable to grasp the file, but keeping the blade at a distance.

Emilio, the night orderly, ran into the room, an alarmed look on his face. "Cosa c'è?" he asked. "What's wrong?"

"It's Miss Penelope," Adele explained. "She must have had a nightmare. She thinks I tried to kill her."

"Easy, Miss Penelope," he said, his English broken, his voice soft. "Everything all right. No-one hurt you."

"Stay away," Penelope threatened. "I won't let you kill me."

Emilio lunged forward and wrapped his arms around her, holding her close. "No-one hurt you," he whispered.

Adele grabbed the file and pried it from Penelope's fingers. "It's all right, Miss Penelope. We'll protect you."

As Emilio kept Penelope subdued, her arms pinned to her side, Adele rushed to the nurse's cart in the hallway and returned with a pill. "Take this, Miss Penelope," she offered. "It will make you feel better. I promise."

"No," Penelope argued, turning her face away, continuing to struggle. "It's poison, I know it is."

Adele shoved the pill into her mouth and clamped her hand over Penelope's lips. "It's not poison," she insisted. "It will calm you."

Penelope fought, moving her head back and forth, trying to spit out the pill, but was unsuccessful. Emilio held her tightly and Adele kept her hand clamped over Penelope's mouth, waiting for the pill to dissolve.

"Look at her bed," Adele said, motioning to the sheets and blankets in disarray, the pillows on the floor. "It looks like she struggled. It must have been a horrible dream." When she was satisfied Penelope had swallowed the pill, she quickly remade the bed, putting the pillows at the head.

Emilio held Penelope for several more minutes until the fright in her eyes began to fade and the sedative started to take effect. He cautiously relaxed his hold and he and Adele led her to the bed. "Lie down, Miss Penelope," he said softly. "You feel better."

Penelope stopped struggling, her eyes starting to glaze, and they helped her onto the bed. She sat upright, staring vacantly around the room. "You tried to kill me," she mumbled.

""I'll get you some water, Miss Penelope," Adele said. She went in the bathroom and returned with a glass and put it to Penelope's lips, helping her sip it.

"Is she all right?" Emilio asked.

"Yes, I think so," Adele replied warily. "But you better get Dr Barnett."

Chapter 5

A loud knock on the front door awakened the Barnetts at 2 a.m.

"Who can that be?" Rose asked sleepily.

"It must be the hospital," Barnett said as he looked at her warily.

They got out of bed, put on their robes and hurried to the entrance.

"Who is it?" Rose called as she helped Barnett, his crippled leg stiff and sore.

"Dr Barnett? It's Emilio, the orderly."

Barnett opened the door. "What's wrong?"

"It's Miss Jones," Emilio said. "She acting crazy."

"Is she all right?" Barnett asked, fearing another suicide attempt.

"I don't know," Emilio said, his accent thick. "She tried to stab Adele with nail file."

"Is Adele hurt?" Rose asked.

"No," Emilio replied. "File not sharp. Adele upset."

"What happened?" Barnett asked, fearing the worst. He hadn't considered Penelope might be violent. But why attack her nurse? And what triggered it?

"Penelope had nightmare," Emilio explained. "Says someone tried to kill her. Smothered her with pillow."

"Have you given her a sedative?" Barnett asked.

"Yes, she calmer. Keeps talking but don't make sense."

"I must go to see her," Barnett said. "Please wait while I get dressed."

Barnett hurried to the bedroom, pulling on his clothes as Rose handed them to him. Once he was dressed, she helped him with his shoes. It was hard for him, his leg was so stiff.

"Shall I wait up for you?" she asked, worried.

He kissed her. "No, my love, go back to sleep. Everything will be fine."

Barnett and Emilio hurried to Penelope's suite and found her still sitting up in bed, muttering, staring vacantly at the ceiling and walls. She wore a pastel nightgown, the bedcovers bunched around her waist. Her eyes were dull, her face expressionless, probably from the sedative.

Barnett watched her for several seconds, wondering if she was even aware of his presence. He turned to Emilio. "Please remove any sharp objects she might have."

"I already did," the orderly replied. "I give to Adele."

"I had no reason to think she was violent," Barnett said. "I suppose we'll have to be more careful."

"Is all right."

"Thank you for your help. I'll take care of her, now."

Emilio nodded. "Call if you need me," he said as he left the room. A moment later the door to the suite closed.

Barnett sat on the bed. "Are you all right, Penelope?"

She looked at him emptily, as if wondering who he was. Then she started to sob.

"It's all right," he whispered. "There's no danger. It was only a nightmare."

"No, it wasn't. It was real."

He studied her closely, but she was too groggy to make much sense. "Tell me what happened," he said. "And we'll make everything all right."

"Adele tried to kill me," she stated firmly.

He moved closer and asked softly, "Penelope, why would Adele try to hurt you?"

"There must be a reason. Ask her."

"Adele would never hurt you. I think you may be mistaken."

She shook her head. "No, I'm not," she insisted. "She tried to smother me with my pillow."

"Maybe you were dreaming," he offered. "Maybe it only seemed like someone was trying to kill you because the images were so vivid."

"No, I wasn't dreaming," she replied. "Adele tried to smother me. I was scratching and scraping, trying to push her away."

"Penelope," he said, speaking tenderly. "How can you be so sure it wasn't a dream?" He wanted to calm her, to reassure here, to persuade her Adele would never harm her. Then he could gradually convince her that no-one else would either.

"It was real," she insisted.

"Maybe it wasn't Adele," he suggested, trying to show belief but to still cast doubt. "I know she doesn't harm people, she takes care of them, she makes them well. And she always has."

"It was her," Penelope said. "I kept fighting with her but I couldn't get away. I scratched so hard my fingers started bleeding."

"Penelope, the door to your suite was closed. No-one could have entered," he said, speaking in a monotone, hoping to calm her. "Adele was in the hallway. She came in when she heard you scream. It was just a nightmare. Nothing more."

"Only a dream?" she asked harshly.

"Yes," he said, hoping to convince her. "Just a dream."

"Then explain this," she snapped. She held up her hands. The tips of her fingers were torn and bleeding.

He was shaken, but tried not to show it. He took her hands in his and consoled her while he furtively examined the wounds. They were real. Her fingers were scraped and tender, the edge of her nails torn and pulled. The bleeding had stopped but dried blood marred her fingertips. He couldn't explain it. He had never seen anything like it. How did she harm herself? He saw no blood anywhere.

"Don't worry," he said gently. "Everything will be all right. I promise."

"No-one ever believes me. Everyone thinks I make it up."

"I believe you," he said.

She took a deep breath. "I need help," she said. "Someone has to protect me."

"The images are very vivid, aren't they?" he asked, ignoring her pleas.

"I can smell edelweiss on the breeze," she said. "Just by leaving my window open."

He knew she changed the subject when she didn't want to answer his questions. "In the dream, you could smell edelweiss," he said, emphasising her nightmare, minimising the possibility of an alleged attack. "The flowers haven't bloomed yet."

"I'm sleepy," she said, rubbing her eyes.

"Do you dream of other forms of death?"

"I always have a window open," she said. "It doesn't matter how cold it is. I can't tolerate being closed in."

He looked at the opened window. It should be closed; it was too dangerous. He looked outside. There was a tree near the building and a stout limb stretched almost to the window, brushing the wrought iron railing that bordered the slender balcony. He could imagine an aggressive reporter climbing the tree and taking photographs of a suicidal socialite. He studied the window a moment more, suddenly suspicious. Someone could also climb the tree, reach the balcony, climb in the window and hold a pillow over Penelope's face. Or, more likely, Penelope just had a nightmare. He closed the window and locked it. He would ensure the staff checked in nightly.

"Penelope, how often do you dream of death?" he asked.

"I want to go to sleep," she said.

He had hoped to continue, but knew it best not to. Her sedative was having its desired effect. "Of course," he said. "You need your rest."

"I'm afraid," she whispered, her speech slurring.

He couldn't deny the child housed in the woman's body. He had to protect her. "There's nothing to be afraid of," he said. "Nothing will happen to you. I won't let it."

Chapter 6

Joseph Barnett sat in his office, sipping an espresso and reading the biographical information that Olivia, his receptionist, had prepared on the Jones family. The report was detailed, providing historical timelines as well as insight regarding the current generation.

The Jones family had several famous ancestors, all of whom made contributions to further the aims of the British Empire. Sir Jonathan Jones made a fortune in the China trade in the 1850s and the family business was still dominated by Asian real estate, banking and shipping, all spawned by this adventurous forebear. One ancestor, Lord General Thomas Jones, fought beside Marlborough in the early 18th century, while another lost his life exploring the African interior near the end of the 19th century. Other relatives were instrumental in shaping British dominance of the Indian subcontinent, while an aunt married a German count and sided with the enemy during the Great War.

Wellington Jones ran the family empire with the assistance of two brothers and three cousins and a contingent of advisors scattered around the world. The conglomerate was well established in a variety of industries; Wellington's primary responsibility was global real estate. The corporation owned properties located throughout the British Empire: the United Kingdom, India, Singapore and Hong Kong. He also oversaw charitable foundations established by the company. Although the main focus was funding medical advances, especially after witnessing the horrific wounds of the Great War, the foundation also supported a global network of kitchens that fed the poor. His hobbies were history and archaeology, as well as botany, and his estate in the English countryside was known for the beautiful landscaping and exotic plants that originated in other areas of the world. He had a penchant for architecture, classical music, fine literature, Paris and red wine.

He didn't remarry after the death of his wife, although he had been romantically linked with a number of socialites throughout the years. Apparently, at least according to newspapers, his current love interest was Claudine Bonnet, a French writer who lived on the Île de la Cité, one of two natural islands in the Seine River that intersected Paris. He was rarely seen with her in public, but he owned a Parisian townhouse conveniently located a few blocks from hers.

Penelope's mother had a different story. Born Annabelle Dundee in New Delhi, India, supposedly of English parents, she had dark hair and eyes complimented by olive skin. Her parents were aristocrats from London, although rumours abounded that her mother had a torrid love affair with an Indian cavalry officer, the product of which was Annabelle. Wellington Jones met her during a business trip on the subcontinent and, even though ten years her senior, they married two months later. Oxford arrived within the year and Penelope three years later, inheriting the olive complexion and dark hair and eyes of her mother.

Barnett skimmed through other details of the report – the Jones family was among the top fifty richest in Britain. Wellington seemed to be estranged from the rest of the family although no reason or explanation was provided, and he spent considerable time in Bombay and New Delhi. But what Barnett found most interesting was that Jones seemed to rate his responsibilities as father first, his business empire second.

Jones arrived an hour later, eight minutes early for an 11 a.m. appointment. He was a handsome man with blue eyes, his black hair streaked with grey and perfectly combed, his face rugged and chiselled with a small cleft in the chin and an athletic build either earned or inherited. He was probably mid-fifties but looked much younger, almost passing for Penelope's older brother rather than her father. He smiled as he approached but it didn't seem genuine, more a smile that came easily to a businessman, probably produced when the situation warranted.

"Wellington Jones," he announced.

Barnett strolled across the room to meet his outstretched hand, always conscious of his limp. "Doctor Joseph Barnett," he said. "Please, sit down."

"War wound?" Jones asked.

Barnett was uncomfortable discussing the war. It only brought back the memories: pain, screams, bombing, wounded, dying and lost loved ones. "Yes, it is," he said curtly, clearing his throat.

"I served as well," Jones informed him. "I could have taken a position in strategic command, comfortable and cosy in London, but that's not me. I insisted on a commission. I was colonel of an infantry regiment. Served under Allenby. I led the main charge at the Battle of the Somme. Some of …"

Barnett started to tremble ever so slightly as Jones's words faded and were replaced by the ever increasing crescendo of battle …

… The bombs burst with a deafening whine as the earth quaked when they exploded and left a lifeless landscape pitted and scarred. Barnett pushed over the top of the trenches with thousands of other men in a single wave as machine guns clattered and body fell upon body. Screams drowned screams as blood flowed into the mud and turned the puddles crimson. Boys not yet men yelled Barnett's name over and over as they begged for help, their agony intense, increasing as each second passed. Barnett rushed forward, ignoring bullets and bombs, propelled to the pleas, trying to treat the wounded. Twenty metres away, the ground between littered with bodies, was a young soldier named Jimmy Spangler trapped in barbed wire, standing limply as the wire held him upright. He was a boy Barnett had mentored, seventeen years old from the farms of Somerset, a lad who never knew pain, a boy struggling to be a man like thousands of others that littered the battlefield.

Barnett scrambled over the bodies and fought to reach him as bullets burrowed into the ground and bodies continued to fall. "I don't want to die!" Jimmy cried, the scream ringing in Barnett's ears, louder than the bombs and machine guns and cries from thousands of wounded and dying. Jimmy's body was riddled with red, blood dripping from bullet holes and staining his green uniform. Barnett yanked the wire away as the ends cut his hands, steel shards tearing his skin.

"Help me," Jimmy pleaded as his strength faded. "Please, help me." Jimmy's face was pale as blood dripped from his body, his eyes vacant as Barnett wrenched a lifeless body from the barbed wire, a boy whose family would never see him again; a man who would never have children, never pass the family name. Barnett carried him to the trench, obsessed with preserving the body, protecting it, even though it had breathed its last, dragging it over bodies, mangled and maimed, dying or dead, and just as he reached the edge of the trench a shell exploded and shrapnel pierced his face, penetrated his outstretched arm and hand and punctured his left leg with fragments as hot as the fires of hell. He fell forward, contorted in pain, engulfed in a kaleidoscope of acrid smoke and tortured cries as grey sky twirled around him and he tumbled into the trench …

"Doctor Barnett?"

"Yes, I certainly understand, Mr Jones," Barnett stammered, his flashback fading. Somehow, he heard both Jones's explanation and the tormented ramblings that consumed him. "I was wounded at the Somme. But I don't like to talk about it."

"Honour the dead and rejoice with the living," Jones said, mouthing a popular phrase used by the war's survivors. "A lot of good men fell at the Somme." He removed a pocket watch from his vest and glanced at the face before returning it to his pocket.

"Yes, they did," Barnett said softly, his mind returning to Jimmy Spangler. "A lot of good boys fell, too."

"Penelope's husband was there," Jones said. "He led an entire regiment. A war hero, you know. He took a bullet eleven months later. Lucky to be alive. You were Medical Corps?"

"Yes, I was. I tended the wounded."

"Rank?"

"Lieutenant."

"Well, Lieutenant, Penelope likes you. She told me herself. And she has decided to stay."

"I prefer to be called Doctor," Barnet told him.

"Yes, of course. How long will a diagnosis take? And a treatment programme beyond that."

"I think after a week or so I can make some preliminary assumptions. But I am concerned about one of Penelope's insistent claims."

"Which is?"

"She's convinced someone is trying to kill her."

He frowned. "A recent development, Doctor," Jones explained. "These delusions have existed for three or four weeks now. A major reason why she's here, among others. Penelope has been to several doctors through the years." He paused, reflective, a saddened glaze consuming his eyes. "She got much worse after her brother was killed. I thought her wedding, which was a few months later, would help her but it didn't. Her decline continued."

"A breakdown is difficult to predict," Barnett said compassionately, watching Jones closely. He suspected the hard exterior hid an emotional interior, tortured and alone. "What was the diagnosis of her other doctors?"

"They reached various conclusions," he informed him. "But she had different problems when she was younger. Depression, mostly. She was very unhappy. Then there was a rapid descent after Oxford died. They were very close."

Barnett could feel his pain, see it in his eyes, written on his face, hidden by the words of a strong man who was just as weak as everyone else. "I'll continue my discussions with Penelope," he said. "I'm sure I can accurately diagnose her condition and provide treatment."

"You don't have much time, Dr Barnett," Jones said gravely. "Penelope tried to take her own life. I can't let that happen again. Especially after her nightmare last night."

"We'll do everything we can to help her."

"What do you think is wrong with her?"

"I need more time before I draw any conclusions."

"But I don't have more time," he said. "I almost lost her once. And I will not risk losing her again. She's my whole life. Do you understand that?"

"Yes, Mr Jones, I do understand," Barnett said, recognising how desperate the man was. "But Penelope has only been here for one day. What is it that you expected me to do?"

"What's your initial assessment?" he asked impatiently.

Barnett studied Jones for a moment, a desperate man trying to hold his world together while it was in the midst of falling apart. "I think we need to attack her inner conflict first," Barnett said. "We can address her symptoms later."

"I'm not sure I understand."

"My priority is to target the conflict," Barnett clarified, "the fear that someone is trying to kill her. Her symptoms can be alleviated through treatment."

"How long will that take?"

"I can't estimate the duration of her treatment."

Jones sat back in the chair, his eyes trained on Barnett. He seemed to recognise strength and he now looked at Barnett differently. It seemed that few people challenged him, but he appeared to respect those that did. "One week," he said. "That's all the time you have to map her road to recovery."

"That's not very long."

"I didn't ask for a cure, only how you will do it. And I don't care how little time it is. I need to protect Penelope."

A knock on the door interrupted them. Olivia, middle-aged, slender with black hair and glasses, poked her head in. "I'm so sorry for the interruption, Doctor," she said. "But I have an urgent telegram for Mr Jones."

Barnett nodded for her to enter. "That's quite all right," he said.

She handed the envelope to Wellington Jones and quietly left.

"Excuse me," Jones said. "This must be important." He tore it open and removed the message. He frowned as he read it, his face pale.

Barnet watched his reactions. Whatever was in the cable appeared to be very disturbing. "Is everything all right?" he asked.

Jones nodded, alarm etched in every wrinkle in his face. "Just business," he said. "It can wait." But he scanned the cable again, almost as if he didn't believe what he had read the first time.

Barnett wondered what was so important. It wasn't easy to get a telegram through Olivia; someone had been very persistent. And Jones's reaction proved that, whatever information the telegram contained, it wasn't good.

An instant later Jones raised his eyes, once again focused. "I have a list of other facilities I'm willing to try," he said with no emotion, acting just like any other successful businessman, resuming the conversation where he had left it a moment before. "Dr Fuentes in Barcelona will be next."

"I'm familiar with Dr Fuentes," Barnett said quietly.

"I don't mean to offend you, Doctor. Really, I don't. But I have no time to waste."

"I understand."

"And you agree with the terms?"

Barnett nodded. "I have one week with Penelope," he repeated.

"Good," he said. The smile returned to his face, although it was weaker than before he had read the telegram. "I have complete confidence in you, as does Penelope's husband. After all, you were our first choice."

"Thank you, Mr Jones, I'm flattered," Barnett said, knowing he was the first choice after a dozen others had failed. But he realised Penelope's condition was deteriorating rapidly; immediate action was required. Regardless of the family's reason for choosing him as Penelope's psychiatrist, he didn't intend to disappoint them.

Chapter 7

Wellington Jones left Barnett's office and looked at his watch; he was meeting Penelope in twenty minutes and needed time to think. He touched the telegram in his suit pocket as walked through the hallway, down the stairs and out to the lawn, and found a vacant bench by the lake, hidden by shrubs. He withdrew the cable from his pocket, scanning the words on the page:

BANKS IN BOMBAY AND DELHI MAY CALL IN LOANS – STOP – HONG KONG AND SINGAPORE THREATEN SAME – STOP – ALL LIQUID ASSETS DIVERTED TO EMERGENCY FUND – STOP

Jones folded the cable and returned it to his pocket. The global recession had begun when the war ended and the world's economies shifted from manufacturing military components back to consumer goods. Prices for all products and hard assets plummeted at one of the fastest paces in history, down almost fifteen percent. The recession, now almost eighteen months old, showed no sign of abating.

For a global real estate company that survived on leverage, deflation was devastating. Many of Jones's properties, primarily those most recently purchased, were worth less than he had paid, even after deducting the down-payment, which was always minimal. But that's how successful real estate operations were run – with other people's money. In this case, it was a consortium of banks. Historically, it led to high profits as prices increased. Now with prices dropping, it led to disaster.

Some of Jones's lenders, primarily those on the Indian subcontinent, were uncomfortable holding mortgages on properties worth less than the lien. They threatened to invoke a little-used clause in the Asian commercial mortgage industry to request payment in full.

Jones and his family had substantial assets. They could sell properties to pay for others, but that took time and he needed money quickly. They could shrink other aspects of the family business, like shipping, to absorb the losses in real estate. Or they could cut the subsidiary loose and let it fail. If they did, Jones would fail too. He didn't have enough money to support his lifestyle, at least not for long. All liquidity had been diverted to an emergency account dedicated to loan repayment in Bombay and Delhi. Reserves were also increased in Hong Kong and Singapore, further starving his funds.

It was a frightening thought. If one bank called in a loan, the rest would likely follow, like a stampede, desperate to salvage whatever percentage of their investment they could, frantic to minimise their loss. Jones had to convince them otherwise. He had to prove that a temporary setback caused by a deteriorating global economic climate had no impact on the financial health of his company. And he had to illustrate that, like all other economic cycles, the current climate was temporary.

He sighed, pensive, waiting to meet Penelope, and studied the rippling waters of Lake Como tickling the shore. The scenery was dramatic, breathtaking – mountains stretching to the water, mansions and hotels and cottages and villas spread out along the coast. It was a different world – the best that Mother Nature had to offer accented by the greatest Italian architecture. He had always loved Como. Almost as much as London.

Even though the situation in India demanded his personal presence, he couldn't leave Penelope, not now, and maybe not for some time. He had to somehow demonstrate that he could repay the loans on their original amortisation schedules, the economy would recover as it always did, and that the value of the real estate he owned would increase to greater than its purchase price. And he had to do that from half a world away. He got up from the bench, determined to succeed. He had problems before and he always solved them. And he would find an answer now – even if it seemed none existed.

Chapter 8

The Cavendish family estate was a lavish four-storey mansion in Chelsea, brick with white marble trim, bay walls and balconies, all framed by lush landscaping. The interior was constructed with the finest material the continent offered: Belgian tile, Flemish wallpaper and Italian tapestry. Built by gifted craftsman a century before, the estate stood proudly in one of London's finest neighborhoods, an inspiration to the peasant who passed and dared to dream.

The heart of the dining room was a long walnut table, a rich grain winding down its length. A matching buffet sat along one wall, bronze sconces above it, and a glass chandelier, reflecting light like facets in a diamond, hung from a plaster ceiling patterned with cherubs. Alexander Cavendish sat at the table, his mother Cora across from him, his father Jackson at the head – all dressed for dinner. Cora wore a lavender evening gown, the men wore three-piece suits. Two servants in long formal jackets and white bow ties served their meal: curried pheasant with rice salad, tomatoes and artichokes.

"I hope Penelope's health improves," Cora Cavendish said with concern. A woman with blonde hair and blue eyes, her son's looks favoured hers.

"I'm hopeful the sanitarium will sort things out," Alexander said. "She seemed a bit better after her discussion with the doctor. Still confused, but I think she understands she needs help."

"Who's the doctor?" Jackson Cavendish asked.

"He's actually an Englishman," Alexander informed them, sipping his wine. "He served with my regiment at the Somme. His name is Joseph Barnett."

"I've never heard of him," Jackson remarked. "He can't be very good."

"Darling, you don't know that," Cora scolded. "He might be a fine psychiatrist. Just because he isn't in London doesn't mean he isn't talented."

"I'll make some inquiries," Jackson said, clearing the last remnants of pheasant from his plate. He motioned for the servant to take it.

Dessert was apple charlotte served with a dab of cream and a cup of tea. The diners eyed it for a moment – it seemed too perfect to eat – before marring it with a fork.

"How long are you staying?" Cora asked her son.

"Just a few days," he replied. "Maybe a week. I have a charity event for war widows and I promised to visit some friends. But I have to get back to Penelope."

"How long is she under Barnett's care?" Jackson asked.

Alexander shrugged. "For several months, I would think. Maybe longer."

"I suggest getting her back to London," Jackson advised. "I'll get the names of some reputable doctors."

"I'm sure Wellington has already done that," Alexander said.

"Then why Como?" Jackson asked. "She could be treated here, near family and friends."

"Maybe that's precisely why," Cora pointed out. "She needs privacy. Family and friends could be part of her problem."

"Nonsense," Jackson scoffed. "Familiar surroundings would help, I'm sure."

The men retired to the parlour after dinner, smoking cigars complemented by a glass of Scotch. This was the moment Alexander had been waiting for, since there was a delicate matter he had to discuss with his father, but he realised it was also the moment his father dreaded, for he suspected a favour was about to be asked.

After several minutes of awkward silence, punctuated by the exhaled smoke of expensive cigars, Jackson broke the impasse. "What sort of trouble do you have yourself in now?" he wondered aloud.

Alexander took a sip of whisky. "What makes you think I'm in trouble?"

"Because I know you," Jackson replied. "Don't pretend you came for a congenial visit, because I know you didn't."

Alexander was quiet for a moment. His father was right, just as he always was. "The horses," he said softly. "I've had a streak of bad luck."

"What exactly is a streak of bad luck?"

"About fifteen thousand pounds."

Jackson's face reddened. "Fifteen thousand pounds? Good God, man, what has happened to you?"

Alexander paused, not sure how to reply. "I don't know," he finally admitted. "I think it's the war."

"The war? What does that have to do with anything?"

"I need to escape, to forget the memories. Whisky, women, gambling – whatever takes my mind off it. I know it's a sickness and I have to stop, but I can't."

"You better find a way to stop," Jackson warned, "before you end up with Penelope in the lunatic asylum."

"I'll be all right. Just help me get through this and I'll change."

"I don't see how," Jackson argued. "You lost fifteen thousand pounds on ponies and it isn't the first time. What about the rugby and cricket bets? How much did you lose there? It's always something. You bet, you lose, I pay. But not any more."

"It'll never happen again," Alexander vowed.

"A promise isn't the same as a plan," Jackson said. "Maybe you need to earn your keep, start working at one of my businesses."

"I'm just going through a difficult time," Alexander said, his head lowered. "It won't last forever."

"Alexander, it's an endless string of failures," Jackson complained. "It started with ten thousand pounds to pay the girl you got into trouble. And it hasn't stopped since."

"Help me this last time and it won't happen again," Alexander pleaded.

"I know it won't," Jackson told him. "Because I'm not giving you the money. It's time you learned your lesson."

"Don't make me beg," Alexander said. "I promise to change. Just give me a chance."

Jackson Cavendish wasn't convinced. "Consider all the money I've given you as an investment in your future," he said. "Now it's your turn to pay."

"I don't have any money," Alexander reminded him. "And I have no way of getting it."

"What happened to the allowance from your trust?"

"Already spent for the year, I'm afraid."

"Then this sounds like your problem, not mine."

"You don't understand how serious this is," Alexander whined. "It's one of the reasons I'm in Italy."

"What are you talking about?" Jackson asked, exasperated.

"I convinced Penelope and her father to see Dr Barnett in Como because I served with him in the war and he's a great psychiatrist."

"And he's not?"

Alexander shrugged. "I have no idea," he replied. "I remember him, but I really know nothing about him. A friend of mine said he saw him in Italy, so I convinced Penelope and Wellington to try the sanitarium there. It was quite easy, actually. They were familiar with Como; they used to go there on holiday before the war."

Jackson's irritation grew. "You're not making sense."

"I can't stay in London," Alexander pressed, "because my life is in danger. Don't you understand that? Bad men are after me. They already tried to collect and I didn't have the money. So now I'm hiding in Como."

Jackson Cavendish smirked. "I wouldn't call it 'hiding', not with Penelope's photograph in all the tabloids. The whole world knows where you are."

"But I doubt they'll go to Italy to find me," Alexander said, desperation in his voice. "Can't you give me the money? I'll repay you from my trust."

"I'm confident you'll find the money," Jackson said firmly. "It just won't come from my wallet."

"They already threatened to kill me," Alexander warned, using sympathy as a weapon.

Jackson Cavendish rose from his chair and started walking toward the door. "Ask your wife for the money," he suggested. "Or your father-in-law. This bank is closed."

Alexander sighed with despair. "I already tried to get money from Penelope," he said. "More than once and with different methods."

Jackson Cavendish turned as he was about to exit the room. "Maybe you need to try a little harder."

Chapter 9

"Penelope, I would like to discuss your nightmare," Dr Barnett said.

"It wasn't a nightmare," she insisted. She sat in a plush leather chair in his office while he sat behind her taking notes, just out of sight. "Adele tried to kill me."

"Maybe it was just a nightmare and you woke, confused and disoriented, and only thought Adele tried to kill you."

"How do you know she didn't?"

"Doesn't it seem strange?" he suggested, not willing to confront her but expressing doubt to help her reach her own conclusions. "Adele has been a nurse at this sanitarium for almost ten years and she never tried to kill anyone. She has an impeccable reputation. She also has nothing to gain by your death."

"You're assuming Adele has nothing to gain," she pointed out. "But you don't know that. You're a psychiatrist, not a detective."

"Then I'll ask you again, what does she have to gain?"

"Maybe someone paid her to kill me. Money is a powerful motive. Read the newspapers."

There were discrepancies in her story that he decided to exploit. "How could she have tried to kill you if you were by the door, waiting for her to enter your room?" he asked.

"She tried to smother me with my pillow," Penelope explained, "but left when I started screaming. When no-one came to my aid, and she knew it was safe, she came back."

"I suppose that might have happened," he admitted, pretending for her benefit that it could have. "But if she wanted to kill you, why didn't she make sure you were dead?"

"I kicked and screamed and punched her and she ran away. I was only protecting myself. When she came back, I was waiting for her."

He decided to explore her family dependencies. "Should we discuss this when your husband comes to visit?" he asked. "We need to keep him informed of threats on your life."

"He left for London," she said abruptly.

"I thought he just arrived?"

"He did, but it was a commitment he had made prior, a charity event for war widows." She paused, perhaps reminiscing. "He's always there for me," she continued. "I never would have got through this without him."

Barnett didn't reply. He knew a different Alexander Cavendish than Penelope did. But he wasn't willing to discuss it with a patient. He changed his focus. Maybe by repeating prior discussions, he might get different answers. "Is that the only time someone tried to kill you?" he asked.

"No, I told you someone made me take pills in Monte Carlo. I had been drinking and my mind wasn't clear."

"But Adele wasn't in Monte Carlo," he pointed out.

"I never said she was."

"Then who tried to kill you?"

"I don't know."

"Is it more than one person?"

She thought for a moment before replying. "There might be more than one killer, but it's orchestrated by the same person."

He listened to her, searching for sincerity. She believed emphatically that someone was trying to kill her. He had to somehow persuade her to unravel the mystery and conclude that it wasn't true.

"Penelope, let's identify the killer's motive. Then, perhaps, we'll reach a different conclusion."

"The first step in my recovery is to make everyone realise my life is in danger," she said, switching their roles. "What are you doing to guarantee my safety?"

"I have taken extra security precautions," he assured her. "The night staff will ensure your window is locked when you retire for the evening and they'll watch the area more carefully. And our security personnel will patrol the grounds, making sure no-one threatens you or any other patients."

"Do you think that will work?"

"Yes, I want you to be safe so we can concentrate on making you well again."

She sat back in the chair, arms folded across her chest. She seemed sceptical, even confused. "I'm only here for one reason," she said. "My life is in danger."

"There are other issues we need to address," he reminded her. "Mood swings and depression. The threats on your life are recent; your other issues are not."

"We talked about this before," she said. "I've been seeing psychiatrists for years and none did anything. If they failed, why would I ever think you can help me?"

He didn't have an answer. At least not yet. But he knew that, in time, he would. "That doesn't mean we'll walk the same path you already travelled. Give me the opportunity. Work with me."

She sighed, pensive. After a moment passed, she spoke. "Fine, I'll work with you. What do you want?"

"Tell me when the problems started. Was it when your mother died?"

She paused, hesitant, and a moment of awkward silence elapsed. "Yes, I suppose," she finally admitted.

"Can you tell me about it?"

"It was a train accident," she replied softly. She turned and looked out at the lake, as if willing the images away, just as he often did. "I was sitting next to her, but wasn't hurt. But I did watch her die."

"Unable to help her," Barnett added. "Because you were a child and you didn't have the skills."

"There was nothing I could do."

"Where were your father and brother?"

"My father was supposed to come, but had a business meeting to attend. He planned to join us the next day with my brother, who was away at prep school. We were going on holiday."

Barnett could feel her pain twenty years after the event occurred. "As horrific as the accident was, you surely don't think you're in any way to blame?" he asked.

"I could have helped her. I could have done something. But I only cried, confused and afraid."

"Which is what a child would be expected to do," he said, consoling her. "You have to understand that. Do you in any way blame your father?"

"Not really," she said. "But if he had been there, he might have been able to save her."

"But he wasn't there and we need to understand that. He wasn't trying to avoid anything. He didn't know there was going to be an accident. He was addressing the demands of his business. Just like any other day he wasn't there."

"He was much different after that," she said, her voice soft and far away, her eyes vacant. "I don't think he ever left my side, at least it didn't seem that he did."

"Does that bother you?"

She shrugged slightly. "Sometimes I feel like I took both their lives. I couldn't save hers and I ruined his."

Chapter 10

Penelope left her session and sat in the parlour of her suite, looking through the glass doors at the lake beyond. She liked Dr Barnett. He was kind and compassionate and seemed to want to help her, even though he didn't believe that her life was in danger. He also failed to recognise that any issues she might have were temporary. She knew that. But nobody else did, including him.

The void formed by her mother's death could never be filled; she realised that. But she thought of her often, usually daily, and as she got older the happy memories overshadowed the sad ones. She sometimes wished she could have a few more minutes with her – just so she could tell her how much she loved her.

It had been difficult growing up, since she was the only girl in school who didn't have a mother. She knew people felt sorry for her, always a bit kinder, more compassionate than they were to other children. She appreciated it, but it only made her feel different, as if she didn't belong and never would. And now that she was an adult, she realised she didn't quite fit with anyone or anything, even her husband.

Just when the pain of her mother's death began to fade, she lost her brother Oxford. He was the only person in the world that shared her pain, understood her loneliness, felt her loss. His death had come at the most terrible time, just as the war was coming to a close. The enemy was retreating, the light visible through a long tunnel of darkness, when Oxford's plane was shot down. The pain she felt when her mother died returned, sharper and deeper, and she couldn't cope. She drank, she took pills and looked for escapes that led nowhere. Her downward spiral gained momentum and, in a kaleidoscope of dreams and nightmares, fantasy merged with reality and she somehow lost track of who she was.

"And now no-one believes that someone is trying to kill me," she said loudly.

She heard a noise in the hallway, someone near the door, listening. She walked toward the French doors and studied a boat on the lake. It was anchored, two men standing, fishing poles in their hands. She watched to

46

see if they were catching any fish when one man pointed toward the sanitarium.

"I see them," she said to an empty room. "They're watching."

She moved away from the window and stood against the wall. She waited a few minutes and peeked around the drapes, looking at the boat.

There was a knock on the door and it opened tentatively. Maria, one of the nurses, leaned in. "You all right, Miss Penelope?" she asked in broken English, studying her curiously. "I hear you talk."

Penelope parted the drapes and pointed to the lake. "Look," she hissed.

Maria looked out and then back to Penelope. "What do I look at?" she asked, confused.

"The men in the boat are only pretending to fish."

"Why?" Maria asked, baffled.

"Because they're really watching my room," Penelope explained. "They want to kill me."

"Miss Penelope, no-one wants to kill you," Maria assured her. "I tell security about boat. They make them go away."

"You had better hurry," Penelope warned.

Maria looked at her watch. "I see other patients," she said. "But come back to see you. Make sure all right."

Maria closed the door but Penelope didn't hear any footsteps on the tiled floor. She suspected Maria stood in the hallway, listening. Someone was always listening. Penelope closed the drapes, inching them across the doors with a drawstring. The sunlight was gradually filtered until blocked completely, the drapes covering the glass and hiding the eyes of a prying world.

"I'll hide," she said loudly and then listened, as if waiting for a reply. "If they don't see me, they'll give up and go away."

She remained at the edge of the door, peeking between the jamb and drape, watching the boat. Whenever one of the men glanced toward the sanitarium, she ducked against the wall, closing the drape.

After ten minutes elapsed, one of the men put down his fishing pole and went to the helm. He started the engine, a wisp of grey smoke curling away from the vessel, and turned the wheel. The boat moved away from the shore, chugging farther out into the lake.

Penelope watched the image grow smaller until she could barely see it at all. She wasn't positive the men were watching her. They could have been studying the building, admiring the architecture, or watching a patient in another room. There was no way she could be sure. But she couldn't take any chances.

"It's safe," she said to an empty room. Maybe someone was still outside her door listening. Or maybe they weren't.

She left the drapes closed and went into her bedroom. She unlocked the window, studying the limbs of the juniper tree that stretched so close to the balcony railing. She opened the window and stood with her hands on the sill. The vertical windows were long and slender, the wall beneath them less than half a metre high.

The people at the sanitarium had taken her nail file; she had no weapon. Then she laughed. It seemed as if everyone thought they knew her. But none of them really did.

Chapter 11

Rose Barnett was raised in Clovelly, a cramped fishing village attractive to tourists because it was so picturesque – etched into the cliffs of Devon, a steep set of flagstone steps leading to the road that wound along the hill a hundred metres above the town. Her father was a fisherman, a kind man with weathered hands and a taut face who was close to his three daughters, spoiling and protecting them like fathers had done for thousands of years. Her mother managed a small souvenir shop for the many tourists that found the town so enchanting, and cared for her family, rarely seen without a smile.

Her mother was an avid reader and encouraged Rose to pursue her education, and she was a conscientious student devoted to the pursuit of knowledge, rarely seen without a book. She enjoyed asking the village elders about their lives, scribbling notes in a journal and promising to someday write a book about their adventures. Gifted with a generous intellect, she had the ability to use words to evoke emotion, to grasp readers' hearts and wrench them from their body, make them sing with joy, or force their mind to journey down a road it had never travelled. She published her first short story at the age of fourteen and several other successes followed through her teenage years. But just as adulthood approached and her career was about to be launched, the war intervened and the idyllic hamlet she called home was shattered, as were so many others. The young men volunteered to fight, leaving many of the fishing boats that provided the lifeblood of the town's economy empty and ghost-like.

For a young woman with a vivid imagination and a fascination for the unknown, the world stage suddenly seemed far more exciting than a charming village. And even though most of the civilised world would have been grateful to call Clovelly their home, Rose felt compelled to participate in the global calamity. She volunteered for nursing, even though she knew she might be assigned to a dangerous location, and postponed her writing career, knowing the experience would fuel future endeavours. She was trained in London, like so many other young women, and then sent to

France, totally unprepared for what she confronted: horrendous wounds, deadly diseases, life in the trenches, never-ending bombing. It was more than a kind heart could ever hope to bear but Rose endured, like millions of others, suffering silently and vowing to make the world better.

Her compassion for her fellow man, already deep-rooted from caring parents, grew exponentially and she developed a passion for those less fortunate, those impaired, wounded or disabled, those that couldn't fend for themselves. She fought for them, acted as both care-giver and protector, viciously attacking any threat posed, real or imagined. Protecting them, as she now protected Joseph Barnett.

She sat at her writing table in Como, wearing a lavender dress, her auburn hair pinned high on her head. She moved her pencil across the page, forming words in fluid cursive writing that was an art in its own. A black cat with a white face named Jack sat by her feet, and a white cat with a black face named Jill lay curled in her lap. They were her constant companions.

"How do you manage to work with those two wrapped around you?" Joseph Barnett asked as he leafed through a psychological journal.

She smiled and paused, petting each cat. "I'm used to it," she replied. "I can't think unless I hear them purring."

"What are you writing? Another book of war poems?"

"No, I want to try something different. The world needs to forget the war. Maybe we should welcome tomorrow and let go of yesterday."

He was quiet for a moment. "I think that's a marvelous idea," he agreed. "We all need to dream, to be optimistic. What's your new project?"

"It's called *Poems of Love*," she replied. "I just finished the first one. Would you like to read it?"

"Of course," he said, getting out of his chair and walking behind her. He looked over her shoulder and read the words so delicately jotted on the page:

'Through a misty morning after
Sprinkled with the night-time's dew,
I can see the bare horizon
And the path you point me to.
There could never be another you.

Through the haze of distant ages

Long since gone then born anew,
I can see the shapeless shadows
And the world you take me to.
There could never be another you.

Through a dark and stormy night,
Cursed by most but blessed by few
I can see the distant future
And the road you take me to.
There could never be another you.'

His eyes misted and he leaned over and kissed her on the top of the head.
"It's beautiful," he said. "Just like the author."
She turned, looking up at him, and smiled. "It's for you," she whispered.

Chapter 12

"Penelope and Oxford rarely left my side after their mother died," Wellington said sadly. "I played the role of both mother and father. Or at least I tried to."

"I think any parent would have done the same," Barnett said.

"I did have their nanny, Mrs Thistle," Jones said. "She was absolutely wonderful, a substitute mother, confidante, playmate, babysitter – whatever the situation demanded."

"You were very fortunate," Barnett agreed. "She must have been a tremendous asset."

"She was," he said, his eyes vacant. "But maybe I didn't do as well as I thought I did, especially given Penelope's current condition. And you know about Oxford. We lost him a week before the Armistice."

"I'm so sorry for the loss of your son." Barnett said sympathetically. "It was a horrendous conflict and the sacrifices offered won't ever justify the successes obtained."

Jones shrugged. "Victory at any cost," he murmured.

Barnett pondered his gnarled hand, his limp, and his disfigured face, the death and destruction that impacted continents. It was a hollow victory.

"We did what had to be done," Jones continued, "and the world is a better place for it."

... The stench of gunpowder soaked the trenches, the landscape littered like a cratered planet of limbless trees blotting the horizon, barbed wire stretching across it for miles with rotting bodies randomly scattered to decompose wherever they fell. When the bombing subsided, haunted screams punched the night as enemy and ally co-existed in zombie-like states of confusion and shock. The respite was brief; the battle waged once more and Barnett ran through pockmarked fields dragging his medical bag behind him. Injured lay on the moonscape with jagged gashes born by bullets and bombs, shrapnel and shells. He haphazardly spread bandages to stem the bleeding but boys still died in his arms, begging a merciful God
...

"Don't you agree, Doctor?"

Barnett smiled meekly. "I'm sorry, Mr Jones," he said. "The war ended three years ago, and I still don't know why it had to be fought."

Jones looked at him callously. "We didn't need to understand why it was fought," he snapped. "We only needed to fight it."

Barnett was quiet for a moment, not wanting to argue. He proceeded cautiously. "How did Oxford's death impact Penelope?" he asked.

"It devastated her," Jones replied angrily, "just as it devastated me. Oxford was our life – past, present and future. Now he's gone and nothing remains."

"I'm sure it was devastating," Barnett said with compassion. "Perhaps I didn't phrase my question correctly. How did his death impact Penelope's mental decline?"

Jones calmed, thought for a moment, and appeared to carefully collect his thoughts. "She always had issues," he admitted, "problems she couldn't solve, nightmares she couldn't forget. But her deterioration was more pronounced after her brother's death, and then steep and rapid during the last few months."

"I don't know what triggered her decline," Barnett said, "although I will in time. But I tend to doubt, even at this early stage, that any of her issues are rooted with you."

Jones rose and started to pace the floor. "I'm not an easy man to live with, I know that," he admitted. "I work constantly. It's my passion, my life. I suppose it's hard to understand. But I did the best I could."

Barnett was pensive, watching Jones struggle to maintain his composure. Some of the world's greatest psychiatrists had researched inner conflicts. An outward extrovert was often balanced by an inner introvert; outward logic stabilised inner emotion. Wellington Jones was conflicted. An outer logic overwhelmed his inner emotions. Maybe he had yet to grieve his son or maybe he never forgave himself for his wife's death but, whatever the reason, Wellington Jones needed help, probably as badly as his daughter did. He might one day break with no explanation, attacking a world he didn't understand or rambling incoherently about enemies that no longer existed. Or he might live the rest of his life broken and shattered but utterly harmless.

"Let's discuss Penelope's childhood," Barnett said. "I recognise the demands on your time, given your business and varied interests, and I was wondering if Penelope and Oxford went with you on your jaunts around the globe."

"Not at first," he said, his mind seeming to wander. He stood abruptly and paced the floor, either impatient or perhaps hiding his emotions. "But as Penelope got older, I did take her with me."

Barnett watched closely, fully aware of the man's internal struggle. "Give me some examples," he requested quietly.

Jones thought for a moment. "We started to take extended holidays when she was about eleven years of age," he said. "I thought it would be good for her to see different cultures and customs. Oxford normally went with us. As did Mrs Thistle, their nanny."

"How long were you gone and where did you visit?"

"The longest trip we took lasted three months," he replied. "We spent three weeks in Egypt studying tombs, a week in Tanzania observing an active volcano, and a week in Ethiopia examining primitive cultures. Then we did some mountain climbing in Switzerland." He smiled, a distant memory apparently returning. "That's where Penelope bested Oxford. She could climb anything."

While Jones was speaking, Barnett remembered a comment Penelope had made. She had to have a window open. She was a bit claustrophobic, as if she had lived in a cage, real or imagined. He wondered what prompted it. Egyptian tombs, perhaps?

"Were there any other extended holidays or business trips?" Barnett asked, again focused on the conversation.

Jones continued pacing. The discussion seemed to help him; pleasant memories clouding the pain. "At the age of thirteen, Penelope, Mrs Thistle and I went on a three-month trip to Asia," he said. "Oxford was in school so he didn't come with us. I enjoyed it very much. I think she did also."

"Which is all very interesting, Mr Jones, but hardly the life of a typical teenager."

"No, I suppose not," he agreed as he returned to his chair. "Although she led a charmed existence when compared to most. I ensured she and her brother wanted for nothing. And I was very protective."

"Where did she spend her childhood?" Barnett asked.

"At my estate in the English countryside," he said. "Just outside of London. She still spends a good bit of time there." He looked away, as if reminiscing. "I only wish we could be there now. And everything was like it used to be."

Chapter 13

"He's a good doctor," Wellington said as he sat in Penelope's suite. "I think you'll improve quickly and we'll be home in no time."

"I do like him," she admitted, "but he's no different to the others." She peered out of the French doors to the lake beyond, anxious and distracted.

"Give him time," Wellington suggested, studying her closely.

"If you think it's best then I'll cooperate."

"What are you looking at?" Wellington asked, unable to contain his curiosity.

"I'm looking for the men."

"What men?"

"The men that were in the boat the other day."

"What were they doing?"

"They were pretending to fish," she said. "But they were really watching me. They were trying to see into my suite."

Wellington's eyes misted, sad that his daughter could be so sick. "Why would they do that?" he asked, feigning confusion.

"Because they were waiting for me to go on the balcony. Then they were going to kill me."

He was sickened, but fought not to show it. He forced a weak smile. "Maybe they were just simple fisherman," he offered with a shrug. "There are many boats on the lake. And many people fish, both commercially and as a hobby."

"I don't think so," she said. She sprung from the couch and leaned against the wall beside the door, peeking through the drapes.

"What are you doing?"

"I thought I saw them," she said. "But it's a different boat." She turned and looked at him with alarm. "Do you think they would change boats?"

"I think they were fisherman," he emphasised. "They may have been discussing the sanitarium or something around it and since you were watching them it seemed as if they were interested in you."

She hesitated, appearing to digest his logic. "One of the men pointed toward my suite," she insisted. "That shows more than mild interest."

Wellington sighed and pensively looked away. After a moment, he invented a diversion. "I think I know who they were," he declared.

"Who?"

"Reporters," he explained. "They assumed you would have the best accommodations, so they surveyed rooms with balconies."

"I hadn't thought of that," she admitted. "But I guess it makes sense. There were reporters near the entrance on the day I arrived."

"I'm sure that's it. Your life isn't in danger, but we need to guard your privacy."

"They follow me everywhere," she said. "They were in Monte Carlo, too. But at least I feel safer now, knowing what's happening."

Wellington smiled, walked to his daughter and gave her a hug. "Good, I'm glad we solved that. Now, I really must go. I have some work to do."

****

Wellington Jones drove to his rented villa a few kilometres from the sanitarium. It was a large stucco building, beige with white trim, a stone patio abutting the lake with a bulkhead protecting it. Flagstone steps led into the water, for those that liked to swim. Jones had rented the villa several times throughout the years. It came complete with staff, some of whom had served him since he first arrived in Como almost twenty years before.

After he arrived, he grabbed his briefcase and went out onto the patio, sitting in the spring sun and watching the water. A butler appeared and set a glass of red wine on a wrought iron table beside his chair. Jones mumbled his thanks and studied the papers he had removed from his case. He had written his business plan for the banks in India in neat cursive writing, detailing the strengths of his global real estate empire and minimising its weaknesses. He included statistics on global economic cycles, impacts to real estate assets, and the average duration before downturns reversed. The report summarised extensive data in the concise, factual format he favoured. After reviewing the document twice, he added instructions to type the report and include company operating information before presenting it to the banks. He then sealed the report in an envelope and left it for the butler to take to Milan where it would be dispatched to Bombay.

He sipped his wine and looked at the envelope, bold letters identifying the address. The contents were critical to his company; they would dictate his future. Would his business survive and prosper, as it had for generations? Or would it collapse around him, divisions of the corporation falling like snowflakes meant to melt and disappear. At this point, he couldn't tell. But he needed resolution quickly. His liquid assets – cash and bonds easily converted to cash – were dwindling rapidly. He only had a few months' expenses remaining. Disaster waited on the horizon.

Chapter 14

There were several dimensions to Alexander Cavendish. He was an admired war hero, devoted husband and debonair aristocrat, but he also had a shadow – the Alexander Cavendish who had returned from the war. This silhouette thrived on danger and deceit, was immersed in forbidden pleasures like women, whisky and gambling, and suffered privately, seeking refuge in the sordid underworld few knew existed.

He stepped out of Mary Westcott's London townhouse just after midnight and cautiously looked in all directions. The woman was married to John Westcott, a member of Parliament who represented Liverpool, and she was Penelope's closest friend. But that didn't prevent the furtive, forbidden liaisons she often enjoyed with Cavendish.

Cavendish's marriage to Penelope had been built on a stable foundation, encouraged by their families, two similar dynasties joined in the interest of both parties like a business arrangement. It wasn't engulfed in the raging passion that ruled his affair with Mary, a stunning blonde with blue eyes, well educated, popular and vivacious. Cavendish found her so alluring, so irresistible, that he somehow managed more time with her than Penelope. Since Mary's husband was often in Liverpool, they usually met in the London townhouse. And when Westcott was in London, the lovers sometimes went to Liverpool. They even arranged exotic holidays – Paris, Monte Carlo, Barcelona – often with an unsuspecting Penelope only metres away.

He hurried down the street, hunched over, avoiding the prying eyes of the few pedestrians who wandered the streets that late in the evening. He was comfortable in the darkness, eluding the muted glow from street lamps, walking through worlds that most avoided. But as he delicately disappeared from his mistress's bedroom, he failed to notice two men who watched him closely. One was dressed well, his clothes expensive. The second was much larger than his companion, casually dressed, more like a working man.

Cavendish walked fifty metres, almost to the corner, when he looked over his shoulder and saw them. He altered his route and turned at the junction, increasing his pace, destined for a park that spread across a city block. A well-lit thoroughfare ran opposite it, a street he would normally avoid, but where he could hail a taxi and escape.

He wasn't sure who they were. But he knew he wasn't safe in London, not with the gambling debts he owed or the married women he wooed. It could be a jealous husband seeking revenge or an angry debt collector, he didn't know for certain. But he didn't want to stop and find out.

Cavendish again glanced over his shoulder, his heart beating a bit faster as the two men turned at the junction just as he did. He crossed the street and hurried through a wrought iron arch that marked the park's entrance, walking along a cobblestone path, hiding among trees and shrubs that bordered it. He quickened his pace, almost running. Thirty more metres and he would be safe, back on a main street with pedestrians and policeman, taxis and trolleys. Then he could vanish into the streets.

He was almost there when he heard footsteps. They were faint at first, barely discernible, but they grew louder with each second, like a drizzle turning to hail. He started running but managed only a step or two before a hand roughly grabbed his shoulder and spun him around. He was punched in the gut, the wind forced from his lungs. A second punch smashed into his face.

"Stop," he hollered, struggling to breathe. "What do you want?"

The larger man had hit him, and he now pinned Cavendish's arms behind his back. The smaller man faced him, standing in the shadows in a tailored suit. He had an ordinary face, could be mistaken for a dozen other men in the immediate vicinity, but had one trait that made him easy to identify: he wore white spats that covered his ankles and part of his polished black shoes.

"I want my money, Mr Cavendish," demanded Billy Flynn, a London gangster and loan shark. "I think I've waited long enough."

"I need more time," Cavendish said, his chest heaving, his breathing laboured. "Another week, maybe ten days."

"You're out of time," Flynn said. "I've been very patient."

"I bought the insurance policy," Cavendish reminded him, "just as you asked. That shows I'm good for the money."

"Yes, you did buy an insurance policy," Flynn agreed. "But that means someone has to be dead before I get my money. Although I prefer not to collect that way, I will if I have to."

"Two weeks and you'll have it," Cavendish promised.

"Jocko, can you persuade Mr Cavendish to pay his debt?" Flynn asked.

Jocko nodded, spun Cavendish around and punched him in the stomach, just below the sternum.

Cavendish groaned, crumbling to his knees, coughing and vomiting. "Stop!" he begged. "I'll get the money."

Jocko reached into his coat pocket and withdrew a short nightstick. He swung it forcefully, smacking Cavendish on the side of his head, raising a welt and breaking the skin, watching with a sick grin as blood oozed down Cavendish's face. Jocko then landed a second blow in the same location as Cavendish yelped with pain.

"Does that help you understand?" Billy Flynn asked.

"Yes, it does," Cavendish said, his head pounding as if his skull had been broken. He held his hands up in surrender. "Please, stop. I'll have the money in a few days. I promise."

"Not good enough, mate," Billy Flynn said. He flung his foot forward, the toe driven into Cavendish's face, his nose crunching.

Cavendish rolled to the ground, barely conscious, and lay in a foetal position. Jocko stood behind him, kicking him in the back, near the kidney.

"Stop, I'll get the money," Cavendish gasped as blackness overwhelmed him. "I promise."

"Make sure that you do," Flynn said. "Be here tomorrow night at 10 p.m. or I'll come find you. And I'll cut you when I do." He withdrew a slender knife from a sheath in his right pant leg and put the blade against Cavendish's check, letting him feel the coldness of the steel.

"Hey, what's going on over there?" a policeman called. He was leaving the main street and hurrying toward them.

Flynn put the knife away and he and Jocko started to flee. "Tomorrow, Mr Cavendish," he hissed. "It's your last chance."

Neither Cavendish, his attackers, nor the approaching policeman noticed another man, older, slim, well dressed, who stood in the shadows. He watched, not intervening. Just as he had been doing for days.

Chapter 15

Penelope sat in the leather chair, Barnett just behind her, as their session started. He watched her get comfortable, looking around the room and briefly fixing her gaze on the bust of Shakespeare. He waited a moment more for her mind to stop wandering and then began.

"Penelope, I want to discuss some of the trips you took with your father," he said, initiating their discussion. "Do you remember watching an erupting volcano?"

"Yes, I do. But the volcano didn't erupt. It only rumbled and spewed some ash. It was actually very boring."

"Any trips to Hong Kong, Singapore or India?"

"Yes, they were interesting, especially India, but nothing unusual happened, assuming that's what you're looking for. I spent most of time with Mrs Thistle, my nanny."

"Did you like Mrs Thistle?"

"I love Mrs Thistle," Penelope clarified. "She still lives on my father's estate. She was as good to me as any mother could be." She turned in the chair and looked at him.

"Is anything wrong?"

"Yes, you're asking the same questions as the other psychiatrists. We'll get nowhere if that's your approach. We need to find out who's trying to kill me."

"I need your background information to assess trauma," he explained. "We need to understand why certain events have been repressed, eventually leading to the emergence of your symptoms."

She yawned and then spoke. "Yes, I know. The others said the same thing."

"How about your trip to Egypt?"

"There were several, primarily the Valley of the Kings."

"What is the Valley of the Kings?" he asked. It was a term he hadn't heard.

"It's an area near Luxor where pharaohs were buried during a period known as the New Kingdom," she informed him. "Most people are more familiar with the pyramids, which are in northern Egypt and from an era known as the Old Kingdom."

He was impressed with her intellect, as he was when they first met. "Did you like going in the tombs?" he asked.

"No, I hated it," she said, shivering noticeably. "They're dark, cramped and scary."

"Why was it scary?" he asked, noting her reaction.

"It felt like death," she replied. "Think about it. They are tombs."

"Do you have any specific memories about the tombs?"

"Yes, I do," she said, folding her arms across her chest.

He watched her movements, perhaps subconsciously protective. "And what might that be?" he asked.

She uncrossed her arms and sighed, as if tiring of the conversation. "No-one tried to kill me there," she said sarcastically. "But someone tried to kill me here."

He hid a smile, impressed with her determination, and wrote some notes. He thought about her mild claustrophobia, the need to have a window open while she slept. "Do you think the tombs caused nightmares," he asked, "or maybe the need to have windows open when you sleep?"

She turned and eyed him strangely. "Why are you asking me all of this?" she asked. "Do you think I have some dark secret to reveal? The tombs were no worse than the trenches during the war."

... Minutes seemed like months in hell as time and space merged in never ending ticks of a pocket watch until three years in trenches of mud and putrid water with rats and lice and the stench of an abstract, underground city covered with earth and sandbags and protected by barbed wire had slowly passed.

The smoky haze never dissipated, hanging heavy on a cratered landscape of destruction – dead trees, limbs blown away, leaves long gone devoid of all aspects of life. Many endured and adapted while others did not and never would and created cocoons within the walls to escape what could never be escaped, hoping for seconds of precious silence or overwhelmed by months of manic warfare.

He tried to help them, he tried to help them all, but the vacant eyes of the corpses came to haunt him through the days and into an endless string of nights causing a tortured agony that never waned, its strength replenished by a determined enemy and the seemingly unlimited supply of innocent bodies. Even the stillness, that eerie silence punctuated by bombing at both ends, created an obscene world so surreal that it seemed a different place and time, an era yet to come or long since left behind. And then the fighting resumed and boys died and men cried and wives had no husbands and children had no father and mothers and fathers had no son and ...

"Doctor?"

"I'm just trying to understand what traumas you may have experienced," he said in a soft, measured cadence, struggling to control his own anguish.

She paused and took a deep breath. "That's fine," she said. "But talk about something else. My childhood was different. Just accept it. I have."

"Shall we talk about your brother?" he asked

"No, we shouldn't," she replied sharply. "I don't want to discuss my brother's death. It was hard enough when it happened, I don't want to re-live it."

"It might be helpful to discuss it."

"No, it wouldn't."

He paused, reflective, considering another of her life-altering events. "Why don't we talk about your wedding?" he suggested. "You experienced several changes in a short period of time – your brother's death, the end of the war and your wedding."

"There's not much to talk about," she said softly. "We've known each other most of our lives, fell in love and got married."

"Are you happy?"

"I have a devoted husband, a war hero, a man so dedicated to helping others that he's in London at a charity event for war widows. How could anyone be unhappy with such a marvellous man?"

He paused. She didn't answer his question. He made remarks on his pad and moved on. "Let's discuss how you felt the day before your wedding," he requested.

"Let's not," she said curtly. "I want to talk about whoever is trying to kill me. Someone was watching me the other day, from the lake."

"Yes, I know. Maria, one of the nurses, told me about it." He paused, wanting to phrase his questions delicately. "Did they approach the sanitarium?" he asked.

"No, they pretended to fish," she replied. "After a while, they went to a different part of the lake. My father said they were probably reporters."

"Yes, they probably were," he said, although he knew they were fisherman. But if she thought they were reporters, and not someone trying to kill her, he wouldn't dispute it. "Let's discuss some of the other doctors who treated you. I'm interested in their methods and opinions."

"I don't know why. None were successful."

"I understand that. But if we don't want to waste our time together, we should avoid revisiting what they may have done."

"They talked about the same issues we do. My mother's death, how my father coped, was it difficult travelling around the world with him, was I afraid in the tombs. They talked and talked and talked and nothing happened. I never got better. I got worse. And then Oxford died and I spiralled out of control."

"It was a time of tremendous turmoil for you," he observed. "You lost Oxford but you gained Alexander."

"Alexander had already been part of my life."

"Except he was gone during the war," Barnett probed. "Many men were different when they returned from the war."

"At least they returned," she said. "Oxford didn't."

Barnett scribbled more notes on the pad. He found the confluence of emotions interesting, a triangulation of death, new life, the war's finalisation with friends returning, some not, some the same, some different. He may have stumbled on the trigger to her decline, hidden somewhere in that tangled web.

"What about your relationships," he continued. "Were you involved with anyone prior to your marriage?"

"There were a few men in my life before I met Alexander."

"Was there anyone you thought you might marry?"

"Yes, a Scot named Ian McKinley. He was the love of my life."

He thought her choice of words interesting. Why wasn't her husband the love of her life? He wanted to learn more. "Tell me about him," he said.

"He was devilishly handsome and in tremendous physical shape." She laughed and added, "If you know what I mean."

"I think I read something about that in the tabloids. He was quite a bit older than you, wasn't he?"

"Age is irrelevant. Some people are old at thirty, others are young at fifty."

"That's true," Dr Barnett admitted. "Why did that relationship end?"

"It doesn't matter. But we were very well matched – intellectually, culturally, traditionally. We were perfect together."

"What happened?" he asked. "We need to talk about it."

"No, we don't," she insisted. "Let's talk about your relationships before you were married."

Barnett ignored her. "Tell me about your last relationship before you met your husband. What was the man like?"

"He was a bullfighter," she said. "I met him on holiday in Spain."

"Were you terribly upset when the relationship ended?"

"No."

"Depressed?"

"Not really." She started laughing.

"What's so funny?"

"I was thinking of a show I saw in London. It was a comedian who was a ventriloquist. Everything the comedian said was nice, but everything his dummy said was nasty."

The conversation had strayed. He let it continue. "Did the bullfighter like comedians?" he asked.

She turned and looked at him strangely. "How would I know?"

"I assumed it was a close relationship and that you shared your experiences, your likes and dislikes, thoughts and dreams. I assumed you were devastated when it ended."

She laughed and then said, "You assumed wrong. He was Spanish. We didn't even speak the same language."

"Did you think he was trying to kill you?"

"No, of course not," she replied. "Why should I?"

"Then why do you think someone is trying to kill you now?"

"Because someone is."

Chapter 16

"Alexander!" Penelope exclaimed as she rushed to greet him. "What happened?"

His face was battered, purple bruises under each eye, a narrow bandage across the bridge of his broken nose. He limped toward her, holding his side, and hugged her.

"Darling, you look horrible," she said as she led him to a sofa. "Are you all right?"

"Yes, I'm fine," he said, flinching as he sat down. "I had a nasty motor car accident after leaving the charity for the war widows. The police said I was lucky to live through it."

She sat beside him. "My poor darling," she whispered, kissing him. "Is it painful?"

"Yes, just a bit. Nothing too serious. It looks worse than it is."

"Why did you risk travelling?" she asked. "You should have stayed in London. Your parents could have looked after you."

"I considered it," he admitted, "but I was worried about you. And I can recover here as easily as London."

"Are you absolutely certain you're all right?" she repeated. "You look ghastly. Should Dr Barnett have a look at you?"

"No, it's better now than it was, although the pain can be intense."

"Oh, my poor Alexander," she said, holding him. "I can't even help you. I'm locked up in a lunatic asylum."

"Don't worry," he said. "I'll be all right."

"What happened?"

"Some scoundrel ran me off the road, right into a building."

"You're lucky you weren't killed!"

"It was horrible," he told her, "but it could have been worse. Some pedestrians were injured, too, but not too seriously. There was a lot of property damage, though, especially after the fire."

"Fire? What fire?"

"The petrol tank," he explained. "A bystander had dragged me from the car by then, or I would have been burned alive."

"Alexander! My Lord! What a disaster! What happened to the other driver?"

"I don't know," he said with a shrug. "That's the sorry part of it, especially with all the damage."

"He drove away?"

"Yes, and very quickly," he told her. "And, of course, there were no witnesses. A crowd gathered after the crash, but no-one saw what caused it."

"Did you summon the police?"

"I didn't. I was unconscious. But the man who rescued me did."

"And they couldn't arrest the person responsible?" she asked sceptically.

"I'm afraid not," he replied. "He was long gone by the time the authorities arrived. And with no witnesses, the police even doubted my story."

She sat back on the sofa and shook her head with disbelief. "At least you're all right," she said, relieved. "That's all that matters. What else did the doctor say?"

"He said there are no serious injuries and I'll recover fully in a few weeks."

"Oh darling, this is horrible," she sympathised, tenderly touching his face.

"But it's more than the injuries," he said sadly.

"I suppose your automobile is damaged beyond repair."

"Absolutely destroyed," he said. "And the building was severely damaged, especially with the fire. It housed three storefronts, so all the merchandise was ruined too,"

"How dreadful," she said, caressing his arm. "It's fortunate no-one was killed."

"It is," he agreed. "What a horrible scene, with glass and bricks everywhere. And then the fire destroyed what was left. That's what makes the damages so horrendous."

"What damages?" she asked.

"I'm liable for all the costs."

"Alexander, that's ridiculous," she said, appalled. "How can you be responsible for damages? Another driver ran you off the road. Surely there's something you can do."

"I don't think so," he told her. "At least that's what the police said. And I already went around to my solicitor."

"What did he say?"

"He agreed with the police," he said. "I have a week or so to raise fifteen thousand pounds to cover the damages."

"Fifteen thousand pounds?" she asked, shocked by the amount. "That would pay for a tremendous amount of damage."

"It's more than the stores and merchandise," he continued. "The flats above them were also ruined. The fire and smoke, and then with the building collapsing."

"I still don't see how you're responsible. The building must be insured."

"It is," he said. "Fifteen thousand pounds is for damages not covered. At least that's how my solicitor explained it. I was nauseous when he told me."

"Are you going to pay?"

He paused, hesitant, as if reluctant to confide in her. "I can't," he said softly, "I've already spent the allowance from my trust this year. I gave far too much to the war widows' charity fund. I have no idea how I can come up with that much money. Unless I ask my father."

"Maybe he can loan it to you. At least until you get more from the trust."

He turned and looked at her, as if struck with an idea. "Maybe you can give it to me?" he suggested.

She sat back in the chair, pensive. "Alexander, I don't know," she said warily. "I just gave you money for that old gambling debt." She eyed him sternly, suddenly suspicious. "But only after you swore you would never gamble again."

"And I haven't," he assured her. "Not after that; it almost destroyed our marriage. I won't let anything like that happen again."

"Ten thousand pounds is a lot of money to lose gambling," she scolded.

"I promised you I would never gamble again," he reminded her. "I just need to get through this mess and then I can devote all my efforts to making you well."

She studied him closely, still finding the explanation unusual. "The damages shouldn't be your responsibility," she insisted. "I think we should talk to my father about it. His solicitor can investigate."

"I'm not sure that's a good idea," he said. "Besides, my solicitor already has."

"Why not get a second opinion?"

"The damages have to be paid within ten days or additional penalties may be assessed. I don't want your father bothered with it. I need to solve my own problems."

"I think we should ask him."

"No, that's all right," his said, appearing overwhelmed. "I'll think of something."

"I'll get the name of another solicitor and we'll get this fixed. I can't fathom you owing fifteen thousand pounds because someone ran you off the road."

"Hopefully you're right," he said.

She paused, briefly wondering if he was lying before discounting it. "How was London otherwise," she asked. "Are your parents well?"

"Yes, I dined with them on my arrival. Both are fine."

"Did you happen to see Mary?" she asked. "I miss her terribly. I wish she would come visit me."

He shifted in the chair. "No, I didn't," he said. "I forgot to check on her. But I'm sure she's well, enjoying the life of a politician's wife."

Chapter 17

Rose Barnett sat just outside her cottage with Lake Como sprawled before her and the mountains stretched behind her. Flowers peppered the property, beds spaced carefully throughout and accented by trellises, all defined by stone walkways. Red roses climbed a white wooden trellis near the roadway; yellow roses scaled an arched trellis beside a stone patio. Beds of flowers boasted lilies, daffodils and leontopodium, or 'lion's paw', a woolly bud with white hairs, the colours all carefully mixed like a rainbow.

Joseph Barnett was an avid gardener. His ability to nurture flowers and plants from seeds to maturity, splashing the landscape in a kaleidoscope of colours, was a gift that few could match. He brought life to the Italian countryside after enduring death in the French trenches. Beautiful flowers that twisted on trellises had replaced grey faces that lay straight upon stretchers. His gardens gave him solace; they were his sanctuary. And he spent many an hour with his hands in the soil or pruning shrubs and vines, shaping his creations into a simple beauty all could admire.

Rose loved her husband and had from the minute she met him. She had fixed a broken man, nurturing him just as he fostered his flowers. He had blossomed from a bedridden shadow, drowning in nightmares that killed the innocent to an active doctor chasing his dreams to cure the afflicted. But just when their goals were reached, with Rose an award-winning poet and Joseph a renowned psychiatrist, their war-time nemesis Alexander Cavendish had come back from hell. He upended the quaint serenity of Como, reviving a world both had willed away, storing it with memories that were best forgotten. They despised the man, having every right and reason to do so.

Joseph had changed since Cavendish arrived. Once calm and compassionate he had gradually become irritated and impatient. He probably hadn't noticed, but Rose had. But he was such a good doctor, his patients always paramount, that he sometimes searched for goodness when only evil existed. Rose offered no reminders; if Joseph wanted to believe Cavendish had changed, then she would let him. But she would never be convinced. She searched for ways to erase Cavendish from their lives, even though she knew she couldn't. She gained comfort knowing his presence was temporary; Penelope would eventually be well and they would go. But for the present, he was a threat to their very existence. Just as he always had been.

She thought of England and how much she missed it. Even a paradise like Como, with breathtaking scenery, peace and tranquility, couldn't replace her home. She missed her parents and her sisters, her friends in Clovelly, her neighbours, some of the fishermen who were friends of her father. But she couldn't return. She knew that and so did they, but they didn't know why. She didn't want them to. Still, she had much to be thankful for. A loving husband, a successful career doing what she had always wanted, loyal readers, a loving family even if she couldn't see them, and many friends in her adopted home. But there was still something missing. She felt it in Joseph, too. Como had been good for them. It had healed them, or at least started the process. But it wasn't a destination. It was part of the journey. And it was time to move on.

She picked up her notepad from the tiny oval table that sat beside the wooden chair. She had written several pieces for her book, *Love Poems,* and she was excited about her new project. Unlike her haunting war remembrances, her current work was still emotional but in a strong, tender way. It celebrated the bond between two people who devote their lives to each other. She would dedicate her book to Joseph.

She heard footsteps and saw Joseph coming towards her, a leather briefcase in his hand. "How was your day?" she called, smiling as he approached.

"It went well," he announced.

"How's Lafite?" she asked, referring to the French artist who had severed his ear.

"Tiptoeing forward," he replied. "But I'm afraid he could be with us for quite some time. I was also given a new patient today, an American."

"An American?" she asked. "Why did they come all the way to Italy?"

"I'm not sure," he replied with a shrug. "I suppose his family can afford it. And it's so peaceful here."

"What's wrong with him?" she asked as she stood, stepped around the cats that lay by her feet, and hugged him.

"He suffered long episodes of heavy bombing," he explained, "and he's had some sort of reaction, a nervous affliction. His entire body continually trembles. His name is Bobby Taylor, from Bath, Maine."

"That sounds serious," she said as they both sat. "What's his prognosis?"

"I think it's too early to tell. But his recovery will be challenging."

"How's Penelope?"

"She's making progress, but slowly."

"Maybe her stay at the sanitarium will be short," she said, secretly hoping it was.

"I am optimistic," he admitted.

"She has the best psychiatrist on the continent," Rose pointed out, proud of the man she had married. "I'm confident she'll be well soon."

"I hope you're right," he said. "If nothing else, we've defined the beginning. And that's the first step taken to reach the end."

Chapter 18

Wellington Jones fired his shotgun for the twentieth time, watching the clay pigeon burst in mid-air.

"Punteggio perfetto, signore," announced the attendant at the shooting range. Perfect score, sir.

"I'm impressed," Alexander Cavendish declared. "I'm no competition."

"You're injured," Jones said, smiling at his son-in-law. "You have an excuse. If you hadn't had the accident your score would match mine. It usually does."

"Non molti sono perfetti," the attendant informed them. Not many are perfect.

"Ho sparato tutta la mia vita," Jones replied in accented Italian. I've been shooting my whole life.

"Sei molto bravo," the attendant praised him. You're very good.

Jones nodded and switched to English, his Italian limited. "Thank you. My whole family is. Oxford was the best. He never missed. And then the war …"

"Sì, signore, la guerra," the attendant agreed. Yes, sir, the war.

"I served with Allenby," Jones stated proudly. "A front-line command. No London office for me."

"Sì signore," the man said, apparently not understanding. Yes, sir.

"Not for a minute. I went to France as soon as I could. I led my men over the top, through no-man's land, and straight into the enemy trenches."

The attendant only nodded.

"Alexander was there, too," Jones informed him. "He's a war hero."

"Different regiment," Cavendish clarified. "Same theatre."

"Honour the dead and rejoice with the living," Jones declared. He looked at the attendant, knowing he didn't understand what they had said. But he politely listened anyway, catching a word or two. Jones reached into his pocket and withdrew some lira and handed it to the man.

"Grazie, signore."

Wellington Jones and Alexander Cavendish left the shooting range and climbed into a chauffeured automobile. They had spent the afternoon there, shooting target and skeet, rarely if ever missing, Jones not missing at all. He knew guns as well as he knew business. And he was a perfect shot.

"I have a rather delicate matter to discuss," Cavendish related as they drove back to Como.

"What is it?" Jones asked.

"It's a financial dilemma," Cavendish explained, "due to the accident I had."

"What sort of dilemma?"

"Significant damage to buildings, merchandise, personal property," Cavendish replied. "I'm liable for some of it. Fifteen thousand pounds."

"That's a lot of money," Jones said warily. The situation seemed strange, but he didn't know the details. His son-in-law was a good man and, if he was in trouble, Jones would try to help him.

"I was hoping you could loan it to me."

"What happened to the money from your trust?"

Cavendish sighed, looking sheepish. "I was a bit too generous with the war widows' charity fund," he replied.

"A good cause," Jones muttered, thinking. He was in no position to lend money, especially with his current liquidity crisis. "What about your father?"

"He initially offered to help," Cavendish said, "but then declined. He's trying to teach me to better manage money prior to inheriting the entire trust."

Jones tried to think of a solution that he wasn't involved in. He couldn't afford to give fifteen thousand pounds to his son-in-law. "Alexander, I don't understand how you're liable for anything," he said thoughtfully. "You told me someone ran you off the road."

"Yes, and witnesses verified it. But my solicitor confirmed my liability."

"I'll have my solicitor take a look. It wouldn't hurt. Get all the information together and give it to me. Then we'll decide what's best."

The driver dropped Cavendish off at the cottage and Jones directed him to a café in the centre of Como, picturesque and known for fine food. The building was several centuries old, constructed of timber and stucco, and overlooked a small square. A dozen white, wrought iron tables were perched along a railing, offering a generous view of the quaint village. He sat at an outdoor table and ordered a mug of beer, watching people as they passed by. He liked Como. It symbolised peace and tranquility as well as strength, the sheer force of nature somehow transposed on those that lived in the mountains' shadow.

Twenty minutes later a man joined him. He was slender, well dressed, a few years older than Jones. He removed his hat and put it on the empty chair, exposing silver hair, short and manicured. His name was William Cain. He ordered a beer.

"How was your trip, Mr Cain?" Jones asked.

"Uneventful, Mr Jones," he replied. "The trains run well."

"Will you be staying for a while?"

"I hadn't planned to. But after arriving I think a few days might be nice. Unless you need me to stay longer, sir."

"Tell me what you've discovered and then I'll decide."

William Cain withdrew a notebook from his shirt pocket. "I'm afraid this will be a bit disconcerting," he warned.

"In what way?"

"Shocking, sir."

"What did you find?"

"I found a man that lives two lives," Cain explained. "One in the light, the other in darkness."

"I don't understand," Jones muttered. "I only asked you to investigate some minor suspicions."

"I'm afraid I've uncovered much more."

Jones was stunned. He sipped his beer, wondering what Cain could have possibly discovered. "Please, continue," he said quietly.

"Where shall I start, sir – the women or the gambling?"

Jones felt his world unravelling. He thought his perfect daughter had the perfect husband. Now he was about to learn otherwise. "Start with the women," he said softly.

"Mr Cavendish is currently having an affair with Mary Westcott, the politician's wife."

Jones frowned, the revelation like a knife to the heart. "And my daughter's best friend," he informed him. "She was chief bridesmaid at her wedding."

"Yes, I know, sir. A delicate situation."

"How often does he see her?"

"Quite often, I'm afraid. Whenever he's in London, which has been frequent lately. Last week he was at her townhouse three of the four nights he was there. They also met in Hyde's Park, an apparent picnic." He leaned across the table and whispered, "I witnessed some sexual activity, sir. Even in a public place such as that."

Jones's face hardened, his eyes lit with anger. "If Cavendish were here I'd strangle him with my bare hands."

"Careful, sir. There's better ways to handle the situation, if that's the path you choose."

"Previous to last week, how often have they been together?" Jones asked, still hoping for a minor indiscretion.

"According to some of my sources, it's been going on for at least two years, sir, and probably prior to the wedding. When he's in London, he manages to see her daily. Usually at her townhouse, so I have no report on what actually occurs there. But I'm sure you can imagine, just as I can."

"I don't think I need to," Jones said with disgust. "Especially after what you saw in the park. John Westcott is a friend of mine. Do I tell him?"

"No, sir. I think not."

"What else?"

"I'm afraid there are others, sir. One in London, a Miss Helen Wentwick, who has actually given birth to a child, a boy named Harold. Although Mr Cavendish no longer sees the woman, or the child for that matter, he does provide a thousand pounds a year for the boy's welfare. And his father made a one-time payment of ten thousand pounds. To keep the woman quiet, I suppose, sir."

Jones's face turned crimson. "I heard rumours, but they were never substantiated," he mumbled.

"They are now, sir."

"Are there more?"

"Yes, sir. A woman in Paris and one in Monte Carlo, casual acquaintances, but secretive meetings."

"Is it safe to assume Cavendish never intended to honour his wedding vows?"

"Quite frankly, sir, I don't think he ever wanted to marry Miss Penelope. Not for love, anyway. I'm sorry, sir. But you asked me to observe him."

"Yes, I know," he said, "and I appreciate the work you've done. I just didn't expect the results. Perhaps a few dalliances, but not what you've described." His emotions shifted from anger to despair. Poor Penelope. She had enough problems, just getting well. She didn't need this. He had to help her; he had to find a solution.

"I understand your concern," Cain continued. "It's a difficult situation."

Jones considered Cavendish's loan request. "How are his finances?" he asked.

"He receives funds from a trust, as you know. His living expenses are paid and he receives an annual stipend of twenty-five thousand pounds. When he reaches the age of thirty, he receives the entire trust. And it's a sizeable amount, sir."

"That's certainly enough for a man to live on."

"I'm afraid not, sir. Not with his gambling issues. He spent his annual allowance already and I'm afraid he's in debt to some nasty characters."

"Then his father can solve his problems," Jones said angrily, "just like he did with the girl he got in trouble."

"I believe that's why he went to London," Cain informed him. "But something went wrong. His father didn't cooperate and I'm afraid young Cavendish paid the price."

"What do you mean?"

"He never paid his debtor. I observed two thugs beat him pretty badly. I heard one say he had a week to come up with the money, I think it's about fifteen thousand pounds."

Jones shook his head, disgusted. "He tried to get it from me," he said, "and I'm sure he'll try to get it from my daughter. He had a phoney story about an accident."

"I think he came to Como to escape his debtor, or the thugs they have leaning on him. But they'll find him. And when they do, I'm afraid it'll be a sorry day for Mr Cavendish."

A smile suddenly crossed Wellington Jones's face. "Maybe these thugs will solve my problem for me," he said and then paused, pensive. "Tell me something, Mr Cain."

"What's that, sir?"

"What happens to the trust should Alexander Cavendish die?"

"I believe Miss Penelope inherits it, sir."

Chapter 19

Penelope's next session was at 10 a.m. When 10:30 arrived and she had not, Barnett asked Olivia, his receptionist, to summon an orderly to find her. At 10:50, Penelope Jones walked into his office, her eyes wide, her face pale.

"Are you all right?" Barnett asked.

She hurried to the French doors and stood by the wall, peeking through the glass. She studied the lake, the shoreline and even mountains visible in the distance. She turned after a moment had passed, apparently reassured, and plopped on the sofa, propping her feet upon the table.

"What were you looking at?" he asked, baffled by her behaviour.

"I wanted to make sure it was safe."

He frowned. "Penelope, you're safe here," he insisted. "We've discussed this many times."

"I'm not sure I agree with you," she grumbled.

"I also expect you to be on time," he said, lightly scolding her. "I have other patients. You need to be considerate of them and me."

"I can't worry about other people," she said nonchalantly.

"Why not?" he asked, realising it was going to be a difficult session.

"Because someone is trying to kill me. I need to worry about myself."

"Penelope, I'm trying to help you," he emphasised. "And so are many others who care about you. Be considerate of them; they're considerate of you."

She frowned and looked away, apparently not interested. "Except whoever is trying to kill me," she muttered softly.

"Why were you late for your appointment?" he asked, ignoring her.

"I was followed by a strange man. I had to lose him before I came here."

Barnett looked at her curiously. "Why do you think he was following you?"

"Because he was."

"Where did you first see him?"

"He was in the corridor when I left my suite, well dressed, tall with grey hair."

"Maybe he was visiting a patient," he suggested.

"He wasn't acting like a visitor," she said.

"What did you do when you saw him?"

"I went it the opposite direction."

"How did he react?"

"He followed me," she replied, "so I walked to the end of the hallway and ran down the back steps. I sat in the lobby, near the arched window, and hid behind that broad-leafed plant."

"Did you see the man again?"

"Yes," she stated emphatically. "He came down the stairs a few minutes later. He stopped by the receptionist, pacing the floor."

"Maybe he was waiting for someone," Barnett offered.

"I'm sure he was," she said. "He was waiting for me. He wanted to kill me."

"Penelope, even if the man did want to kill you, he wouldn't do it in the lobby. Why didn't he do it in the rear stairway?"

"I'm not sure," she replied. "Maybe he couldn't catch me."

"What did you do next?"

"I waited as he paced the floor, staring at his watch. After fifteen minutes, he went back up the stairs."

"And what did you do?"

"I hid for ten more minutes and then came to your office."

Barnett decided to placate her. "I'll have my receptionist find out who he was."

"I'll feel much safer knowing he won't be back."

Barnett jotted down some notes and then looked back at Penelope. "Can you give me a better description of the man?"

"My husband returned from London," she said, ignoring him. "He was in a motor car accident and badly injured."

Barnett studied her closely, jarred by the abrupt change in the conversation. "I'm sorry to hear that," he said, even though he wasn't. "How severe are his injuries?"

"Mostly cuts and bruises, but he did break his nose."

"I would be happy to recommend a physician."

"Thank you, I appreciate that but it's not necessary."

Barnett paused a respectful amount of time, as if showing compassion for Cavendish, before continuing the session. "Penelope, how many times have you felt like someone has tried to kill you?"

She gazed out the French doors. "The snow on the mountaintops is melting," she observed. "Only a little is left on the peaks."

He studied her closely, the changing expression on her face, the inability to concentrate on any given topic for more than a few minutes. Something wasn't right; he just didn't know what it was. "I want to discuss the attempts on your life," he said.

"Yes, but I don't."

"You discussed nothing else at our last session."

"So," she argued. "Now I don't feel like it."

"Fine," he said. "What shall we talk about? How about Shakespearean England?"

"We already discussed it," she said sullenly.

"When were you first aware that you had lived in Shakespeare's time? Was it after writing your position paper in college?"

"Yes, I think so."

"Maybe you felt familiar with the time period because of your research and only thought you had lived during that time."

"I don't think so," she replied. "I was drawn to that era because I had been there before."

He could see the conversation leading nowhere. He tried another topic. "Let's talk about your nightmares," he suggested. "How often do you dream of death?"

"I don't remember."

"Penelope, how could you not know?" he asked sceptically. "That's not a difficult question. Is it often? Once a month? Twice a year?"

She yawned and said, "I don't want to talk about nightmares."

He paused, wondering what she was thinking and why she wouldn't share it. "I've developed some theories about your condition," he informed her.

She leaned forward, as if sharing a secret. "I'm crazy, aren't I?" she whispered and then grinned.

He smiled, pleased her mood was improving. "No, I don't think so," he said. "Difficult at times, like now, but not crazy."

"Then what's wrong with me?"

"I must probe a bit further," he said. "I think your condition is rare, but something we can address."

She frowned. "Doctors have studied me my entire life," she reminded him. "Whatever you discovered has already been found."

"Perhaps," he said. "But I don't think so. Especially since your condition has worsened in the last few years."

"Tell me what my problem is," she requested. "You have my attention, now."

"I had best not say anything until I'm certain," he said. "I have a bit more research to do."

"Is this ailment curable?"

"I believe so," he answered without making promises. "Although it's only recently been identified in psychological circles."

"Do you know how many doctors have told me they can cure me? Forgive me if I don't believe you."

"You'll believe me when you start to improve."

"Give me something to believe in," she said. "I want to know who's trying to kill me, I really do. And I want it to end."

He was quiet for a moment, wondering whether to continue. He finally decided to share his conclusion, observing her reaction as he did so. "I think we're dealing with two separate issues," he said.

"Wonderful," she replied, rolling her eyes. "I can't wait to hear them."

He smiled, amused by her reaction. "Your life has been marred by trauma," he continued, "tragic deaths that anyone would find difficult to accept."

"I don't want to talk about my mother or brother," she reminded him.

"I understand," he said, leaning forward and lightly touching her arm. "But recognise the impact they had on you. Your mother – your protector, the most important person in your life – died in front of you. Your older brother, who in many ways replaced her, was tragically taken by a war that didn't need to be fought."

"I've thought about that many times," she said. "I understand it better than you do."

"Maybe not," he countered. "I'm talking about defence mechanisms your subconscious created to cope with these traumas. They let you escape."

"I don't understand."

He paused, hesitant. "I'll give you my theory," he offered. "Don't get angry or dismiss it. Only agree to consider it."

She studied him for a moment. It seemed she wanted to believe, but was struggling to do so. "All right," she said softly. "Tell me."

"I think you've developed delusional thought patterns, inventing episodes that never occurred, both to escape from the present and protect yourself from the future."

"Enlighten me."

"The belief that you've lived in other times only lets you escape from the present," he clarified.

She looked at him strangely, either unable to comprehend or seeing a path she never knew existed. "I'm not sure I agree," she said softly.

"And your second escape is the relentless fear that someone is trying to kill you," he explained patiently. "Because someone killed your mother – a careless train conductor or maintenance man, perhaps – and someone killed your brother – an evil enemy pilot."

She stared at him, her eyes vacant, appearing a bit overwhelmed. "I think I've had enough for today," she said, smiling weakly as she stood to go.

"Don't leave," Barnett said, standing. "We're making marvellous progress."

There was a light knock on the door as Penelope approached him. Just as the door opened, the hinges creaking, she clung to him tightly and kissed him on the lips.

Olivia, the receptionist, stopped in the entrance with eyes wide and mouth open before retreating and quietly closing the door behind her.

Chapter 20

"Lieutenant Barnett," Alexander Cavendish said warmly as he strolled across the office floor. "It's good to see you again."

"Likewise, Captain Cavendish," Joseph Barnett replied, although there were few men he despised more. He saw Cavendish wince when he walked, his broken nose and the bruises on his face, but he felt no compassion. "Please, sit down."

"I'm sorry I'm so delinquent in getting re-acquainted," Cavendish offered. "I was summoned to London shortly after Penelope was admitted."

"She told me about your motor car accident," Barnett said, aware that Cavendish had returned to Como over a week before. "Is your condition improving?"

"Yes, it is," Cavendish replied, wiping the blond hair from his forehead. "I was rather sore for a few days, but I think I'm starting to mend."

Barnett nodded, finding the conversation awkward. They weren't friends and never would be. "I'm sure you're wondering how Penelope is doing," he said.

"Yes, I am. Has she made any progress?"

Barnett paused, reflective. He wanted to phrase his response carefully. "She's still convinced someone is trying to kill her," he replied. "I'm sure she told you about the last incident."

"Yes, she did. She claimed a nurse tried to smother her."

"It was likely a nightmare," Barnett said, "or a delusion. She's actually had several imaginary episodes. Although she's convinced they're real, they exist only in her subconscious."

"Can she be cured?"

Barnett hesitated, phrases from psychological journals coming to mind. "Treatment for this type of mental illness is still in its infancy," he explained, "but tremendous advances have been made in the last decade. I'm hopeful she experiences a full recovery."

"And if she doesn't respond to treatment?"

"She'll be institutionalised for the rest of her life."

Cavendish seemed stunned. "Are you confident she'll recover?" he asked.

Barnett sighed, reflecting on patients he had treated and cases he had studied. "I would say her odds are even at best," he replied.

"That's not very hopeful."

"It's all I can offer right now," Barnett said.

"How long will her treatment be?"

"Months rather than weeks, potentially years."

Cavendish frowned, burying his head in his hands. After a brief pause, he looked up and spoke. "I want her to have the best treatment available," he stated firmly, "for as long as she needs it. But I can't always be here for her. I'm often in London for business and charity events."

"I realise you have commitments," Barnett assured him. "And Penelope does, too."

"Thank you for understanding," he said as he rose, preparing to leave. "I'm at the cottage on the edge of the grounds should you need to contact me."

"It's fortunate you're nearby. Visiting will be much easier."

Cavendish started for the door but stopped and turned. "I hope there's no hard feelings," he said.

"For what?"

"The Somme," he replied, as if a weak apology could erase horrors housed in hell. "The war was horrendous; we all did things we weren't proud of. And for me, regret isn't enough. I'm considered a war hero, constantly reminded of days best forgotten. I only did what any man would do, even though … "

… Grey clouds wept as they studied the carnage below, passing serenely as raindrops fell to the ravaged earth in a vain attempt to wash away the blood, leaving pink puddles marring the mud with ruddy streaks. Foxholes filled, the ponds floating with debris: discarded cigarettes, half empty cans of food, letters with blotted ink running across the page and pools of blood from the corpses that lay in the hole before the rains came and covered them to leave no trace that they ever existed. Swollen and infected feet, rats and lice, days of boredom, and then the rain stopped and the killing came back, death after death after …

"Don't you agree, Doctor?"

"Yes, Captain, we all did things we weren't proud of," Barnett murmured, his mind clearing. "And many men died because of it."

"Honour the dead, rejoice with the living."

Barnett sighed, his head pounding, his vision clouded by images he wished he could forget. "I never liked that phrase," he said. "And I never will."

Chapter 21

Rose Barnett pedalled her bicycle down the dirt lane that led to the cottage with the rustic rail fence along the rear of the property. It sat behind a grove of trees, twenty metres from the lake, a hundred metres down the hill from the main road. She leaned her bicycle against the fence and walked through the gate to the entrance and rapped on the wooden door.

A moment later the door opened and a man stood before her, fading bruises on his face. "Rose, it's so good to see you," Alexander Cavendish said slyly. "It's been too long."

"I got your message," she said curtly. "What do you want?"

"Rose, darling, is that any way to treat an old friend?" he asked, smiling. "I'm surprised. Where are your manners?"

"We're not friends."

"Please, come in. Let's talk. We're off to a bad start."

"No, I'm not coming in. Tell me what you want. You have three seconds."

He sighed, shaking his head. "Fine, Rose, we'll skip the niceties," he suggested. "We'll keep it all business." He pointed to two wooden chairs perched under a sprawling chestnut tree, a square table between them. "Let's sit outside."

She wondered how his nose got broken but she didn't ask; she didn't want to prolong the discussion. It was already distasteful. She watched as he walked to the chairs, holding his side and cringing. It was nice to see him suffer. She wished it was worse.

He sat down and motioned to the chair beside him. "Sit," he said, more of a command than a request.

She reluctantly complied. "Let's get to the point," she said, removing a piece of paper from her pocket. "Your note said to meet you at this address, that you're in trouble and I can help. Why do I find that hard to believe?"

He grinned. "Maybe I exaggerated a bit," he admitted. "But you're here, so it worked."

"What do you want?" she demanded.

"I'm short of funds."

"What does that have to do with me?"

"I need fifteen thousand pounds."

She laughed. "As if I had it?" she asked. "And if I did, why would I give it to you?"

"Rose, you're a famous writer. Fifteen thousand pounds is nothing to you."

"Fifteen thousand pounds is a tremendous amount of money," she argued. "And whether I have it or not, is none of your business."

"I disagree," he said, his tone serious. "I need money and you have it. That makes it my business."

She looked at him, disgusted. "Income from my books is deposited in a London bank. Some of the proceeds are distributed to my family, some are saved, some are sent here. The largest percentage is used to help those who survived the war but can't help themselves."

"I'm not interested in where you get it," he told her. "I'm really not. But I need the money in a week."

She leaned toward him, her face close to his. "Absolutely not," she insisted.

Cavendish frowned, apparently not expecting the reply. "Doesn't your husband have money?" he asked. "Get it from him."

"Even if my husband did have money, which he does not, you're the last person on earth he would give it to."

His face hardened. "Why are you so defiant?" he asked. "It's very simple. I need money and you will give it to me."

"You're wrong," she said and started to rise.

"Wait," he said, motioning her back down. "If you don't come up with fifteen thousand pounds, I'll tell your husband we were lovers."

"That's absurd!" she declared. "We're weren't lovers. And no-one will ever believe we were. There are other names for what you did, even though you got away with it. And it wasn't just me. There were others."

"A young, attractive nurse stuck in a battlefield hospital in France, lonely and afraid," he said, provoking her. "You were so vulnerable, so in need of love. Hospital beds filled with men, damaged and dying, mere shadows of what they used to be. And then I came along, wounded but functional, strong, virile, wealthy – everything you ever wanted in a man. Who wouldn't believe it?"

"Everyone," she retorted. "Because it's not true."

"You're word against mine."

"If you ever say anything, I'll tell my husband what really happened," she said, her eyes fiery. "And then he'll kill you."

"The cripple?" he asked, laughing. "I don't think so. But he can try."

She stood and started to leave. "Leave me alone from now on," she threatened, "or I'll contact the police."

"No, you won't, Rose," he said sternly, "because you have too much to lose. You know that and so do I."

She walked out the gate and climbed on her bicycle.

"I have an idea, Rose," he called. "Get me the money or I'll kill the cripple."

She stopped and turned to face him. "If you ever come near me again, I'll kill you myself," she said icily. "I promise."

Chapter 22

"A woman went to his cottage today, but she didn't stay long," William Cain informed Wellington Jones. They sat at a corner table in the tavern in Jones's hotel, sipping beer. Potted plants shrouded them from other guests, the adjacent tables vacant.

"Don't tell me he has a woman in Como, too," Jones said with disgust.

"I haven't made a determination yet. Like I said, the visit was short."

"Can you find out who she is?"

"I already did. It's Rose Barnett. The doctor's wife."

"I don't believe it," Jones said, stunned. He rubbed his forehead, as if willing away the stress. "How long have they been seeing each other?"

"I don't know that they are, sir."

"What do you know about her?"

"She's the poet," Cain said.

"The poet?" Jones asked. *"Poems of the Great War*, that poet?"

"Yes," Cain replied. "She's got quite a following, although I doubt anyone knows she's in Como. She's English, from Devon, but was in France during the war. She was a nurse at the hospital in Amiens that treated Cavendish. Barnett was there, too."

"That was five years ago," Jones said. "Have they been lovers all of this time, even though she married Barnett and Cavendish married my daughter?"

"I don't know that, sir. I only know he saw her briefly today."

Jones lifted his mug to his lips, reflecting on the battles, the murdered and maimed. "Cavendish was only in the hospital a few months," he remembered. "He was a captain at the Somme, wounded in the stomach, a war hero – all of Britain knows who he is."

"I suspect that's where they met," Cain added. "I doubt if they knew each other before that."

"How long was Barnett a patient?"

"For two years. He married Rose when he got out, just as the war ended."

"What could the connection between Rose and Cavendish be," Jones mused aloud, "assuming it isn't an affair?"

"Maybe it's financial," Cain suggested. "She has the money to pay his gambling debt; she is a famous author."

"But why would she give him anything?"

"That's the mystery, but maybe there's a reason why Miss Penelope was admitted to Lakeside Sanitarium," Cain speculated. "Cavendish may have persuaded her to come here so he could be with Rose."

Jones frowned. "Cavendish did suggest she be treated here, but I had something to do with that, too," he admitted. "We spent some holidays in Como and I knew about the sanitarium. After Penelope tried to take her life …" He turned, emotional, and looked out the tavern window and watched a woman passing, a freshly baked loaf of bread in her arm. "At first I wanted her back in London, but I eventually agreed with him."

"How did he convince you?"

"He said the hospital's reputation was impeccable, which it is, and that the secluded location would ensure her privacy, which it does."

"Did you know that Barnett had served with Cavendish?"

"Yes, Cavendish told me," he replied. Jones paused, looking at the suds in his beer. "Have you seen Barnett yet?"

"No, I haven't."

"He was badly wounded. He limps, his face is scarred and he has little use of his left hand. The man paid a heavy price to serve his country." He paused, reflecting. "Do you think he knows about Cavendish and his wife?" he asked.

Cain shrugged. "We don't know for sure that anything is going on," he pointed out, "although it may have at one time."

"I don't think Barnett would tolerate it. Sometimes I think he's like a volcano about to erupt. I think he would go after Cavendish, maybe even kill him."

"If he served in France, he has some military experience, even if he was a psychiatrist," Cain said.

"He was actually in the Medical Corps, in the trenches tending the wounded," Jones said. "Although I'm sure he can take care of himself, if he had to."

"Let me offer a theory, sir," Cain suggested. "And I have no proof, just a suspicion. But let's just say that Cavendish and Rose were lovers and have been since the Somme."

"I'm listening."

"Should anything happen to Miss Penelope, I assume her money goes to Cavendish."

"Yes, of course, he's her husband," Jones said. "Why, what are you trying to say?"

"I think we should watch Cavendish very closely."

Chapter 23

Joseph Barnett led Bobby Taylor, his shell-shocked American patient, out of his office and into the reception area. "Olivia, can you bring Mr Taylor back to his room?"

"Of course, Doctor," she said, her English accented but functional.

Just as they were leaving, Penelope Jones walked in. She nodded politely, cringing when she saw the trembling American.

Barnett took a pocket watch from his vest. "Thank you for being on time, Penelope," he said.

She ignored him and walked into his office, sitting on the leather couch. Barnett followed and sat in a straight-backed chair across from her.

"Penelope, we need to discuss the kiss that ended our last session," he said sternly. "There will be no more displays of affection. Our relationship is professional, not personal."

"You seemed to enjoy it," she said slyly.

He ignored her, having made his point, and shuffled through his notebook. "Penelope, I need to hypnotise you," he said. "I have to explore your subconscious to confirm my theories."

"How ingenious," she replied sarcastically. "That's what the other psychiatrists did."

"To paraphrase a Chinese proverb, just because I take the same first step does not mean I have the same destination."

"Very clever," she admitted. "But don't forget that, unlike you, I've actually been to Asia. I'm not as gullible as you think."

He enjoyed when she poked fun at him. "I'll start slowly," he assured her. "If this first session is productive, we'll try it again. If it isn't, we won't."

"Try whatever you like," she suggested, "but that doesn't mean it'll work. I'll lie down. That's what the other doctors made me do."

"As long as you're comfortable," he said as he moved his chair closer. "This will be easy. Are you ready?"

"Yes, I am."

"Then let's begin," he said, pausing to collect his thoughts. "Isn't Como a charming city?"

"It is pleasant."

"Let's envision lying on the edge of the lake, watching the water shimmer in the sunlight. The scent of edelweiss tickles your nostrils as sail boats drift lazily in a gentle breeze. It seems like another world, so calm and peaceful ..."

It was more difficult to hypnotise her than he expected. She resisted at first, but gradually succumbed to his suggestions and five minutes later her eyes closed, her breathing slow and regular, and she seemed prepared to accept his commands.

"Are you completely relaxed?" he asked when convinced she was ready.

"Yes," she murmured, "I am."

"And now I want to turn back the calendar, month after month, year after year, until you're a small child again. Do you understand?"

"Yes," she whispered. "I'm a small child."

He studied her for a moment to ensure she was actually hypnotised. He was confident in the diagnosis he had recently made, but needed to verify the traumas she had experienced. Since she refused to discuss them, hypnosis was his only available path. He also needed to find what led to her suicide attempt.

"I want you to tell me about your mother," he said softly. "Start with your earliest recollection and continue from there."

The session lasted almost fifteen minutes. Penelope described her childhood memories: her mother, her father and brother, Christmas, birthday parties and friends. She seemed a happy child until her mother died. Initially she blamed herself for not being able to save her, not that any child could, but through psychiatric treatment she later learned to cope with her loss and forgive herself, which is often hardest to do.

Her emotional distress eased as she grew older, voids filled by her nanny Mrs Thistle to whom she was very attached, her father and her brother, close friends like Mary Westcott, boyfriends, her studies. She seemed on the path to recovery, her emotional needs sated, her grief no longer consuming, her emptiness not as vast. And then came the war and Oxford died.

He had been three years older, a surrogate parent, someone she admired. When his life ended so abruptly, the anguish was deeper, the pain harsher, the second death of a loved one that she had to endure. At some point the delusions began, created to escape her inner conflicts, fantasy trampling reality, gradual at first and then more pronounced. Even her marriage failed to ease her pain and, as each day passed, she slipped deeper into darkness. Three years later, she attempted suicide.

Barnett listened closely, taking notes, probing but protecting. He learned nothing new – it was just as he assumed when he offered his tentative diagnosis. But there was still something missing, a clue he hadn't uncovered, but he didn't know what it was or where to find it. Her descent had been gradual at first, but then steep and rapid over the last few months. What had triggered it?

"And now we'll bring the session to a close," he said. "When you awaken, you'll feel rested, refreshed, and free of torment. Your eyes will open on the count of three. Do you understand?"

"Yes."

"One, two, three."

Her eyelids fluttered and then opened. She sat up, her face flushed. After she glanced around the room, her eyes met his and she smiled. "Did we accomplish anything?" she asked.

"Yes, we did," he said. "Do you remember what we discussed?"

"No, I don't," she admitted.

"How are you feeling?"

"Fine," she replied. "I've been hypnotised many times before. It has no effect on me whatsoever."

"Good," he said, smiling. "I'm glad the session didn't disturb you."

"No, it didn't. But you don't look very well. Did you make me normal and drive yourself crazy?"

He chuckled. "I wish it was that simple," he said. "I really do."

"Did we make any progress?"

He studied her for a moment and then continued. "We confirmed my theory. I told you before that the root of your problems are traumas and the escape mechanisms your subconscious developed to cope with them. I'm now convinced that theory is correct."

"Then we're finished?"

"No," he said, smiling. "It's not that simple. And there's more, reactions I still can't explain. Our efforts to find the inner conflict must continue."

She was quiet, reflective, her eyes examining the contents of the room. She seemed confused and afraid. "When do we get to who's trying to kill me?" she asked.

He sighed in surrender. After exploring her subconscious, dissecting the traumas that tortured her, never once did she mention someone trying to kill her. "That's the topic of our next session," he promised. "I think you've had enough for today."

Chapter 24

Penelope left Barnett's office and returned to her room. She assumed he had been satisfied with her hypnosis session, at least he seemed pleased with the results and that's all that really mattered. She smiled, thinking of him scolding her. He had been so surprised by the kiss, but he didn't resist or push her away. He clung to her as tightly as she clung to him. And then the embrace ended and he blushed, his face a mask of remorse. She had turned and left, knowing he watched her walk from the room, too shocked to say a word.

Sometimes she wondered how he coped. The war must have been so horrific for him, but he never discussed it. He limped, sometimes cringing with pain, his left hand paralysed, his face scarred. She suspected that if he had been that battered physically, he must have suffered psychologically. Maybe they should switch roles; she should play doctor and he could be the patient.

She knew she was making progress, starting to understand her mind's intricate web of twists and turns, avenues and avalanches. Dr Barnett's probing questions, asked so softly and delicately, were taking her in different directions – but in places she needed to go. Although he was focused on subconscious traumas and other phenomena that must be terribly exciting for him, it was painfully dull for her. He was a good psychiatrist, but no matter how hard he tried he still didn't believe that her life was in danger – that someone was trying to kill her.

She got up and walked to the French doors, studying the lake stretching into the horizon, the mountains descending from heaven to greet it. Her hair was a bit mussed, as it always seemed to be, and she tried to smooth it with her hand. There were dark circles under her eyes from lack of sleep, not easily noticeable, but she could still see them.

She saw a man on the sanitarium lawn, trimming the shrubs with a pair of shears. He seemed intent on what he was doing, fussing with the bushes until they were perfectly shaped. He trimmed for a few minutes more and then stepped back, admiring his work, ensuring it was just the way he wanted it.

She thought of her father's estate near London, the grounds beautifully manicured, laced with exotic plants he had collected in his travels around the world. She realised how much she missed it. And then, with a stab of loneliness, she realised how much she missed Mrs Thistle. Her nanny, her surrogate mother, her confidante and friend, Penelope was closer to Mrs Thistle than any person on earth. Suddenly Lake Como and the majestic Italian Alps weren't as attractive as they once were. Maybe she should return to London. She could live in her childhood home; Mrs Thistle would provide much needed support and she could still receive the treatment she needed. There was really no reason to stay in Como, except for Dr Barnett.

Penelope stood at the glass door, watching the gardener, when he looked up at the building and waved. She stepped back from the door, surprised. Was he waving at her or someone in the room adjacent to hers? She then heard voices in the hallway and the door to the neighbouring room closed.

"I know you're there," she said loudly.

The patient in the next room was a Spanish singer whose name she couldn't remember. Maybe she knew the gardener? Or maybe someone else was in her room. Penelope hurried to the door and listened as the talking continued, louder and closer. She heard a woman's voice, soft and sensual, that she recognised as the Spanish singer. Another woman spoke, the voice deeper.

"You had better leave me alone," she called.

After a hushed whisper, the hallway got quiet. A moment later the door to the neighbouring suite closed and there was a knock at Penelope's door.

"Miss Penelope," the deeper voice said, the English broken.

It was the cleaning woman. Penelope stood by the door, hesitant.

"Miss Penelope?"

"I saw the gardener wave to you," she said through the door. "Has he been watching me?"

"No, Miss Penelope," the cleaning woman replied. "We on balcony and he see us. Just wave hello."

"I'm sure he was watching me," Penelope insisted. "He wants to kill me."

"No, Miss Penelope. Is not true. He nice man."

"I know what he's doing," Penelope said. "He's with them."

"He with who?" the cleaning woman asked. "He works in garden, no hurt anybody. Do you want me to get nurse?"

"He's trying to kill me."

"I get nurse, Miss Penelope," the cleaning woman said. "Is all right."

Penelope went back to the glass door and looked at out the gardens. The man wasn't there. "He's gone," she called to the cleaning lady. "I'm safe. At least for now."

Chapter 25

Alexander Cavendish sat on a rock at the edge of Lake Como, the boulder polished by the wind and rain it had defied for decades. His cottage was just behind it, elevated above the water, the banks of the lake climbing to the mountains that dwarfed all that lay in their shadows. Hidden from the road by a grove of trees, he contemplated his future and tried to forget his past, watching ripples in the water tugging to and fro from shore.

His body still ached, the cuts and bruises from the battering he had taken in London a painful reminder of what happened when you didn't pay your debts. The tape on the bridge of his nose that held the broken bone in place was dampened with sweat the spring sun created. He touched it gently, wondering how long it would take to heal.

He had to change; he had to again become the man he was before the war. But it was easier to wish and want than actually accomplish. He was destroying himself, day by day, vice by vice, with whisky, women and gambling. He swore that if he ever escaped his current cage, he would never get back into it. His future would be bright, just as it had been before the war, and he would once more be counted among Britain's elite, a gifted intellectual who helped guide the nation forward, helped govern a global empire. But first, he had to fix what was broken, and that began with paying a fifteen thousand pound debt.

He regretted returning to Como. He had left London immediately after his beating, fleeing Billy Flynn and his henchman Jocko Jakes, panicked and afraid. In hindsight, it would have been so much better if he had gone to his parents, letting his mother see that he was severely injured, getting her to beg his father to relent and give him the money he so desperately needed.

It was still only a matter of time before Flynn found him. It was easy to do, especially with the press coverage Penelope received when admitted to the asylum. They wouldn't be far behind, finding the records of his travel to Como. Before they did, he had to get the money. They would kill him if he didn't.

He decided to send his parents a telegram. Maybe he could add a doctor's assessment, claim he had been injured in a motor car accident like he told Penelope. Just word it cleverly so his father understood what really happened. Somehow connect his injuries with the need for money, stating that he was staying in Como to recuperate and provide support for Penelope. His father would pay his debt and might even add a little extra. It was a good plan. But his father wasn't stupid. Or sentimental. He would probably be angry that his son had manipulated his mother, using her emotions to get what he wanted. It was worth the effort, but unlikely to succeed.

He had expected Penelope to give him the money. But she was guarded, cautious, very prudent when it came to expenditures, even for someone who was half crazy. His first attempt was made before he went to London, claiming he was involved in an investment with fellow officers from the war, some real estate in Brighton, the seaside resort. But he made two mistakes. He asked for much more money than he needed – thirty thousand pounds – planning to play the ponies and recover his original losses, which he would then use to repay Penelope. He had a sure thing with a horse called Just A Bit Faster, a great name, a tip he had gotten from a friend at the stables.

His second mistake was inventing a real estate venture, which was Wellington Jones's forte. As soon as he mentioned it, Penelope wanted her father consulted. Once Cavendish was trapped, he told her the deal fell apart. Then he went to London and had his unfortunate meeting with Billy Flynn. Upon his return, he invented the motor vehicle accident, playing on her sympathies. Again, she deferred to her father, and again he was unsuccessful. He then got other ideas in regard to Penelope, harsher but more effective. He just hadn't been successful implementing them – at least not yet.

He knew from the war that you always needed more than one plan, and Rose Barnett provided another path to success. She would get the money – if not from royalties then from her husband. She had too much to lose. He was surprised how upset she was when he threatened to kill Barnett. He was a crippled lunatic in the hospital during the war, overwhelmed with nightmares, his tortured screams waking all the men in their wing. Cavendish had been across the aisle and a few beds down, quietly watching, but he doubted Barnett remembered. He was too badly wounded, physically and mentally. He only saw the battlefield in his demented mind – not doctors, nurses or patients.

Rose probably thought she was rid of Cavendish forever. But she couldn't have been more wrong. He knew all her secrets, some kept from her husband and the rest hidden from the police. After putting the pieces together, he realised she offered his best chance for success. He planned to visit her when she least expected it, describing her life and detailing every mistake she had ever made. Then he would blackmail her. If that didn't work, he would again threaten to kill her husband.

He was pleased with his plans: a telegram to his father; approach Penelope for the money again but with the option of taking more drastic action; and then there was Rose, his old friend who wasn't quite what she seemed. Maybe he would use all the options and get more money than he needed. He could pay off Flynn and play the ponies. But only to get enough money to start over, to change, to end the downward spiral that was sucking him under and suffocating him.

He smiled, comforted by his cunning. There was also his father-in-law, the pompous jackass Wellington Jones. If anything happened to him, Penelope would get all of his money. And Wellington was very rich. What a sweet pot of gold that would be. Fifteen thousand pounds wasn't much given the riches he had. Maybe an accident could solve all of his problems. And Cavendish was just the man to arrange it.

He rose from the rock and went back into the house, a joyful gait to his walk. He had several plans to put in motion. It was time to get started.

Chapter 26

"How is Penelope doing?" Rose asked, watching her husband as he sat in his leather chair, browsing through files he had taken from his briefcase.

"I'm not sure," he mused aloud, distracted. "I thought I had found the root to her conflicts – the deaths of her mother and brother – but that's so obvious that any of her other psychiatrists would have reached the same conclusion."

"Why didn't they treat her somehow, through therapy or hypnosis?" she asked.

"I'm sure that they did," he muttered, looking up from his papers. "So there has to be something else, something I'm missing."

Rose hesitated, not sure whether to voice her opinion. A moment later she spoke, quietly and measured. "She married Cavendish shortly after her brother's death – the Cavendish you and I know. She now knows him, too."

"I've been thinking about that," he said, "although she appears to love him very much. It's still something I need to consider."

"I realise she's always had issues," Rose continued, steering her husband in a new direction. "But when did her steep decline actually begin?"

"Her condition rapidly deteriorated about six months ago."

"And what was the catalyst?"

He bit a finger nail and said, "It must be something she hasn't discussed or perhaps doesn't even recognise."

Rose thought for a moment, trying to put herself in Penelope's position, but knowing how difficult it was to replicate a demented mind. "Why not confront her?" she asked. "Emphasise that she's not being rational, expose her delusions, define them, make her aware of them and continually correct them."

"It seems a reasonable approach," he agreed, "but she is absolutely convinced that someone is trying to kill her. I'm not sure why and neither does she."

"Can't you use the Monte Carlo police report to convince her?"

"It's not that simple," he explained. "She insists the police were wrong."

Rose thought of Cavendish, capable of doing anything, and in desperate need of money. "Maybe they were," she suggested softly.

"But the police report is very convincing," he said. "That alone makes me think she's delusional, although there are some discrepancies."

"Like what?"

"Apparently, the barbitone dose she took wasn't enough to kill her."

"Maybe she thought it was," Rose concluded. "Or whoever gave it to her thought it was."

"All involved are certain it was a suicide attempt – her family, her doctor and the police."

"I probably shouldn't say this, but her husband is capable of anything. You know that and so do I."

Barnett frowned. "I realise that," he admitted. "But there's no apparent motive or evidence, so it doesn't seem logical." He paused, quietly reflecting. "I can't accuse the man of attempted murder because of what he did during the war."

Rose recognised his inner turmoil, the desire to do right, as he wrestled with a gnawing suspicion he couldn't ignore. "Just consider it," she said. She paused and studied him lovingly. "You always find the good in people, even where there's evil."

"Not with Cavendish," he assured her with distaste. "He's the only human being I've ever despised."

"I share your assessment," she added bitterly.

"He actually scheduled an appointment to discuss his wife's progress," he told her. "I had hoped never to see him again."

Rose was anxious, protective, not wanting her husband exposed to hurt or danger. "What did he say?" she asked tentatively.

"He told me he left for London shortly after Penelope arrived," Barnett said. "Some business matter."

"It must have been important if he disappeared right after she was admitted."

"He also said something about the war forcing people to act far differently than they really are," he said, "almost like an apology. Sort of a cryptic statement, don't you think?"

"It was hell on earth," she replied softly. "We all did things we wish we hadn't."

"I understand that. But it doesn't mean I'll ever forgive him for sending boys to their deaths."

"I saw him in town a few days ago," she said tentatively. "He was in a nasty motor car accident."

"You spoke to him?"

"Yes, but not about Penelope. He just talked about his accident."

"I saw the bruises when he came to see me," he told her. "It looked like his nose had been broken and he winced a bit when he moved. Did he say how long he was in the hospital?"

"I didn't think to ask," she admitted. "And I didn't really care."

"I'm told he comes from a good family," Barnett said. "I suppose he and Penelope are a good match. Maybe I am wrong about him."

"I don't think so," she replied. "Alexander Cavendish is a despicable human being. I know that and so do you."

"He certainly was in the trenches," he muttered, as if willing away an image he didn't want to see.

"And he was at Amiens Hospital," she added. She decided to delicately reveal what had really happened, especially if Cavendish was planning to do so. Joseph had to know. "He was horrendous, rude, demanding and condescending."

"That describes half of the British officer corps," he said with a nervous laugh, as if suspecting he was about to be told something he didn't want to hear.

She looked at him, her face hard, her eyes angry. "He also made advances on the nurses," she confessed, "unwanted advances."

He looked at her, his eyes wide. "I'm shocked," he said slowly, the inference slowly absorbed. "Which nurses?"

"All the nurses. I don't think any were spared."

"Including you?"

"No-one was spared."

He quietly got out of his chair, moved to a closet, and reached behind some winter coats and boxes and withdrew a rifle. He grabbed an En-bloc – a magazine with six bullets – from the top shelf and loaded it.

"Joseph!" she exclaimed. "What are you doing?"

"I'm going to confront him," he said, his voice detached, devoid of emotion. "He's in the cottage next to the sanitarium."

She stood in front of him, blocking his path to the door. "Joseph, stop! Don't do this!"

"I'll kill him if I have to," he declared. "I should have done it in the trenches." He moved her aside, rougher than he intended to.

She grabbed his arm. "Joseph!" she pleaded. "Put the gun away."

He pulled away, moving relentlessly toward the door. "He deserves to die," he insisted.

She ran past him and stood in his path, her back against the door, her hand on the rifle. "Joseph, give me the gun and sit down," she said, softly but sternly, her eyes trained on his.

"No, I want him dead," he muttered, his eyes vacant.

"You don't have to kill him," she said softly, gazing into his eyes, "not for me. I can take care of myself."

"What do you mean?" he asked, pausing, his breathing erratic.

"I took care of myself then," she said, her words expressed calmly, in a measured monotone. "Because nothing happened. And I can take care of myself now, if I have to."

He hesitated. "I need to protect you," he said.

"It's all right," she assured him, her hands still on the rifle. "He isn't a threat to me. If he comes near me, I'll kill him. I'm just afraid I'll enjoy it."

He calmed, lowering the rifle, and closed his eyes tightly. "I'm sorry," he said softly. "I acted like a crazy man."

"It's all right, darling," she whispered, her hand leaving the rifle and caressing his face.

"I won't be able to control myself if anyone ever hurts you," he said, still breathing heavily.

She kissed him lightly and took the gun from his hands. "I know, darling," she whispered, "but everything's all right." She led him to the chair.

He sat down, his eyes wild, as if a bottled rage had been uncorked. He took deep breaths, gradually letting his heartbeat slow to a regular rate, calming himself.

Rose unloaded the gun and put it away. Then she sat beside him. "I told you that story not because I need you to protect me."

"Then why did you tell it?"

"Because I think you should reconsider Penelope's claim that someone is trying to kill her."

"And why is that?"

"Maybe someone is. And it might be Cavendish."

Chapter 27

William Cain sat in the driver's side of the sedan, Wellington Jones beside him. They were parked just off a winding mountain road, over a hundred metres above Lake Como. Nestled twenty metres from shore below them was the bungalow Penelope had rented for Alexander Cavendish.

They parked there for over an hour, smoking cigarettes, watching the charming cottage for a sign of its occupant. They knew Cavendish was there; they had watched him arrive, driving up in a rented convertible. But he had gone inside the cottage, received no visitors, and not emerged. Now their patience was starting to ebb.

"I'm tired of waiting," Jones said warily.

"I'm used to it, sir," Cain replied. "I spend most of my time watching him."

"He's a despicable sneak," Jones said with disgust. "How can a man live two lives for three years without anyone knowing it – even his family?"

"Most men have secrets," Cain offered. "Some get found out, most don't."

Jones removed the watch from his vest pocket and looked at the time. "What are we trying to accomplish?"

"I thought Rose Barnett might come," Cain replied. "I wanted you to see them together. I still think they might have something planned. We just don't know what it is."

"Do you think Penelope is in danger?"

"Yes, I do," Cain answered. "Cavendish has a lot to gain if anything happens to her."

"But why take the chance?" Jones asked. "It would be too obvious; he'd be sure to get caught. His family has money anyway, if that's the issue. He inherits the trust, rather than an allowance, as soon as he turns thirty."

"I would just be very protective of Miss Penelope," Cain advised. "Cavendish is up to something. And whatever it is, it isn't good."

"Let's get out of here," Jones said. "I'm too busy to waste the day hoping I'll catch him up doing something he shouldn't be."

"Of course, sir," Cain obliged, starting the engine.

He backed the car and turned onto the mountain road. Another car approached, passing them, climbing higher, as he negotiated the winding road down towards Como. They drove a half kilometre, gaining speed, when a bend approached. Cain tapped the brakes. When the vehicle didn't respond, he applied more pressure.

"Slow down," Jones said, irritated. "I want to get back alive."

Cain forced the pedal to the floor. "The brakes aren't working," he said, the car gaining speed.

Jones braced himself, a hand on the dashboard. "Pump the pedal," he suggested, eyeing the road ahead.

Cain pushed the pedal up and down and then forced it to the floor. The car slid as the turn approached, the tyres kicking up dust, a plume forming behind them. They hugged the outer rim of the road, no barrier to protect them. Two wheels barely touched the ground, almost floating as Cain spun the wheel, the car sliding towards the edge of the cliff. They negotiated the turn, barely on the road, the rear wheels skidding. A straight ramp downward started just after the curve and they started to rapidly gain speed.

"Turn the engine off," Jones yelled. "And try the emergency brake."

Cain turned the ignition key off. The engine coughed and rattled but stopped, the vehicle still plunging downward. He applied the emergency brake with no response. They approached another curve travelling much faster. Cain turned the wheel, the rear of the vehicle sliding uncontrollably.

"Brace yourself!" Jones hollered.

Cain fought to keep the car from flipping over. They sped into the curve sideways, barely on the road, no cars coming from the other direction. They raced through the turn, the tyres only centimeters from the edge of the cliff. A cloud of dust billowed behind them as they descended down another straight run of road, the terrain starting to flatten.

"Drive off the road," Jones shouted, holding onto the dashboard, warily watching the speedometer. "See if that slows us down."

They hurtled onto the field, bouncing over ruts and gullies and running over bushes and shrubs. Cain lost control and the car spun sideways, spiralling faster and faster, slamming into the mountain with the screech of crumbling metal, spitting dirt and dust, bouncing off and spinning forward fifty metres more before smacking into the trunk of a tree.

Wellington Jones slowly lifted his head, blood dripping from a cut near his hairline. He moved tenderly, found nothing broken, only cramped and aching muscles.

"Are you all right?" he asked Cain.

"Yes, I think so," Cain replied, twisting and turning to make sure.

"What happened?" Jones asked as he opened the smashed door, squeezing out past the tree.

"I don't know," Cain said, climbing from the vehicle. "Let me check."

He slid under the vehicle, examining the front and rear undercarriage. After a few minutes of inspection, he emerged. "The brake lines were cut," he announced grimly.

"How?" Jones asked. "Everything worked on the way up the mountain."

"They're cut at the rear wheels," Cain answered. "And it was done while we watched the cottage."

Chapter 28

Barnett sat in his study after dinner, reading *The Tempest*. He had such a penchant for Shakespeare that he could re-read the same play several times, finding new meanings each time he did. Shakespeare had kept him company on many a lonely night, especially in the trenches during the Great War.

"Don't you ever tire of Shakespeare?" Rose asked. She sat across from him, pen to paper, writing and revising the poems that would form the foundation of her next book: *Poems of Love.*

"How could anyone tire of Shakespeare?" he asked with amusement. "It's an evolving process of enlightenment. The more you read, the more you discover."

"I do recognise his genius," Rose admitted.

"Penelope thinks she knew Shakespeare, or at least the man who really wrote the plays and sonnets."

"Yes, you told me. Edward DeVere was the man you mentioned."

"It's an interesting theory," he continued. "She's a true Shakespearean expert. She taught at Cambridge during the war – Shakespearean literature, Elizabethan theatre, creative writing."

"She seems extremely intelligent," Rose said.

"Yes, she is," Barnett agreed. His mind wandered, reflecting on his patient, her behaviour, her diagnosis, and he was struck with a thought. "Sometimes I feel like I'm playing a part in a play Penelope wrote."

Rose looked up from her papers. "Maybe you are," she said.

Barnett considered the matter a moment more: the delusions, claims her life was in jeopardy, the belief that she lived in other times. Penelope could be subconsciously acting out a script. Or maybe she wasn't.

Rose returned to her writing. She seemed focused, as she somehow always managed to be, ignoring sights and sounds or any other distractions, including her cats. She had a unique ability to shut out the world while sitting in the midst of it. She wrote continuously, poems and short stories mostly, purging her subconscious on a daily basis, scribbling any thought she might have down on paper. She wasn't a good writer, her initial drafts almost a random collection of thoughts, but she was a fabulous re-writer, painstakingly working revision after revision until she achieved perfection.

The tranquility was interrupted by a knock on the door. Rose answered it, finding Millie, one of the nurses from the sanitarium, standing on the step.

"I need Dr Barnett," she announced, her English crisp, the accent slight. "It's Miss Penelope."

Barnett went to the door, looking at his pocket watch. It was only 8 p.m.. "Millie, what's wrong?" he asked. "It can't be another nightmare."

"I'm afraid it's much worse," she replied.

"What happened?" he asked, his face pale, fearing the worst.

Millie had an anguished look on her face. "I think she tried to commit suicide again," she explained. "I came to get you as fast as I could."

"Is she all right?" Rose asked, alarmed, wrapping her arm around her husband.

"Yes, she seems to be," Millie replied. "Although she gave us quite a fright."

"Joseph, be careful," Rose said, as if knowing he was flustered and would try to hurry. That's when he was most at risk, given his crippled leg.

As they moved quickly along the path that led to the sanitarium, Barnett wondered what could have gone wrong. Penelope had been progressing well, or at least she seemed to be. There wasn't any indication her condition had deteriorated.

"Do you know what happened?" he asked.

"She jumped from her balcony," Millie told him.

"My Lord," he gasped. "How badly is she hurt?"

"She's bruised, but she didn't break any bones."

"How did she survive?" he asked, shocked. "She's on the third floor."

"She landed in the juniper tree near the balcony," she answered. "The branches broke her fall, but she was injured when she hit the larger limbs on her way down."

"Have her husband and father been notified?"

"Yes, Emilio is contacting them now."

They continued to the sanitarium, climbed the sweeping staircase to the third floor and rushed down the corridor toward Penelope's suite. It was quiet, like a surreal silent movie. No patients lingered; no orderlies waited. It was unusual given what had just occurred.

Adele, the nurse Penelope accused of trying to kill her, greeted them at the door. "She's resting now," she assured them, her English accented.

"Any serious injuries?"

"Just some bruises," Adele told him. "More on her right side than the left. Must be the way she landed."

"Any broken bones?" he asked.

"No, nothing is broken," Adele clarified. "Her right arm is swollen and there are bruises on her legs. She's very fortunate."

"After she gets some rest, we have to put her in a different room," Barnett said. "Somewhere safer."

"We tried to before," Adele reminded him. "But she wouldn't go. She says she'll leave if we move her."

"Then we have to make the room more secure," he said. "Maybe we'll seal the balcony doors closed. We have to protect her from herself."

Barnett walked into Penelope's bedroom, leaving Adele and Millie in the sitting room. As he walked in, he saw the window opened fully, the branches of the tree just beyond it. The evening was pleasant, even if a bit chilly. He went over and closed the window, then locked it securely.

"Leave it cracked open," she said softly. "I don't like it closed."

"It's supposed to be locked," he said as he sat on the edge of the bed, watching her closely.

Her eyes were glassy from a sedative, but there were no bruises on her face. There was a purple blotch on her right forearm, the rest of her body hidden by bedsheets.

"What happened?" Barnett asked softly.

"I was standing on the balcony, looking at the lake. Someone came up behind me and threw me over the railing."

He covered his head with his hand, sad that he hadn't been able to help her. Their last session had been so productive – no evidence of delusions, only therapeutic discussions on the tragedies she suffered. Penelope had been in good spirits, light-hearted. And now this.

"Penelope, who tried to kill you?" he asked softly.

"It may have been the same person that tried the last two times. Adele tried to smother me. It was probably her. I know you don't believe me, but who else would it be."

"Adele couldn't have thrown you off the balcony. She doesn't have the strength."

"Maybe you should call the police," Penelope suggested.

He considered Rose's advice. Maybe someone really was trying to kill Penelope. It would be prudent to have the police investigate. If they determined no foul play was involved, it might make her understand that she was sick, confusing fantasy with reality. If the police found evidence of an intruder, he would suggest a likely suspect – Alexander Cavendish.

"You're right," he admitted. "We should call the police."

****

Two Como policemen arrived twenty minutes later. Barnett gave them a description of the events, at least as he could explain them in his limited Italian, and gave them permission to examine the property. They first inspected the grounds, scribbling in a notebook, looking up at the balcony, and then the juniper tree that had broken Penelope's fall. They spent some time on the lawn, crawling on their hands and knees in the grass where she had fallen, checking the location's proximity to the balcony and the damage to the tree. They carefully conducted their investigation, but were unable to determine anything other than a body had landed in the juniper tree, breaking branches and falling to the ground.

Barnett then led them to Penelope's suite. They examined the door, to see if entry had been forced, and then the balcony, searching for signs of a struggle. They checked the sitting room and the bath and finally the bedroom. After a thorough investigation, they found no indication of foul play.

Penelope sat up in bed, watching them curiously, but not speaking

"Hai visto l'intruso?" a policeman asked. Did you see the intruder?

"No," she replied, apparently understanding Italian.

"Può dire se era un uomo o una donna?" he asked. Could you tell if it was a man or woman?

"No," she replied, shaking her head.

"Un modo per identificarli? Un anello o guardare, forse?" he asked. Any way to identify them? A ring or watch, perhaps?

"No, l'intruso mi ha sorpreso," she told them with a shrug. No, the intruder surprised me.

"The window in her bedroom was open," Barnett informed them. "I closed it when I arrived."

One of the policemen swung the halves of the window open, studying the tree that grew beside it. He then turned his attention to the sill, examining it closely.

"Dottore, hai visto questo?" the policeman wondered aloud. Doctor, did you see this?

Barnett walked the window. "What is it?" he asked.

"Ci sono tracce di sangue sul davanzale della finestra," he said. "There are traces of blood on the windowsill."

Chapter 29

Just after the policeman left, Wellington Jones barged into Penelope's sitting room. "What happened?" he asked, flustered.

"I'm not sure," Barnett replied. "It appears that she fell from the balcony. Fortunately, she landed in that juniper tree. The branches broke her fall and she avoided serious injury."

"Is she all right?"

"Yes, she is," he replied. "There's nothing broken, but she is bruised and battered. She's actually very fortunate."

"Did she say how she fell?"

"She claims she was pushed, that someone tried to kill her."

"What were the police doing here?"

"I called them. I wanted Penelope's claims investigated."

"And what did they find?"

"No evidence of foul play, but they did find some smeared blood on the windowsill in her bedroom."

Jones was confused. "Where did the blood come from?" he asked. "An intruder?"

"Possibly," Barnett replied. "The policemen didn't reach any conclusions, but they did say that the tree could provide access to Penelope's bedroom."

"Then Penelope could be telling the truth," Jones countered. "Someone may be trying to kill her."

Barnett studied Jones closely, a man normally so composed now frantic. He seemed to know more than he was willing to share. "It's possible," he speculated, "especially with the blood on the windowsill."

"If the intruder entered her bedroom window, as he probably did when she claimed she was being smothered, he could have sneaked up on her while she stood on the balcony and pushed her off."

"That's certainly plausible," Barnett said. He glanced in Penelope's bedroom, not wanting her to hear. "Unless she did imagine it, which is more likely. The blood on the windowsill could be hers. After the last alleged attempt on her life, her fingertips were torn."

Jones studied Barnett, as if weighing both possibilities. "I understand your diagnosis, Doctor," he said, "and it certainly makes sense. But events you're not privy to give credence to Penelope's claims."

"Then we certainly need to entertain both options," Barnett said, with no prejudice or hesitation.

"Are the police taking any action?"

"I'm not sure they have grounds to take action," he said.

"I think they should do something."

"It might be wise to assign Penelope to a different room," Barnett said delicately, ignoring the comment. "I suggested she move after the last episode, but instead we increased security and the staff ensured her window was locked. Now we know that Penelope unlocks it after they leave."

"No, she's not moving," Jones said as he glanced toward his daughter's bedroom. "She wants to stay here. And I'm not sure that a new room would make any difference."

"Whatever you wish, Mr Jones," Barnett said. "I only fear for her safety."

"I'm sure we can compromise," Jones offered. "Maybe I'll hire a watchman to supplement the sanitarium's security. He can patrol the grounds after dark."

"Let me discuss it with the staff," Barnett said. "There may be alternatives."

Jones glanced around the room. "Where's her husband?"

Barnett went to the entrance and poked his head in the hallway. "Has Mr Cavendish been notified?" he asked Emilio.

"No, I'm sorry, Doctor," Emilio said. "We weren't able to locate him."

"That's not surprising," Jones muttered. "Where's Penelope?"

"She's resting," Barnett said. He led him towards the bedroom. "Don't be alarmed by her appearance. The injuries aren't as bad as they look."

Jones knocked on the door and started to open it. "I'd like to talk to you after I see her, Doctor," he requested.

"Of course," Barnett said. "I'll wait in my office."

****

Twenty minutes later, Wellington Jones entered Barnett's office. "She's sleeping," he said softly, sitting in front of the desk. "She's very sore. Are you sure she isn't badly injured?"

"Yes, the bruises will heal quickly, probably in a week or so. The same for the abrasions."

"Has her husband been to see her at all?"

"Yes, he has. I think they have breakfast together every morning."

"What do you think of him? You served with him."

Barnett shrugged, not wanting to get involved in a family dispute, but deeply despising Cavendish. "I don't know him well," he said evasively.

"Has he asked you about Penelope's condition?"

"Yes, he has, in general terms. Nothing specific. He may have talked to one of her nurses, I'm not sure."

"Do you remember him from the Somme?"

"Yes, I do. I wasn't in his regiment, at least not initially. It got confusing after the battle started. Especially with all the bombing."

"The artillery was horrendous," Jones agreed.

... Bombs dropped for days with a deafening roar in and around the trenches as the earth quaked and flung mud and dirt from where the shell penetrated the surface and hot metal fragments splattered everywhere as rats fled and left only soldiers to suffer. Huddled in holes or surrounded by sandbags men still died grotesquely with limbs destroyed or bodies maimed or blood sprayed on the faces of friends. Screams of agony were drowned by commands to attack and soldiers stepped over the dead and dying to climb the wobbly wooden ladders that led to the top of the trench to rush across the stark terrain to attack an enemy they would never see, falling when pierced by a bullet or retreating back to where they had come when the attack failed and the ground was littered with bodies of men who only minutes before had breathed with life. And then the second wave came over the top and ...

"Don't you agree, Doctor?"

"Yes, it was," Barnett said, a pasted expression hiding the pain. "Chaos, confusion, destruction and death."

"But fighting for the king."

"Yes," Barnett said softly, willing the images away. "And dying for the king, as well."

Chapter 30

Alexander Cavendish's cottage was a brisk fifteen-minute walk from the sanitarium. By motor car it was longer, starting on a dirt driveway that led to a narrow road that wound up the mountain and around the lake, to another road that led down the mountain to the sanitarium driveway. Since Alexander Cavendish had other places to go after a planned visit to Penelope, he decided to drive.

He had barely left his bungalow when he looked in the rear-view mirror to see a car behind him, still at a distance, two men in the front. There weren't that many vehicles in Como. It didn't seem likely one would follow him from his cottage to the sanitarium. He continued onto the main road, the car still following him but far enough away that he couldn't identify the occupants.

He shifted in the seat, not sure if Billy Flynn had found him, but hoping he hadn't. As the car maintained a discreet distance, Cavendish got nervous, beads of sweat forming on the back of his neck. Maybe he panicked for no reason; it was unlikely Flynn would come all the way to Italy. But then, fifteen thousand pounds was a lot of money. He realised that, even if it wasn't Flynn, he might still come, and never really go away. Cavendish had to get the money to pay his debt, and he had to do it soon. If he didn't, they would kill him – if only as a warning to others who didn't meet their obligations.

The authorities at the sanitarium hadn't contacted him about Penelope's fall until earlier that morning. They had sent someone to his cottage when it happened, but he had been away for the evening. He had decided to celebrate – he deserved it, with all he had been through. His current distraction was a buxom barmaid from a local tavern, a woman who knew only that he was a rich Englishman. She didn't know he was a married rich Englishman.

He now realised Wellington Jones had someone watching him. Cavendish had been careless, and had never considered being observed. But at least he found out before it was too late. He took action at once, as soon as he saw the two fools watching his cottage from their car, and sneaked up the mountainside and cut their brake line. Although they survived, he was sure they were shaken. And he could do much worse if he had to.

As he entered the circular drive to the sanitarium, he noticed the car that followed him was no longer there. They probably turned toward the city of Como or they could have stopped at any of the villas dotting the shoreline. They also may have been passing through, innocent travellers whose path had crossed his. Or they might be back.

****

"You're as bruised as I am," Cavendish observed as he sat beside Penelope on the sweeping lawn of the sanitarium. He dabbed his lip with a handkerchief. "My lip has been bleeding a bit. Can't seem to get it to stop. Are you sure you're all right, darling?"

"Yes, I'm just sore," she said, twisting in the chair to move stiff muscles. "But otherwise not hurt. I'm fortunate; not many people survive attempts on their lives, especially when they're thrown from a third-floor balcony."

"I'm sorry I wasn't there to protect you," he offered contritely. He paused, reflective, before continuing. "I know you wouldn't try to hurt yourself, but are you sure you didn't fall?"

"No, of course not," she insisted. "Someone is trying to kill me. I'm certain of it. I didn't jump and I didn't fall. Someone pushed me."

He looked at his watch, already tiring of the conversation. He had heard it so many times before. "Did you explain everything to Dr Barnett?"

"Yes, but he didn't believe me."

"Did he do anything?"

"Yes, he contacted the police."

Cavendish looked at her strangely, his eyes wide. "The police?" he asked, surprised.

"Yes," she replied. "They came to investigate."

"Did they find anything?" he asked, subconsciously dabbing his bleeding lip with the handkerchief. "I assume an intruder, if there was one, left no tracks." He tenderly touched her arm. "And I don't mean that in a nasty way, love. It's just that you're sick, at least we think you are, and you may not remember what actually happened."

"The police studied the grounds, examined the tree and the balcony, and then checked my suite. After a thorough investigation, they determined that the tree branches had broken my fall. Brilliant."

"That's all they found?" he asked. "The intruder left no clues? Maybe we should discuss it with Dr Barnett, darling. It could have been one of your episodes."

She thought for a moment, appearing to digest his statement but possibly thinking of so much more. "They did find some blood on the windowsill," she informed him casually. "Although they couldn't determine where it came from."

"Blood on the windowsill?"

"Yes, not a lot. Almost like it dripped there and was smudged with a finger."

He was quiet, his mind racing. "Do they think someone could have entered your suite through the window?"

She shrugged. "I don't know, darling. They really didn't say."

"It just seems like they should be able to determine that."

"Maybe they did," she added, and then grabbed his handkerchief. "Oh, look, darling. Your lip is bleeding again, just a little drip. Can't a doctor do something for that?"

Cavendish was quiet for a moment, delicately phrasing his thoughts. "Has Doctor Barnett discussed the attempts on your life?"

"Yes, we talk about it all the time."

"What do you discuss?" he asked. "Has he ever mentioned me?"

She looked at him strangely. "Why would he ever mention you?"

He laughed nervously. "I don't know. I was just curious."

"He tries to dissect the murder attempt," she explained.

"I'm not sure I understand?"

She paused, as if wondering how to phrase her reply. "We discuss motives," she told him. "Why would anyone want to kill me?"

"And that exposes the delusions," Cavendish surmised. "For example, why would Adele want to kill you?"

"I'm not sure it exposes any delusions," she countered. "More often than not, we discuss the most common motive for murder."

"And what is that, darling?"

She turned to face him, her expression sweet and innocent. "Money," she replied. "Money is the most common motive for murder."

Chapter 31

Rose Barnett sat by the lake, the water shimmering in the sun, the cluster of cabins and cottages, mansions and summer hotels winding along the coast. She held a notebook and pen, scribbling on the page, totally focused. She read a written line but wasn't satisfied with it, the rhyme not working:

'You take my wrongs and make them disappear'

She had been studying the words, mouthing the metre, tapping her pen on the page, admiring the lake, watching birds fly by, observing a boat in the distance with two men casting fishing rods as her two cats, Jack and Jill, sprawled on the grass beside her. Many minutes passed before the answer came to her. She crossed the line out with her pen and re-wrote it:

'You take my wrongs and make them right
Turn my blindness into sight
Steal the daytime from the night'

She smiled, now satisfied. But she had been so engrossed in her work that she hadn't seen him approach. It was instinct or intuition more than anything that told her someone was near. She turned abruptly and he was standing there, just a few feet away.

"Good morning, Rose," Alexander Cavendish said with a disarming smile.

"What are you doing here?" she demanded, her face lit with anger.

"We never finished our chat the other day."

"I think we did," she said firmly. "As I recall, I said if you didn't leave me alone, I would kill you."

"I realised you were joking."

"I wasn't," she insisted. "I meant it. I have a rifle and I know how to use it. Now go away for good, before I act on my threat."

"Oh, my dear Rose," he chuckled, "how dramatic. You aren't going to kill me. I know that and so do you. Because you can't. You're weak; I'm strong. Didn't we prove that years ago?"

"You're disgusting," she smirked. "And you're wrong."

"No, I'm not," he said as he sat on the chair usually reserved for Joseph.

"Go away!"

"Not until we finish our discussion."

"What do you want? Be quick, and then be gone."

"I want money. You know that."

"And I don't have it. I told you my royalties go to a London bank. Much of it is used to help my family, the rest is donated to veterans' charities. We live off my husband's earnings at the sanitarium."

"You could get money from your London bank if you wanted to."

"Yes, but I don't want to. You need to understand that. We live simply. We help people and we don't want to be bothered."

"You can still get fifteen thousand pounds."

"No, I can't."

"Your husband will give it to you," he assured her. "Especially since it's going to a worthy cause."

"Even if he did have it, he wouldn't give it to you. I already told him what a despicable pig you are."

"Like he would do anything about it."

"Don't be so sure."

"I'm tiring of this game, Rose. You have two options: ask your husband for the money; or get it from London."

"You're out of your mind. I'm going to the police."

He started laughing, shaking his head. "The police?" he asked incredulously "My dear Rose, I thought my wife was the lunatic. Maybe it's you. We both know you would never go to the police."

"I think you drove your wife crazy," she replied. She got up from the chair and started walking toward to the house, knowing she could run inside, get the rifle or a knife, and kill him.

He pretended to be hurt. "Rose, you're so cruel."

"Here's what you need to understand," she declared, still edging towards the house. "I am not going to give you any money. Now I'll give you one last chance to leave me alone."

"That's not going to happen."

She darted for the door, running across the lawn. Cavendish jumped from the chair, chasing after her. She had almost reached the house when he leaped forward, catching her ankles. She fell to the ground and he climbed on top of her.

He pinned her face down in the dirt and sat on her back. "That was very stupid, Rose," he scolded.

"Get off me!"

His hands roamed up and down her body, touching and caressing. "Oh, Rose," he moaned. "I forgot how nice you feel."

"Let me up!" she yelled. "I'm going to the police."

"My dear Rose," he said, sliding his hand in her blouse. "You won't go the police. We both know that. You didn't the first time and you won't now."

"Yes, I will," she said, reaching back and clawing at him.

He rolled her over, straddled her chest and forced her hands to the ground. "Listen closely, Rose," he warned. "You have three days to get me the money. If you don't, I will go to the police and tell them a story."

Her eyes widened, her face paled. "No, I'm going to the police," she insisted, but weaker than before. "After I expose you for what you are, they'll throw you in jail."

"You won't go to the police, Rose."

"I will. Now get your hands off me and let me up."

"No, you won't. You can't. And we both know why."

She struggled, trying to push him away. "Please, get off me," she asked politely, trying a different tack.

"Three days, Rose. That's all the time you have. If I don't have the money by then, I'll ruin you. I'll tell the police your secret."

"I have no secrets."

"Yes, you do Rose, we both know that."

"I said to get off me!"

"You're a murderer, Rose, aren't you? Now the whole world will know."

"No-one will believe you."

"Yes, they will," he said, leaning forward and kissing her face. "Because you've killed more than once."

"Get away from me!"

"Three days, Rose. And then the police. If that doesn't work, the cripple is dead."

"I swear I'm going to kill you!"

"No, you're not, Rose," he insisted. "You're going to do what I tell you, so listen closely. I'll be standing outside my cottage every night at midnight, holding a lantern. I'll be easy to find. You just bring the money."

"I'm not giving you any money!"

"Yes, you will. If you don't, I go to the police. If that doesn't work, I kill the cripple," he threatened. "And I mean it." He shoved her head in the soil and the climbed off her and started to walk away.

"Get out of here!" she screamed, shaking dirt from her hair.
"Midnight, Rose. Make sure you're there."

Chapter 32

Penelope tossed and turned, unable to sleep. She kicked the blankets off, rolled on her back and stared at the ceiling. Then she turned on her left side, closed her eyes, and thought about her father's estate outside of London – the lawns, garden statues, flowers and shrubs. She pictured Mrs Thistle, her former nanny, who still lived there with her caretaker husband. They had been exchanging letters, but it wasn't enough. Penelope missed her – the chats they enjoyed over a cup of tea or their long walks through the estate. She realised she wanted to go home.

After fifteen minutes had passed and slumber still eluded her, she got out of bed and walked to the window. She looked at the tree branches that stretched near the building, the sill where the policeman had found traces of blood, and the sanitarium grounds beyond.

She wondered how sick the other patients were. She avoided them; they scared her. Some were celebrities, like the Spanish singer in the next room. And some wanted to be celebrities, like Lafite, the painter who cut off his ear. And there were some from the military, the American who couldn't stop his body from shaking and a French captain with a manic look in his eyes. She had seen other familiar faces: politicians, spouses of public figures, a famous chess player.

She walked into the sitting room, opened the French doors and went out on the balcony. She knew that Dr Barnett had increased the security, but she hadn't seen any signs of it. There was a guard at the front entrance, but there always had been. And she had seen another guard walking the grounds.

After she had admired the stars, twinkling in a clear sky, she went back inside, closing the doors behind her, and sat on the sofa. It was dark and quiet, only the tick of the clock marring the silence. She liked the darkness; it was pure, innocent, yet at the same time, it was sinister. She was starting to get tired and she thought she might sleep on the couch, rolling on her side, not even bothering to go to bed. Her eyes closed.

She heard a noise in the hallway and bolted upright, squinting to see the grandfather clock against the far wall. It was 3 a.m. She wasn't sure if she had been sleeping or not. But regardless, she heard something and, if she had been asleep, it was loud enough to wake her.

It was quiet now, the only sound coming from the hands of the clock moving: *tick, tock, tick, tock.* She sat motionless, listening. Several minutes passed, but there were no more noises. She was just about to get up and go to bed when she heard a hushed whisper from the hall.

"Penelope."

She froze, not recognising the voice. She didn't move, not wanting to make a sound, not wanting whoever it was to hear her. Several minutes passed before she heard them speak again. It was a man who uttered one word.

"Barbitone."

The sedative they gave her to help her sleep. The drug she had overdosed on in Monte Carlo. Why is a man in the hallway talking about her? And why did he mention barbitone?

She slowly rose from the couch, easing her weight off the cushion so the spring wouldn't squeak. Then she moved cautiously across the tiled floor, her bare feet making no sound, one step and then another, pausing, waiting for another word to be uttered. She could see light filtering from the hallway, spilling under the crack at the bottom of the door. She took a tentative step and was barely a metre from the door when she saw the shadow, the light underneath interrupted, the muted glow disjointed, as if someone stood just on the other side of the door.

"Should I check?" a man murmured.

Penelope moved against the wall, waiting for the door to open. Seconds passed, the shadow still blocking the light, until another voice was heard, a woman, farther away.

"… sleeping."

She couldn't hear the whole sentence. Breathlessly she watched the crack under the door. The shape of the shadow changed; she heard footsteps, and the figure was gone, the light flowing uninterrupted. She sighed with relief.

"They're trying to kill me," she said loudly. "First it was barbitone, then they tried to smother me. Then a man followed me, trying to get me alone, but I escaped. Then it was the gardener, and then I was thrown from the balcony. Now it's barbitone again."

"Miss Penelope?" called a woman's voice from the hallway. "Miss Penelope?"

"What do you want?" she asked.

There was a tap on the door and then it opened tentatively, the night nurse standing there. "Va bene?" she asked.

"No, I'm not all right," Penelope replied. "Someone is trying to kill me."

"Hai avuto un brutto sogno. Va tutto bene," the night nurse said. You had a bad dream. It's all right.

She led Penelope into the bedroom, helped her lie down, and covered her with a blanket. "Buona notte," she said as she quietly left the room.

Penelope lay still. The police were suspicious, but not enough to provide protection. Dr Barnett seemed to believe her, at least he listened. And it was the same with her father. She didn't know what Alexander thought, but he did seem to want her well.

She needed a plan. She had to get out of the sanitarium. And she had to do it soon.

Chapter 33

"If someone cut the brake lines to my motor car, someone could just as easily be trying to kill Penelope," Wellington Jones insisted.

"You should have gone to the police," Barnett advised. "At least they could have launched an investigation."

"To determine what?" he scoffed. "That someone is trying to kill me?"

"Could the brake lines have been damaged in any other way? Perhaps from the terrain?"

"No, we were on the road when we lost our brakes," Jones explained. "We had to cross a field to slow the vehicle down."

"Who would have anything to gain by killing you or Penelope?"

"I have a suspicion," Jones said, speculating, "but no proof. My assistant is investigating."

"Let's assume the issues are unrelated," Barnett suggested, "because I'm convinced Penelope is suffering from delusions."

"What about the last attempt on her life," Jones asked, "and the blood on the windowsill?"

"If you recall Penelope's nightmare when she claimed Adele tried to kill her, her fingertips were torn, with traces of blood. Maybe she touched the windowsill."

"That still doesn't explain why her fingers were bleeding."

"It may not," Barnett argued. "or it might. She'll do anything to prove her delusions are reality, whatever's required to legitimise them."

"Even injuring herself?"

"Yes," Barnett replied firmly. "Even injuring herself."

"I'm still not convinced."

"There are too many innocent explanations for what she claims are attempts on her life," Barnett continued. "She had another issue last night. She insisted someone was trying to kill her because she heard voices outside her room. That was at 3 a.m."

"What did you determine?"

"Only that there were voices outside her room," Barnett informed him. "It's a hospital. There's night staff – orderlies, nurses, cleaning personnel, security – any one of whom could have been talking in the hallway."

Jones was quiet, giving no indication whether he agreed with Barnett or not. After a minute, he asked, "Have you determined what caused her rapid decline?"

"I think her problems are related to a series of emotional traumas that have somehow become manifested in delusional behaviour – like thinking she lived during Shakespeare's time or insisting someone is trying to kill her. The delusions are an escape, a subconscious defence mechanism, so she doesn't have to confront reality."

"Her mother's death was horrendous, as you can imagine. Penelope had a very difficult time, but she eventually managed."

"We discussed the tragedy in one of our sessions," Barnett said "I think she's accepted the loss, largely due to the substitute role that Mrs Thistle played."

Jones paused, sighing. "Neither of us dealt very well with Oxford's death," he said softly. "But I'm sure you're aware of that."

"It's difficult," Barnett assured him, wondering if the father needed help as much as the daughter. "The whole continent grieves."

"We did our duty, Doctor," Jones stated firmly. "As we've discussed before."

"Yes, I suppose," Barnett said, looking at his hand, knowing it would never move again.

"Do you link her problems to Oxford's death?"

"I'm not sure," Barnett admitted. "But her steep decline occurred somewhere near that time period." He paused, reflective. "Why did she marry so quickly after the war?"

Jones shrugged. "It seemed the right thing to do," he said. "They had been together since before the war, engaged for two years. There were many marriages when the war ended."

"Yes, there were," Barnett agreed. "But her wedding was only months after Oxford had passed. Death and marriage are both major changes, sometimes difficult for the mind to master."

"I thought the wedding would help her forget," Jones conceded. "And Alexander had an impeccable reputation – kind, caring, compassionate, a war hero. His family is among the wealthiest in England. It seemed a suitable match."

"It *seemed* a suitable match," Barnett said. "I assume it wasn't?"

Jones appeared troubled, as if wondering how to continue. "Alexander was much different when he returned from the war," he said.

"In what way?"

"He was colder, a bit darker," he explained. "He was more of a shadow than a man, a porcelain façade ready to break at the slightest provocation."

"Few people were the same when they returned," Barnett reasoned, even though he despised Cavendish.

"I realise that," Jones admitted. "But this is different. Much more pronounced. He seems to be in a decline as steep as Penelope's."

"That's interesting," Barnett muttered, still having no compassion for the man. "And probably worth exploring."

Jones was quiet for a moment, appearing to study the spines of some leather books on the shelf behind Barnett's desk. After a moment, he spoke. "What's next for Penelope? Is there anything else we should be doing?"

"I've considered a new approach, a complement to our ongoing sessions."

Jones seemed interested. "What is that?" he asked.

"I think we need to emphasise Penelope's superior intellect and give her a purpose. She loves literature and she's one of the world's experts on Shakespeare. Maybe she can teach again, like she did during the war, or critique or edit or write."

Jones was quiet for a moment, digesting Barnett's suggestions. "I'm sure she would be interested," he surmised. "And if she isn't, I can involve her in the business."

"That might help," Barnett said, "but only if she wants to. It should be something she is truly passionate about."

"You really think that will work?"

"I do," Barnett said. "And when combined with effective psychotherapy, Penelope can lead a normal life."

Jones was quiet for a moment, lost in thought. "Don't underestimate her," he said softly. "She's very complex. Somewhat of a genius, actually. And somewhat of a loner."

Barnett was surprised. "She is a genius," he agreed, "but I didn't know she's a loner. I thought she was very active on the social circuit."

Jones frowned. "Not really," he said. "But her husband is. There is only one person outside of family that Penelope really cares about, and I include Mrs Thistle among family."

"Who might that be?"

"Her friend, Mary Westcott. Penelope spends most of her time with her whenever she's in London."

Barnett broached a difficult topic. "The tabloids claim Penelope received a percentage of your estate when she married and that she spends vast amounts of money."

"Not true," he said. "Not true at all. Penelope is very thrifty. Not many people are aware of that."

"I wasn't," he said.

"She inherited a trust fund when she was twenty-one years old," he explained. "Since that time, through a series of shrewd stock and bond purchases, she's tripled her initial investment. Her performance far surpasses any division or individual performance in my entire company. Now she's investing in American real estate. And I'm sure she'll do well."

"I had no idea," Barnett admitted. "She's never given the slightest hint of business acumen."

"She's very modest. And as I said, she's very private."

"Maybe business is, or can be, Penelope's passion," Barnett said as he sat back in the chair. "Maybe she could start a new division in your corporation by investing in American real estate."

"We can certainly pursue that," Jones said. "But please, at least accept that she could be telling the truth, that she's not delusional. Consider her claim that someone is trying to kill her."

Chapter 34

Barnett contemplated Wellington Jones's warning as he sat in his office waiting for Penelope. If someone was trying to kill her, the only viable suspect was Alexander Cavendish. Even though Barnett despised him, he thought it unlikely he would try to murder his wife. He had too much to lose: one of several heirs to a large fortune; an impeccable reputation as a war hero; and a promising future. It seemed far more likely that Penelope suffered from delusions, an escape from traumas either real or imagined.

She had cited several occasions when either an attempt had been made on her life or she suspected someone was plotting to kill her. And although each claim had some merit, they were easily explained, especially fisherman or gardeners or unknown voices – all of which Penelope saw as a threat but were only people living their lives or pursuing their occupations. Her overdose was an exception. She claimed she had been drinking, fell asleep, and vaguely remembered someone forcing her to swallow pills. The police found otherwise. Curiously, the dose administered was not high enough to kill her.

Penelope arrived a short while later, strolling into his office, her arm still bruised, her abrasions healing, the blemishes starting to fade. She paused at the desk and thoughtfully studied a bowl of candy before selecting one and popping it into her mouth.

"I love chocolate," she said as she grabbed another. "This is Swiss; they make the best."

"I'm glad you're enjoying it," Barnett remarked, amused.

"I am, and if you don't take that bowl away, I'll eat every single one."

"Penelope, your sense of humour is one of your finest traits," he said, smiling.

She rolled her eyes. "Yes, I'm absolutely hilarious," she joked. "Just ask the other lunatics."

"That's not funny," he said, lightly scolding her. He paused and picked up his pad, reading over some prior notes. "I was encouraged by our success with your last hypnosis session. I think we should try it again."

"Whatever you think is best," she grumbled, apparently not pleased. "Maybe you can cure my addiction to chocolate."

He laughed, pleased she was in such a good mood. As she reclined on the couch and closed her eyes, he pulled the chair up beside her. After ensuring she was comfortable, he began the process of hypnotising her, speaking slowly and deliberately, issuing commands that had previously proven successful. Once he was certain she was in an altered state, he began his questions.

"Penelope, have you ever felt that your life was in danger?" he asked.

"Yes."

"And when was that?"

"The train accident. When mommy died."

"Were there any other instances?"

"In Egypt. I got lost in the tomb. It took forever for daddy to find me."

"Has anyone ever tried to harm you?"

"Yes, someone has been trying to kill me."

"When was the first attempt?"

"In Monte Carlo; someone pushed pills in my mouth and made me swallow them."

Barnett studied her closely, ensuring she was actually hypnotised. Her breathing was slow and regular. There were no changes to her facial expressions. She gave every indication she was in a deep hypnotic state. He could only assume, given her responses, that she honestly believed someone was trying to kill her. He decided to probe further.

"Have there been other attempts on your life?"

"Yes, Adele tried to smother me with a pillow."

"How do you know it was Adele?"

"She climbed out the window. I tried to grab her."

He was stunned. "Maybe someone else climbed out the window," he suggested. "Is that possible? Maybe it wasn't Adele?"

"Maybe.

"Did anyone else try to kill you?"

"Yes, someone threw me off the balcony."

"Do you know who it was?"

"No, I only saw a shadow. They were behind me. I turned but didn't see them. They pushed me."

"Do you really think Adele is trying to kill you?"

"No, not anymore."

"Who do you think it is?"

"Dr Barnett."

He was shocked, wondering how she ever came to that conclusion. "Why does Dr Barnett want to kill you?" he asked, astonished by her accusation.

"Because I ate all his chocolate," she said.

He didn't think he heard her correctly and simply stared, mouth open, unable to comprehend her response. Why fear for her life because of candy?

After an awkward pause, she opened her eyes and started laughing. "I'm sorry," she said. "I couldn't resist."

When the initial shock wore off, he laughed with her. "I suppose you weren't really hypnotised," he said.

"No, I wasn't. Sometimes it works, sometimes it doesn't. I should have told you. But I couldn't resist playing a joke on you."

"I've hypnotised dozens of patients," he informed her, "but I've never been tricked before. Did you at least tell the truth – even about chasing an intruder out of your window?"

"Yes, I did."

"Did you give the policemen that information?"

"Yes, but I'm not sure they believed me."

He shook his head, still amused. "Penelope, I don't know what I'm going to do with you."

She laughed lightly. "I was just having some fun."

"I can see that," he said. "But I do have to hypnotise you again. We'll have access to your subconscious and know what's driving your delusions."

"They're not delusions," she insisted.

"And then there are two processes that work to affect a cure," he said, ignoring her. "The first is recognition. It's very important that we identify the conflicts."

"And find out who's trying to kill me."

"The second is known as catharsis," he explained, still discounting her assertion.

"It sounds like the name of an insect."

He laughed. "Cathartic memory is a powerful technique," he informed her. "Essentially, a forgotten trauma is identified and exposed. Once the event is remembered and re-lived with associated emotions, it's purged from the subconscious. Sometimes a single session can effect a cure, but more often the process is continually repeated."

Penelope frowned. "It seems complicated," she said. "I think it should work like an eraser. Then you could make the past disappear."

"I think we all would like to erase parts of our past," he agreed, amused be her analogy. "But everyone makes mistakes. They're part of who we are."

"I suppose," she said reluctantly. "I only wish we could fix them."

After the session ended and Penelope had gone, Barnett smiled, thinking about the joke she had played on him. He liked that facet of her personality – the amusing, cheerful component that surfaced so rarely. But then, as he gave the matter more thought, his smile began to fade. He wondered if it was the first time she had fooled him. And who else had she fooled?

Chapter 35

Wellington Jones sat on the verandah of his rented villa, looking out at Lake Como and the mountains beyond, the trees painting them green except for scattered expanses of grey rock and dwindling traces of snow on the peaks. The pastel colors of cottages, villas, mansions and hotels – all staggered along the shore, the residents and guests enjoying the spring day, and the glistening water of the lake splashing sunlight off its surface, almost seemed like a watercolour portrait of a landscape that only existed in fairy tales. He sipped a glass of Amaretto, watching the sun tiptoe across the sky, walking toward the peaks on the distant shore as another day was crossed off the calendar.

It had been quiet in Como, uneventful since his brake lines had been severed. Barnett suggested it was an accident, a manufacturing defect or previous damage that led to failure. Although he might be right, it seemed unlikely. But as far as Jones knew, no-one wanted him dead. Unless they had been trying to kill William Cain instead. They both needed to be careful.

He reflected on his meeting with Barnett and considered Penelope's progress. Could someone be trying to kill her? He wasn't sure. The clues were consistent, the motive apparent. It seemed to him that her husband had both opportunity and need. Penelope's death would solve so many of his problems: money for debts; funds for vices; and availability for Mary Westcott, his mistress and Penelope's best friend. But it was a difficult scenario to believe, even of Alexander Cavendish. Few men plot their wife's death. Even fewer actually attempt it. Jones had to constantly remind himself that he despised his son-in-law. He had to tread carefully, or he might create a case where none existed.

But if Cavendish was innocent, and no other assailant could be identified, he had to accept that Penelope suffered from mental instabilities, delusions that confused fact and fiction. And even though she had recovered from the deaths of her mother and brother, the catalyst that caused the precipitous decline in her mental state lay hidden somewhere in her past, dormant until the last few months, but now very much alive.

Wellington wished he could help her, somehow fix what was broken, but he knew he couldn't. He understood what she'd endured; he had dealt with the same sorrow. He was an adult and still couldn't cope with his wife's death, but had finally managed to accept it; Penelope had been a child. But he would never get over Oxford. The nightmares tortured him; the grief overwhelmed him; the memories haunted him. It was like losing a part of himself that couldn't be replaced. His remaining days would always be dulled, the dawn always dimmer, the days ahead not what he dreamed. It was probably the same for Penelope, but her pain dwarfed his.

A servant walked out on the verandah and handed him a cable, interrupting his thoughts. "This arrived from Bombay, sir," he announced.

"Thank you," Jones said, nodding. He took the envelope and opened it as the servant walked away.

It wasn't what he expected. The information he had given to his associates, proof that his global real estate operation was financially sound, had been rejected by his creditors. They hadn't called any liens or demanded immediate payment, but they threatened to do so, giving thirty days' reprieve pending improved global economic conditions or assessment of any alternatives Jones might have to offer.

He looked out on the lake, so serene as the sun began to set, and glanced about the lavish villa that he had rented. He thought about his mansion in England, constructed by the finest craftsmen of the best material the world had to offer, the grounds beautifully landscaped and superbly maintained. He considered the servants who depended on him for their livelihood, the business associates and employees who gave him their devoted support – all of those whose lives would forever be changed if his business empire crumbled. He needed a solution and he needed one quickly. He stood on a precipice, teetering and about to fall. But he had to remain upright; he had to stand strong. Too many people depended on him.

He sipped his Amaretto, reflective. There had to be a solution, a compromise that both parties could accept. Deflation had made the economic downturn so horrendous, with prices of hard assets – real estate, minerals, agricultural goods – declining by almost twenty percent. His property liens had been secured with debt that equalled large percentages of the purchase price. Now any equity had evaporated, exposing his creditors to unwanted risk.

What if he offered different terms on the liens so they could be restructured? Instead of calling the debt and demanding payment, maybe

Jones could offer his creditors cash for each property that equalled the price decline. If markets had dropped twenty percent, he would provide payment of twenty percent. That should satisfy the banks, re-establish the debt-to-asset ratios, and preserve his real estate empire.

There was just one problem. He owned dozens of properties in India alone. And Hong Kong and Singapore banks would probably demand the same agreement. All of his creditors might request the same terms – regardless of location.

Where would he ever get the money?

Chapter 36

Alexander Cavendish walked in the front door of his bungalow and found two men sitting in the parlour. The first was a big man, casually dressed, wearing a workman's cap, a day's growth of beard. His companion was well dressed in an expensive suit, silk shirt and tie, polished shoes with spats.

"You owe us some money," said Jocko Jakes, pointing a snub-nosed revolver.

Cavendish looked at the barrel, then to the men who watched him so smugly. "I was wondering when you two were going to show up," he said sarcastically, trying to hide his fear. "I've been expecting you."

"We got tired of waiting in London," Billy Flynn informed him. "I thought it might be nice for Jocko and me to take a bit of a holiday. Italy's a wonderful place. I've been here before."

"I asked for a few more days," Cavendish said.

"That was three weeks ago," Flynn reminded him. "Your debt is long overdue. I even paid your father a visit. I thought he might settle it for you. Not quite yet, I'm afraid. But I think if we see him again, he might be more interested. Don't you think so, Jocko?"

"I do," his henchman replied. "Or maybe your mother might be more agreeable."

"You know, I hadn't thought of that," Flynn admitted. "Maybe if Alexander doesn't pay up, we can call on Mrs Cavendish."

"I just need a little more time," Cavendish pleaded.

"That's what you said in London," Flynn recalled. "Did you think we wouldn't find you? Your lunatic wife is in all the headlines. Everyone knows where she is."

"Billy says to me, hey, let's go to Italy," Jocko said. He then leaned forward, his face menacing. "And I told Billy, that's fine with me. I can beat Cavendish to death in Italy just as well as I can in London."

"I intended to return to London as soon as I got the money," Cavendish assured them, his voice quivering.

"Except you never got the money," Flynn said. "Or have you?" He turned to Jocko. "Maybe he lost the money on Italian ponies and forgot all about Jocko and Billy Flynn."

"I haven't got it yet, I swear."

"That's a shame," Jocko said. "Because now we have to kill you."

"No, wait," Cavendish said, coming closer. "I'll get the money. I promise."

"Which means you don't have it," Flynn said.

"No, but I can get it."

"How?"

"I have several different plans."

"What are they?" Flynn asked, his expression wary.

"I can get the money from my wife," Cavendish said.

"The lunatic?" Flynn asked. "Why didn't you do that already?"

"She's been too ill. As soon as she's better, she'll give it to me."

Flynn looked at his companion. "He thinks we're stupid, doesn't he?" he asked.

"I think he does," Jocko agreed. "Do you want me to rough him up a little?"

"I'm telling the truth," Cavendish swore, desperate.

"Except your wife is loony," Flynn said. "She's in the crazy house and for all we know she may never get out."

"Yeah, nice try," Jocko said, chuckling. "But I think you're about to be dead, mate."

"Wait," Cavendish begged. "I have other ways of getting the money."

"Then why haven't you done it?" Flynn asked. "It makes me think you can't."

"No, I can get the money. There's a psychiatrist here. I know his wife from the war; she has money. I'm blackmailing her."

"I'm listening," Flynn said, eyebrows arched. "How badly does she want what you know kept secret?"

"Very badly," Cavendish told them. "She killed some people and got away with it. And she's a famous writer. It'll destroy her if it gets out."

Flynn let out a low whistle. "Very interesting," he said, apparently impressed. "We may want a piece of that action. But you would already have the money if she planned to pay."

"She's thinking about it," Cavendish assured them. "I told her I would wait by the lake at midnight so she can give me the money. But it might take her a few days."

Flynn seemed sceptical. "What if I don't feel like waiting?" he asked.

"I have other options."

"Like what?" Jocko asked.

"I also threatened to kill her husband. He was badly injured during the war. I'm not sure how long he'll be around anyway."

"Do you think she'll pay to protect him?" Flynn asked.

"Yes, I'm sure of it."

"Then why hasn't she paid already?" Flynn asked. "If she's a famous writer, she should have money. And plenty of it."

Cavendish shrugged. "Her money is in London," he responded.

"Maybe if she were dead you could get the money from him," Jocko said. He then smiled. "To ensure her memory isn't soiled, so to speak."

"I wouldn't have to kill her," Cavendish offered, "just threaten to. I served with her husband in the trenches. He couldn't handle losing his wife; he's half-crazy already. He would pay just to make me go away."

"Sounds messy but do-able, I suppose," Flynn said, as if considering the options. "What else?"

Cavendish hesitated, knowing they would kill him if he couldn't convince them. "If my father-in-law were to die, my wife would inherit the family fortune," he told them.

"And since she's barmy you would handle the finances," Jocko surmised.

"Yes, and I could pay you."

"With a premium," Jocko added.

"I see an easier way," Flynn said.

"What is that?" Cavendish asked.

"If your wife was dead, you would get all of her money," Flynn said. "And since you arranged a life insurance policy that names me as beneficiary, I collect if she dies."

"I already thought of that," Cavendish said.

Flynn rose and started for the door. "Come on, Jocko," he said. "Let's get out of here."

"Do you want me to smack him around a little before we go?" Jocko asked.

Flynn paused and looked at Cavendish, watching him tremble, his bruises still fading from the last beating. "Not just yet," he replied. "Let's give him another day."

"I promise I'll have the money tomorrow," Cavendish said, relieved.

"See that you do," Billy Flynn said as he walked out the door.

From a window Cavendish watched them leave. Then he went into the kitchen, got a half empty flask of whisky and, with a shaking hand, took a long swig. He felt it burn from mouth to stomach and then drank more. He walked back into the parlour, whisky bottle with him, and sat down, looking at his pocket watch. He remained in the chair until the whisky was gone and then went into the kitchen and got another flask. When midnight arrived, he lit a lantern and walked to the lake, still carrying the flask.

"Come on, Rose," he muttered to himself. "Don't let me down."

Chapter 37

A simple fisherman found the body. On a shoreline cluttered with mansions and hotels, summer cottages for the well-to-do and the Lakeside Sanitarium, there were still those who lived and worked along the lake, their homes farther down the shore from Como, or climbing the mountains that surrounded the placid body of water nestled so peacefully in the Italian alps.

He had taken his boat out at dawn, moving farther south than normal, almost to the asylum that sat on the outskirts of the city. He cast a small net and three fishing lines and waited, contemplating the ways of the world, watching the sun's rays peek through the mountains and splash warmth upon the water. As the sun rose higher and the light became brighter, he noticed a shadow on the shore. He squinted, at first unable to tell what it was, and then decided to move closer. He navigated the boat to a stone bulkhead fifty metres away, tied it off, and walked tentatively along the bank, the water rippling by his feet. The shadow took shape and, as he approached, he saw it was a body and he ran towards it.

The corpse lay face down in the water, a bloodstain on the back. The fisherman stood transfixed, unable to comprehend that a life had been taken. He turned quickly, frightened, and ran back to his boat. He started the engine, pulled away from shore and sped to the town of Como, docking his boat and hurrying to the police station. He burst into the building, panting, rambling, his eyes wide, and explained what he had seen. For a man who lived a peaceful life, it was a traumatic experience. Finding a corpse was distressing enough, but a victim that was obviously murdered in a town where most had no locks on their doors was absolutely terrifying.

The Carabinieri, the Italian police, listened to his explanation, as startled as the fisherman that a murder had occurred in their jurisdiction. They left immediately, an inspector, a captain, and two policemen half the force that presided over the tranquil communities nestled along the shore. They climbed into a police boat – a bit weathered but functional and used for patrols along the southwestern basin of the lake – and followed the fisherman to the crime scene.

Fifteen minutes later, the police docked beside the fishing boat and the officers made their way to the crime scene. They gathered around the corpse, studying it for a moment – the position of the body, the face submerged in only a few centimetres of water, the shoes anchored to shore. They scanned the area, the mansions, cottages and sanitarium that sprawled around them, and the terrain that climbed from the water to the mountains beyond. It was quiet – no people, dogs or cats – not even the birds that normally soared above the water, waiting for the tiny fish that sometimes strayed too close to the surface or washed upon the shore. It seemed no-one knew about the murder – or maybe they didn't want to know.

Inspector Antonio Falcone cautiously surveyed the landscape before turning again to examine the corpse. An oil lantern lay near his left hand, a flask of whisky by his right. Apparently, the victim stood on shore, probably late the evening before, enjoying his whisky when the bullet entered his back. Falcone looked at the rising terrain, trying to determine where the killer may have been hidden up the hillside. A road looped around the rising mountain, layered into the rock, but it seemed too high given the bullet's path. He suspected the gunman was lower, somewhere in the trees and shrubs that scaled the side of the mountain.

Falcone had been born in Rome, his family rooted there for many generations. He was an older man, olive-skinned, his black hair streaked with grey, his eyes dark. Although he smiled often, it was empty, as if he wanted to be happy but somehow never could be. He had joined the Carabinieri as a young man, rose through the ranks, and then served as a major in the military during the Great War, distinguishing himself against the Austrians during the First Battle of the Isonzo. His family wasn't as fortunate. His son was killed by a chlorine gas attack in the Battle of Caporreto, lingering for days but dying in agony. A gentle boy whose smile never left his face, a lover of animals, a gifted guitar player, his death took a piece of Falcone's heart and soul that could never be replaced. His wife passed less than a year later, just before the war ended, more from heartbreak than anything else. Italian women love their sons above all else, and while Falcone's heart was broken, his wife's was destroyed. The loss of two loved ones in so short a time had stolen his will to live, and for many months after he was more a shadow than a man. A daughter survived but, with too many haunting memories in Italy, she emigrated to America. Now Falcone was alone.

When the war ended, he didn't return to Rome, finding the familiarity too much to bear with no family beside him. He transferred to Como, changing the priorities in his life, accepting far less responsibility, wanting only to live in peace. With a prominent career behind him, skilled in murder investigations, familiar with the study of ballistics, a relatively new science, he was welcomed by all in his new assignment. He loved the lake, home to both wealthy and mundane – merchants, fisherman, craftsman – a slice of humanity that lived peacefully, respecting each other. Como was a quaint village close to Milan, the opera capital of the world, and Antonio Falcone loved opera. It was, perhaps, the only enjoyment he had left. So there, in the sanctity of the Italian Alps, he mourned his wife and son, missed his daughter, and healed from the world war, just as the rest of Europe tried to do.

The Lakeside Sanitarium was perched in the distance, a massive building of Italianate design, the polished façade a pale yellow, the trim a crisp white accented with green. Marble balconies jutted from the building, some wide and expansive, others narrow, more decorative than functional. Falcone estimated the distance from building to body, and then to cottages that sat on the other side of the hospital, and a larger home higher up the hillside. He wondered who may have heard the gunshot. And who fired it.

"It appears to be a single bullet," said Captain Minelli. He was a younger man, had advanced rapidly, a bit gruff and arrogant but in awe of Falcone. Minelli knew he had much to learn. He had spent his whole life in Como and had a talent for making award-winning spaghetti sauce.

"The wound is high on the back," Falcone said, studying the body carefully. "He might have initially survived but lost consciousness and fell in the water. The post-mortem may prove that he actually drowned."

Minelli bent over the body. "It's a clean shot, maybe fatal," he observed, craning his neck to look up the hillside. "And a very difficult one. Not many men could make it."

"No, they couldn't," Falcone said, frowning. "Especially at night."

"There are easier ways to kill."

Falcone was pensive, eyeing the murder scene. "The killer must have been perched on the mountainside. But how could they know the victim would walk out of the cottage, especially late at night."

Minelli shrugged. "They may have waited for hours," he guessed, "or even days."

"I suppose," Falcone agreed, "that they could have been watching him. Was there any identification on the body?"

"Yes, he's an Englishman. Alexander Cavendish, from London."

"Is this his cottage?" he asked, pointing to a building nestled among some trees, thirty metres from the water.

"We don't know that yet," Minelli replied. He looked up and down the shoreline. "I'll question the nearby residents."

Falcone's attention turned to the massive building beyond the cottage. "I'll talk to those in the sanitarium," he said. "But first I want to see where the shot came from."

Chapter 38

Joseph Barnett watched dawn break, the sun shining brighter as it inched higher in the heavens, the soft glow if its rays burning the morning mist off the shimmering water of the lake. He saw a cluster of activity down the shore – a small fishing vessel, the paint faded and weathered, and a police boat. Four men, three in uniform, stood by the water; an elderly fisherman watched from a distance. Barnett squinted, wondering what could have spoiled the tranquility of such a peaceful morning.

He went in the bedroom to wake Rose. He stopped, smiling, watching her sleep, her auburn hair lying in a mound around her head. The blanket partially covered her, exposing her cream-coloured nightgown, a bare foot dangling over the edge of the bed. He leaned over, kissed her on the forehead, and stepped back to admire her.

A moment later, unable to satisfy his curiosity any longer, he kissed her again and shook her gently. "Rose," he whispered, "something happened down the lake. The police are there. I think they may be at Cavendish's cottage."

She stirred and wakened, her eyes fluttering open. "The police?"

"Yes, there's a boat near the cottage on the other side of the sanitarium. Get dressed. We'll go see."

Her eyes opened, showing confusion and then beginning to clear. "I wonder what happened," she said as she climbed out of bed.

He watched as she dressed, removing the nightgown, exposing creamy skin dotted with freckles, the firm swell of her breasts, the curve of her buttocks. She smiled as he watched, stepped into her clothes, and ran a brush through her hair.

They left the cottage, passing the flower beds so carefully cultivated, walking the half kilometre to the sanitarium and then continuing past it a few hundred metres to the cottage where the policemen waited. As the Barnetts approached, a man stepped forward, not in uniform, but wearing a dark suit.

"I'm sorry," he said in Italian. "But you can't come any closer. An investigation is in progress."

"What happened?" Rose said, her Italian marred by an English accent.

"Is this your home?" the man asked, eyeing her carefully, ignoring her question.

"No," Barnett replied, answering for his wife. He turned and pointed to the bungalow further down the shore, barely visible in the melting mist. "We live in that cottage in the distance. I'm Dr Joseph Barnett, from the sanitarium, and this is my wife Rose."

"I speak English," the man informed them. "Is that better?"

"Yes, thank you," Barnett said.

"How long have you been in Como?" the man asked.

"Almost three years," Barnett answered.

"I'm Inspector Antonio Falcone," the man said. "I'm leading the investigation."

"What happened?" Barnett asked.

"Did you hear anything last night?" Falcone asked. "Loud noises or unusual sounds, perhaps a motor car late at night?" He glanced at Barnett's scarred face and then looked away.

Rose listened to the policeman but looked past him, staring at the corpse as policemen prepared to remove it. "Is that Alexander Cavendish?" she asked, her hand moving to her mouth.

"Do you know Alexander Cavendish?" Falcone asked.

"We both do," Barnett replied.

"We know him from the war," Rose clarified.

"And his wife is my patient," Barnett added.

"Do you know who lives in this cottage?" Falcone asked.

"Cavendish is renting it," Barnett replied.

Falcone took a notebook from his pocket. "Does Cavendish have any other relatives in Como?" he asked.

"Yes," Barnett replied, "his father-in-law, Wellington Jones, is renting a villa a few kilometres down the lake."

"Doctor, I assume I can contact you at the sanitarium?"

"Yes, of course."

"I'll have many questions over the next few days."

"I'll help in any way I can," Barnett promised.

"And where can I contact you, Mrs Barnett?"

"Just come to our cottage. I'm usually home."

Falcone paused, looking sheepish. "Are you Rose Barnett, the poet?"

"Yes, I am," she said, surprised.

He looked at her, reflective, and said, "Hollow hearts and empty eyes, the anguish that they can't disguise."

She smiled. "My poem, *The Survivors*," she said.

He looked at her, his heart hollow, his eyes empty. "You captured the emotions of an entire generation," he told her.

"Thank you so much," she replied humbly.

He bowed slightly. "I'm honoured to meet you."

Barnett kept looking at the body, the policemen now carrying it on a stretcher to one of the boats. "Inspector," he said, "I must know if that is Alexander Cavendish. His wife is in my care. I have to tell her if something happened to her husband."

"Dr Barnett, at this point we are not able to release the victim's identity. As soon as we are, the appropriate parties will be notified."

"I can identify the body, if needed," Barnett offered.

"Thank you," Falcone said, "but if such an identification is warranted, a request will be made of a family member. For now, I suggest you return to your home. I will contact you when more information is available."

Chapter 39

"I'm sure that was Cavendish," Rose whispered as they walked back to their cottage. She sneaked a peek over her shoulder, but then turned away when she saw that Falcone was watching them.

"It was hard to tell," he said, taking her hand in his as he limped beside her. "We were too far away."

"Who else has wavy blond hair?" she asked. "And the body was thirty metres from his cottage."

"I suppose it's likely," he agreed, "but it could have been an intruder. I'm sure the man has enemies. Maybe Cavendish is the killer, not the corpse."

She was quiet for a moment, considering what he said. Then she spoke softly, almost as if she was afraid someone would hear. "I hope it was Alexander Cavendish."

He squeezed her hand. "I feel the same way," he assured her. "I know it's horrible to wish he was dead, but we would finally be free of—"

"Amiens," she added, interrupting him. "He was the only one that knew, the only witness."

"We could go back to England," he offered optimistically, as if an impossible dream might come true.

"With no fear of arrest," she said, her face showing guilt. "But we shouldn't gloat over his death, assuming it was him."

"Why not?" Barnett asked harshly. "The world's a better place without him."

They walked past the sanitarium, across the manicured lawns, hugging the lake. They continued through some trees and shrubs where a trail had been cut and onto their own property. Their cottage was perched by the water, nestled among gardens and shrubs and trees nurtured by Barnett, hidden from the prying eyes of the universe, their very own sanctuary.

He paused on the stone walk that led to the cottage entrance and plucked a rose from a bush that bordered the walkway. "For you, my love," he said, smiling.

She took the rose and kissed him, then hugged him tightly. "Each day that comes is better than the last," she said happily. "And that's because I have you to share it with."

They opened the door and walked inside, quickly closing it behind them. They locked in an embrace, their world a bit better, their future more secure. They avoided the urge to celebrate and separated with a quick kiss.

"We should act as we would on any other day," Barnett suggested cautiously.

"I'll make some breakfast," she said.

"And I'll wash and dress, share breakfast with you, and then go to the sanitarium."

"I think it best that you not say anything to Penelope. Not until the authorities confirm that it's Cavendish."

He nodded, reflective. "Wellington should be notified, too," he said. "The authorities should tell them, although I'll be present. But I think they should be together. They survived other losses by leaning on each other. They'll survive this one the same way."

Rose was suddenly concerned for Penelope, the patient. It was a perspective she hadn't considered, so relieved was she her nemesis might be dead. "Will Penelope be all right?" she asked softly.

"I certainly hope so," he replied, "but I'm afraid not. Assuming it's Cavendish, this will be the third loved one she's lost – all well before their time, all suddenly, cruelly, and with no warning. It would weigh on a healthy mind, let alone one so delicate."

He went to dress while Rose made espresso and put fruit and cheese on the table, along with water and biscuits. While she waited for her husband, she went to the front porch, looking down the shoreline. A few moments later, Barnett emerged from the bedroom, dressed in a suit purchased from a local tailor.

"They're searching the grounds," Rose said from the door. "One of the policemen is taking photographs."

"Of what?"

"The area around the cottage," she told him. "And the mountainside."

"What about the body?"

"They're loading it on the boat."

"Come and get your breakfast," he said softly. "We'll learn what happened soon enough."

She closed the front door and walked toward the kitchen, stopping in front of him to straighten his tie. She then shared a secretive glance. "If we don't know already," she whispered.

Chapter 40

Falcone and Minelli slowly walked the trajectory they thought the bullet had travelled, starting at the shoreline where the corpse was found, searching the surrounding area, and then gradually moving upward, following the natural incline that the mountains had made in the millions of years since they were born. They paused behind the cottage, looked up towards the road that was barely visible from their location, and then searched through the grass, combed the trees, and inspected the shrubs and edelweiss that dotted the landscape as they sought signs of an intruder.

"Cavendish's car," Falcone said when they encountered a Fiat, bright red with white trim and spoked wheels, parked just past the trees.

Minelli approached the vehicle and tried the door. It was unlocked. "Shall I search it?" he asked.

Falcone nodded and checked the boot, finding some blankets and a flashlight, the jack and some tools. "Any luck?" he called to Minelli.

"Two empty whisky flasks, a sweater, a roadmap and papers proving the automobile had been leased by Alexander Cavendish," he replied.

They continued on, the elevation increasing, as they poked and prodded but noticed nothing suspicious. Their investigation gradually led them farther up the hillside, the ascent levelling at different elevations, narrow plateaus crowded with trees and shrubs and teeming with wild flowers, the incline subtle for metres before stretching skyward and reaching the peak several kilometres away.

They could see the road, a broad shoulder beside it, a wooden railing abutting the edge where the cliff dropped precipitously.

"The killer could have been in a vehicle," Falcone said. "He may have parked the car, stood at the railing, aimed and fired."

"But it was dark," Minelli countered. "How could he see the victim?"

"The moon was full," Falcone replied. "Assuming the murder took place in the darkness before dawn, the moonlight would reflect off the lake, backlighting the target. The victim also held an oil lantern in his hand, which made it easier to spot him."

Minelli studied the hillside, apparently assessing the climb. "I think we can make it up to the road," he said, "although it may be difficult. There's a path, a bit overgrown, but still passable."

"Then let's give it a try," Falcone suggested. "We can always drive if we can't access it from here."

They followed the path upward as it wound through the foliage, the climb a bit steeper than they'd expected. The road was no longer visible from their location, but they knew it wasn't far away. They inspected the grass and trees and shrubs as they passed, but saw no broken branches or trampled flowers, nothing to indicate someone had been there before them. Eventually they reached the road, a bit winded, and a hundred metres away from where they had first seen it from the back of the cottage.

Minelli pointed to the shoulder. "Tyre tracks and cigarette ends," he said.

They knelt, collecting the butts and putting them in a bag. They studied the tyre tracks and Minelli took a notebook from his pocket and drew the pattern.

"Someone waited here for a while," Falcone observed.

"Long enough to smoke four cigarettes."

"More of the cottage is visible than I thought," Falcone mused aloud as he looked down the slope, "as well as the crime scene."

"It's a good location if you want to watch Cavendish," Minelli noted.

They stood at the railing and looked down at the lake, a serene image that made good postcards – at least not when stained by murder. They could see the shoreline where they found the body, the cottage sitting at the edge of the trees, and some of the path they had just travelled to climb the hillside, but not much of it.

"How far do you think this shot would be?" Falcone asked.

"Probably one hundred and fifty metres, maybe forty-five degrees."

"We have a location where we know someone was waiting, with nothing to look at except the cottage and the crime scene. There's just one problem."

"The shot is nearly impossible," Minelli said grimly.

"Yes, it is," Falcone agreed, "especially at night, even with a full moon." He paused and looked at his partner. "At least I haven't met the man who can make it."

"Nor have I."

Falcone looked down the hillside, scanning all directions, studying the slope, the trees and shrubs and dwellings that all shared the rugged terrain.

He observed the sanitarium, a massive building that dwarfed any other. Four stories high, taking most of the level ground between the slope and the lake, it had been a hospital during the war. He knew it had originally been constructed by a railroad tycoon and, for a moment, he wondered what it was like to live in that world, one he would never have the privilege to do so.

He noticed a small glade tucked within the trees, about thirty metres lower. "That landing below might offer a much better shot."

"We can try to climb down to it, but it's a bit steep."

"Let's use the path we took to get here," Falcone suggested. "Maybe we can reach it from there."

They returned to the path that led them to the road and reversed their steps, walking down the hillside. Again, they carefully surveyed the area, searching for disturbances, anywhere that a gunman could have waited until his victim appeared. It was as difficult going down the hill as it had been climbing up, and it took several minutes, occasionally slipping and sliding in the soft soil. As soon as they reached the slender glade they saw the reeds and grass matted, as if someone had been sitting there for an extended period of time. Maybe for several nights in a row.

"This is where the murderer was," Minelli said.

Falcone knelt where the grass was compressed and looked down at the cottage and the lake that sprawled beyond it. He positioned himself as a shooter might, pretending to sight a target. "Ninety metres, a hundred at most," he observed.

"At a thirty-degree incline," Minelli added, "maybe a bit more."

"It's not easy," Falcone said. "But it's a shot that could be made."

Chapter 41

"I don't understand what's happening," Penelope said warily. She anxiously glanced at her father, then Barnett, and then the inspector, fear flickering across her face.

Inspector Antonio Falcone had learned through the years that there was no easy way to relate a loved one's death. "I'm afraid I have some tragic news," he said delicately.

She looked at him strangely, her face pale. "Can someone please get my husband?" she asked. "I don't think I want to continue without him."

Falcone hesitated, assessed the bewildered look on her face, and then continued. "I'm sorry to inform you, Miss Penelope, that your husband has been killed."

A look of disbelief washed over her face. "Killed?" she asked, her jaw dropping. "How can that be?" She started to cry, shaking her head. "No, I don't believe you."

Wellington moved closer to his daughter, wrapping an arm around her protectively. "It's true, darling," he whispered. "I just identified the body."

Tears rolled down her face. She stuttered, as if to speak, but could only sob. "How?" she finally asked in a hoarse whisper. "Was it a vehicle accident?"

"No," Falcone replied softly. "I'm afraid it wasn't an accident."

She looked at him, confused. "Then what happened?" she asked. "What are you trying to say?"

"Unfortunately, someone murdered your husband," the inspector replied.

"Murdered?" she asked, her voice loud, agitated and unbelieving.

"Yes. Miss Penelope, I'm afraid so," Falcone replied.

"Who killed him!" she screamed, tears running down her cheeks, her body jerking and heaving.

Wellington hugged her tightly, as if trying to pass his strength to her. "The inspector doesn't know yet," he said softly.

"Alexander is dead?" she sobbed. "It can't be true. Tell me it's not true."

"Please accept my condolences," Falcone offered.

Jones tried to comfort her as she sobbed into his shoulder. His face was pale, stern – almost frozen, his eyes vacant. "It's all right," he whispered as he stroked her hair. "The pain will pass and we'll survive, just as we always have and always will."

Falcone stood by passively, compassionate but keenly observing. It was difficult to deliver such horrible news to a family. But it was also a murder investigation and, only hours after the crime had occurred, everyone was still a suspect.

Jones dabbed at Penelope's eyes with a handkerchief and her tears began to subside. They were both in shock, their faces pale, eyes vacant.

"What happened?" she asked finally, her voice muted.

"He was shot," Falcone said. "A single bullet. A good marksman."

She paused, hesitant, and then her eyes widened with fear. "Maybe it's the same person who's trying to kill me," she said wildly. She started crying again, tears falling faster.

Falcone looked at her strangely. "Someone's trying to kill you?".

"Yes," she said, wiping the tears with her hand as they trailed down her cheeks. "Once in Monte Carlo and twice here at the sanitarium."

Falcone's glanced at Barnett, even though he spoke to Penelope. "I will need more information," he said. "There could very well be a link."

"What if they try to murder me," she asked, "just like they killed Alexander? How are you going to protect me?"

"We have security personnel at the sanitarium," Barnett assured them all. "Penelope is safe."

"Maybe not," Wellington said, handing his handkerchief to his daughter. "Whoever killed her husband could be coming after her. Inspector, can you provide additional security?"

"Of course," he said warily. "I'll discuss it with Dr Barnett."

"Was he killed at his cottage?" Penelope asked.

"Yes, he was," Falcone replied.

"Oh, no," she wailed. "I knew it. I rented the cottage for him."

"Penelope, it's not your fault," Jones said. "The cottage had nothing to do with it."

"A fisherman found his body this morning," Falcone added softly.

"A fisherman?" Penelope asked, aghast.

Falcone was confused by her reaction. "Yes, it was a fisherman," he repeated.

She turned to Barnett. "I told you fishermen were watching me," she reminded him. "It's probably the same people."

"Fishermen have been watching you?" Falcone asked, knowing her mental state was fragile and afraid fact was mixed with fiction.

"Yes, they were," she said, wiping tears away. "They were waiting for me to go out on my balcony. Then they were going to kill me."

"They may have been reporters, Inspector," Wellington interjected. "Penelope attracts a lot of attention."

"We don't think this fisherman was involved in Mr Cavendish's death, Miss Jones," Falcone informed her. "Your husband appears to have been shot from higher up on the mountain. The bullet came from near the main road."

"I'm sure they'll kill me next," she moaned. "They've tried three times already. But why kill Alexander?"

"Our investigation has just begun," Falcone said. "We have more questions than answers."

Penelope was frantic, unable to cope, and now seemed afraid she would also be killed. "When will you have answers?" she asked, covering her face with her hands. "I'm so frightened."

"I can't provide a timeline," Falcone said. "Not yet."

"I think we should probably leave the two of you alone for a while," Barnett interrupted. The discussion had taken a turn he didn't think Penelope was ready for. She needed to grieve. "Inspector Falcone and I will be in my office."

Chapter 42

"You're required under Italian law to answer my questions," Inspector Falcone said sternly as they entered Barnett's office. "You can cooperate and it will be easy. Or it can be much harder for both of us."

"I understand," Barnett said as he motioned for Falcone to sit in the leather chair in front of his desk. "Can I get you anything? Coffee or espresso?"

Falcone shook his head and withdrew a small notebook from his pocket. "No, thank you."

"What do you want to know?" Barnett asked, once they were comfortable.

Falcone was quiet for a moment, as if mentally preparing the sequence of questions he intended to ask. "When did Penelope come to the sanitarium?"

"About three months ago."

"Why, specifically?"

"She was admitted after attempting suicide," Barnett explained to Falcone. "She suffers from schizophrenia."

Falcone paused, looking up from his notebook. "What exactly is schizophrenia?" he struggled to pronounce the word.

Barnett hesitated, trying to describe the disease in terms Falcone could understand. "It's a long-term mental disorder," he explained. "The relationship between thought, emotion and behaviour is distorted. The patient's perception is impaired; they sometimes withdraw from reality into fantasy and delusion, which I believe is Penelope's problem."

"She said two attempts have been made on her life since her arrival here," Falcone said. "Are those delusions due to her illness?"

"Yes, I believe so," Barnett replied. "The alleged first attempt was in the middle of the night. Penelope was screaming and, when attended by Adele, the night nurse, she tried to stab her with a nail file."

"What was her explanation?" Falcone asked.

"She claimed Adele was trying to smother her with a pillow," Barnett said.

158

"Did Adele have a valid explanation for her whereabouts?"

"Of course," Barnett replied. "Adele has been an employee for years, since before the war."

"What did Adele think?"

"She thought Penelope had a nightmare."

"And your assessment?"

"I agreed with her."

"Did Adele find any indication that a perpetrator may have entered Miss Jones's suite?"

Barnett thought for a moment, reliving the event. "There was a window open in her room," he said. "She's claustrophobic. She gets upset when she feels closed in."

"Her suite is on the third floor."

"Yes, it is."

"Was there a mechanism to access her room, evidence of a ladder, or any other means of entry?"

"There is a large tree limb outside her window," Barnett explained. "It's possible for someone to gain access."

Falcone was pensive, apparently calculating. "I'll need to examine her suite at the earliest opportunity."

"Yes, of course," Barnett said. "I can certainly arrange that."

"What was the second attempt?"

"She claimed she was pushed from her balcony. She landed in a tree, tumbled to the ground, bruised but not seriously hurt. Most of the bruises were to her right side, which seems to support her story."

"As if she turned to face her attacker when pushed?" Falcone asked, scribbling down the details.

"Yes, that would make sense. But she just as easily could have leapt."

"Was the window in her room found open at that time?"

"Yes, it was."

"Is she in the same suite?"

"Yes, both she and her father insisted she remain there. The window is secured by the staff every evening and security has been increased. The staff also visit her room throughout the night."

"But the window can still be opened?"

"Yes, it can."

"Were the police ever notified?"

"Yes," Barnett said. "They arrived shortly after the second alleged attempt. They found nothing unusual except traces of a substance on the bedroom windowsill which may have been blood."

"Interesting," Falcone said. "I'll have to examine the police report. Who are the fishermen Miss Jones was talking about?"

"She saw two fishermen in a boat on the lake," Barnett explained. "She was convinced they were watching her, signalling to someone inside the sanitarium of her whereabouts."

"And what happened to the fishermen?"

"They eventually left, probably after catching no fish. As I mentioned before, Penelope suffers from delusions. She thinks someone is trying to kill her. She thinks she has lived in other times. She is anxious, afraid, plagued by nightmares. That's why she's a patient here."

Falcone sat, thoughtful. "But maybe her life *is* in danger," he suggested. "Have you ever considered that she may not be delusional?"

"I have," Barnett answered. "And there are many times when I've suspected that, at least in regard to the attempts on her life, she could be stating fact rather than fiction."

Falcone seemed to consider the scenarios, perhaps linking her husband's murder to potential attempts on her life. "Has she shown any improvement since her arrival?"

"She has," Barnett said. "For example, she no longer believes it was Adele that tried to kill her."

"Is that a significant step in her treatment?"

"It is. Her recognition of a delusion, and understanding it wasn't true, is a major accomplishment. Eventually, all of her delusions will be addressed and reconciled."

"And then she's cured?"

"It's a little more complicated," Barnett said. "She'll be cured when she recognises a delusion as it occurs, when her mind is capable of determining fact from fiction, fantasy from reality."

"And how long do you think that will take?"

Barnett shrugged. "I think her progress to date has been encouraging."

"Weeks, months or years?"

"Not weeks or months; perhaps a year but probably longer."

"Has anything else happened to Miss Jones that you might consider suspicious?" Falcone asked. "Other events or claims that were classified as delusional but may have been actual occurrences?"

Barnett paused, reflective. "As I mentioned," he explained, "she often claims to have lived in other times, or to know famous people from previous ages. But then she sometimes makes a joke of it. I haven't yet explored the root of these beliefs."

"Has she ever discussed her husband?"

"Not in any detail. Just casual conversation."

"Did she ever speak ill of her husband, or complain about their relationship?"

"No, not to my knowledge."

"How about her father?"

"They're very close. Penelope's mother died when she was a child. Mr Jones has played the role of both parents ever since, although he's had the help of a nanny named Mrs Thistle. Frankly, I think he's done very well."

Falcone was quiet, still transcribing thoughts into his small notebook with a stubby pencil. When he finished writing he looked up, smiled faintly, and looked around the office, as if seeing it for the first time.

"Any other deaths in her family?"

"Her brother Oxford was killed just before the war ended. He was a pilot. Both Penelope and Mr Jones took it very hard. Quite frankly, I don't think either one of them has coped with the death, even years later."

"That's understandable," Falcone said with a hint of compassion. He looked at Barnett, shrugging slightly. "Maybe no-one ever does."

... So many died with their eyes open, lying on their backs and staring vacantly into an ashen sky that engulfed the battlefield and then the bodies, some still warm with life, were collected and laid side by side and the line of corpses extended sometimes for hundreds of metres. The hideous sight of a thousand eyes searching for heaven and hiding from hell and the journey awaiting their soul. Barnett knew they were watching him, corpse after corpse after corpse, the shock and pain still etched in their chalky faces and some with their mouths open as if to pray for peace and the eternal sanctity of heaven to avoid forever burning in hell. He hated when they died with their eyes open, judging him with an accusing scowl while wondering why he hadn't saved them or done what the Medical Corps was supposed to do or why he couldn't treat their wounds or ease their pain and let them return to their families at home, sons and daughters and wives and brothers and sisters and nieces and nephews and fathers and mothers ...

"Doctor?"

"Yes, I'm sorry," Barnett said. "My mind wandered for a moment."

"I asked how well you knew Alexander Cavendish?"

"We served together during the war."

"Have you talked to him recently?"

"Yes, once. We discussed Penelope's treatment."

"When was that?"

"Shortly after her arrival."

"Was it a good reunion?"

Barnett turned away, looking out of the French doors at the lake beyond. After a few seconds had passed, he replied. "No, I wasn't glad to see him," he admitted. "I despised him during the war and, the second I saw him, I realised that my hatred for him hadn't diminished in the slightest."

"Why do you hate him?"

"He led many men and boys to their deaths," Barnett said, his voice barely above a whisper. "And he got medals for it. A true war hero."

"Did you have an altercation when you last saw him?"

"No, nothing like that."

"Why hasn't he been back?"

"He has, I'm sure. To see Penelope, though. I haven't talked to him."

"Was he here every day?"

"I don't know. He did return to London for a while. Ten days, maybe. But I don't think he's left Como since he came back."

"Where did you serve?"

"In France, the trenches."

"He was in your regiment?"

... Cavendish pointed his gun in the face of a trembling Jimmy Spangler. "Go over the top!" he screamed, waving the pistol.

"I can't!" Jimmy Spangler said, tears streaming down his face. "I can't do it."

Cavendish cocked the pistol, the barrel inches from Spangler's nose.

"Please, stop!" Barnett pleaded. "Just give him a minute. He'll be all right. He'll attack."

Cavendish hollered, "I said now!"

Jimmy Spangler picked up his rifle and turned towards the wall of the trench. Cavendish stood right behind him, the pistol pointed at the seventeen-year-old boy.

"I'm going to count to ten," Cavendish said. "And when I'm done you had better be gone. One, two, three, four ..." Jimmy Spangler took one

step up the rickety wooden ladder, and then another, before pausing, "... *five, six, seven ... I will shoot you, soldier!" Spangler hesitated a moment* *more, and then climbed the remaining rungs. Cavendish turned towards* *Barnett. "I would have killed him." Then he grinned and walked away ...*

"Doctor, are you all right?"

"Yes, I'm fine," he said, smiling weakly. "Yes, in the same regiment. The memories aren't pleasant, I'm afraid."

Falcone looked at Barnett, his face showing compassion. It seemed he knew what it was like when your mind can't forget and your heart can't forgive. "Where were you wounded?" he asked compassionately.

"At the Battle of the Somme."

"What was your involvement with Cavendish?"

"He was a captain, commanded men adjacent to ours in the trenches. As I said, he's a war hero, actually, if you read his records. I don't know how, though."

"Why do you dislike him?"

Barnett paused, wondering if a case was being built against him. Still, the truth should be told. Falcone would find it, whether he shared it or not. "He ordered a boy who was too scared to fight to go over the top," he recalled. "He pointed a pistol in his face, threatened to shoot, and the boy obeyed his order."

Falcone paused, his eyes sad. "I lost a son," he said softly, "in a war that meant nothing. I see his image constantly, as a toddler, a football player, then a teenager, smiling, happy, a boy with a promising future that will never be realised." He looked at Barnett as if sharing his pain. "How I wish I could see him one more time, to hold him, to tell him how much I love him. But I'll never have that opportunity."

Barnett was moved, almost to tears. "I'm so sorry for your loss," he offered compassionately.

Falcone nodded, whispering, "Thank you." He then gathered his pencil and notebook and put them in his pocket.

"Is that all, Inspector?" Barnett asked.

Falcone sighed, maybe preferring the past more than the present. "For now, I suppose it is," he said. He looked at Barnett, his eyes trained on the doctor's. "What happened to the boy?"

"He was killed."

"Were others treated the same way?"

"Yes."

"What happened to them?"

"They died," Barnett said, struggling for control. "They all died."

Chapter 43

"I can't believe he's gone," Penelope muttered, her eyes vacant. "It's like he went to London or Monte Carlo."

"But we know he didn't," Barnett said softly. "We have to accept that."

"I keep waiting for him to come back, to walk in the door."

"It's not easy, I realise that," Barnett said, as he sat in a straight-backed chair behind her. "You're still in shock. In time, you'll cope."

"It's my fault," she said. "I rented that cottage so he could be nearby. I never thought he would die there."

"Penelope, it's not about the cottage. Nothing you did could have prevented Alexander's death."

"That's not true. I'm to blame. He should have stayed in London."

"You're not to blame. Whoever committed this treacherous act probably followed him here. He could just as easily have been killed in London or Monte Carlo."

"I don't think so," she countered. "He was killed because I rented the cottage."

"The cottage had nothing to do with it," he insisted. "Nor did you."

"The cottage had everything to do with it," she argued, her voice louder. "If he wasn't in that cottage, he never would have been killed."

"Penelope, I assure you," he repeated, "the cottage meant nothing." She was linking irrelevant threads to justify conclusions that made no sense. It was a familiar pattern, amplified by her illness, but he didn't know what was driving it. Why was she so focused on the cottage?

"I waited for him this morning," she sobbed, apparently not listening. "We always had tea together after breakfast. But he never came. That's when I realised that I'll never see him again."

He wanted her to talk, to express her emotions and confront her grief. It was part of the mourning process. He knew how badly she hurt, how empty she felt. But it would be best if she memorialised their relationship, at least initially, to mute the pain.

"How did you two meet?" he asked, encouraging happier memories.

She paused, perhaps reflecting. Her hand moved to her face, wiping away a tear. "I've known him for years," she replied, "but not very well. The first time I actually talked with him was at a wedding in London, even though we both had come with other people."

"Your families didn't know each other?"

"Yes, of course they did. They know each other very well. Oxford and Alexander went to the same prep school."

"Whose wedding was it?"

"Mary Westcott," she responded. "She's a very dear friend of mine, my closest. But I haven't seen much of her lately."

"Who did she marry?"

"A Member of Parliament named John Westcott, from the House of Commons. He's a popular politician, some years her senior, but they seem very happy."

"That's when you first got to know Alexander?" Barnett prodded.

"Yes, I suppose, although I had talked to him before, it was usually at my brother's school events. He was with a woman from York – I can't remember her name – and I was with Ian McKinley, the man I had hoped to marry."

"What happened to Mr McKinley?" Barnett asked. "We discussed him at another of your sessions."

"He lives in Scotland, still not married," she replied. "I told you he was the love of my life, but my father never approved of him. He was quite a bit older than me, that's probably why. Eventually, I honoured my father's wishes and Ian and I stopped seeing each other."

"How did your father feel about Alexander?"

"He thought we made the perfect match," she said. "But who wouldn't? He was devilishly handsome, the world's most eligible bachelor, a wealthy war hero – everything a woman could want."

"I thought it odd that your father stayed in a villa while Alexander was in the cottage. Why not stay together?"

"Alexander refused to encroach on my father's privacy," she said. "That's just the way he was – very thoughtful, considerate, always wanting what's best for others."

Barnett was quiet. He knew a much different Alexander Cavendish – a man that forced boys to their death, accosted woman, bullied the weak. How could he be so wrong and Penelope so right? Or maybe, how could he be so right and Penelope so wrong?

"It seems a man as wonderful as Alexander wouldn't have any enemies," he asked delicately.

She hesitated, but then spoke. "He was in some sort of financial trouble. Maybe his murder had something to do with that."

"Did he have unpaid debts?"

"Yes, he owed a lot of money. Something to do with his motor vehicle accident."

"That doesn't sound like a debt that would cost him his life," he pointed out, observing her. She sat motionless, barely reacting, speaking in monotone.

"I wonder if the person who killed him is the one that's trying to kill me," she said. "I should discuss that with the inspector."

"Yes, you should," Barnett agreed, feigning belief in her delusion. "We need to ensure he investigates it thoroughly."

She was quiet for a moment, perhaps reflecting on the past. "He did have gambling debts before we came to Como," she said, "but I paid them."

"Do you think he could have incurred more?"

"I don't know," she replied, her voice tinged with doubt.

"Why did you pay off his last debt?"

"I feared for his life and so did he."

Barnett was alarmed, learning about a world he had never walked in. "Why was his life in jeopardy" he asked, suspecting he knew the answer.

"Because they want their money," she said simply. "And they will stop at nothing to get it."

"Was he a bad poker player?" he asked, wondering what caused the debt.

"No, I think he lost money betting on horses. He always picked ponies he was sure would win. It just seemed that they never did."

"You should also tell that to Inspector Falcone," Barnett advised. "What happened after you paid the debt?"

"I thought they went away," she said simply. "But maybe they didn't."

"Were they the kind of men that go away?" he asked. "And could Alexander avoid them; was he strong enough to stop gambling?"

She thought for a moment before replying. "Probably not," she answered. "Alexander thrived on danger. I think there were parts of him that I never saw. He knew the men were trouble, but he didn't seem to care."

Barnett was taken aback. "Who are these men?" he asked,

"Men you don't want to know."

Chapter 44

"I questioned members of the hospital staff," Minelli informed Falcone.

"Did you learn anything?"

"Yes, I did," Minelli replied. "It seems our good doctor is not what he seems."

Falcone's interest was piqued. "Why would you say that?"

"I interviewed Olivia, his receptionist," Minelli explained. "She walked in on Barnett and Miss Jones during one of their sessions."

"And what did she find?"

"They were locked in an embrace, kissing," Minelli said with smug satisfaction.

Falcone was sceptical. "It could have been innocent."

"She didn't think so," Minelli said him. "It was a clinging embrace, their arms around each other, lips locked. Even though she knocked on the door, they didn't realise she'd entered the room."

"What did she do?"

"She left quietly, closing the door behind her. She suspects they're lovers and probably have been for some time."

Falcone was quiet for a moment, thinking. "If she's correct," he speculated, "it would add a whole new dimension to our investigation."

"Yes, it would," Minelli agreed. "Barnett would have a motive for murder."

****

The following morning Falcone and Minelli left the Como police station and took a motor car to Cavendish's cottage. They intended to search his residence, looking for any clues that may have led to his murder.

"Has the coroner issued the post-mortem report?" Falcone asked.

"Not yet," Minelli said, guiding the vehicle along the mountain road. "But he did send blood samples to a laboratory in Milan."

"When will he get the results?"

"It could take weeks," Minelli replied. "And the coroner won't issue the cause of death until he has the toxicology report."

"I was hoping it wouldn't take that long," Falcone said, images of potential suspects wandering through his mind. "Will he release the body for burial?"

"Yes, in a few days."

They drove behind the sanitarium, winding down the mountainside, the landscape littered with alpine flowers of amber, violet and blue, until they reached the dirt lane behind the bungalow. They came to a stop beside the red Fiat and walked to the cottage tucked behind the grove of trees – the house where Alexander Cavendish had lived.

"Did our officers find anything when they searched the area?" Falcone asked.

"No, nothing. The killer even retrieved the spent shell."

"I keep thinking about the shot," Falcone admitted. "Even with a full moon, it's difficult."

Minelli shrugged. "Someone was able to make it," he said. "We just have to find them."

"Cavendish was holding a lantern. That would have helped."

"We should come back at night and validate the conditions," Minelli offered as he reached into his pocket and withdrew a key. "Are you ready to search the cottage?"

Falcone nodded and followed him to the door. The cottage sat away from the water, simple but grandly designed as were all buildings in Como. They had found the body thirty metres from the door, past the edge of the building. He wondered how long the killer waited for the victim to walk out to the lake. Had it been minutes or hours? Was it the first night or fifth or tenth?

They walked into the parlour, a cosy room with a wooden table flanked by two leather chairs and a stone fireplace with a massive wooden mantel. A writing desk was perched in an alcove by the window, the curtains pulled, light streaming in. A kitchen sat in the rear of the house with a wood stove and simple sink, flanked by cabinets painted white. A small oval table and two chairs occupied the remaining space. Two unopened bottles of whisky and a half empty bottle of Limoncello sat on the table. A door led to the outside, stacks of firewood a metre away.

Falcone tried the back door. It opened. He tried to engage the lock; it didn't work. The mechanism was broken.

"Why shoot him from so far away?" Minelli asked. "The killer could have walked in the back door and murdered him with far less effort."

"If they knew the lock was broken."

"Maybe we can eliminate any suspects who did," Minelli suggested.

They searched the kitchen, finding fresh vegetables in the pantry, peppers and broccoli, some empty bottles in the rubbish, cooking and eating utensils in the cabinets, a pot on the stove used to make his last dinner. It was pasta cooked with tomato sauce, the dirty dishes in the sink.

They next checked a bedroom just off the parlour. The furniture was simple, a bed and bureau with a small wardrobe, but they found only clothes and some personal items, a few books, some baggage, but not much more. The bathroom was adjacent, the tile white with black trim, a pedestal sink equipped with chrome piping. They found nothing unusual there or in a vacant bedroom down the narrow hallway.

They searched the parlour last. There was a letter lying on the table between the two leather chairs, the envelope torn where it had been opened. It was dated February 27, 1921, sent to Monte Carlo, predating Cavendish's arrival in Como by two weeks. It was postmarked London, from Mary Westcott, and left little doubt as to the nature of their relationship:

'My dearest Alexander,

Monte Carlo was heaven, the hours in your arms, sometimes with Penelope so close I could smell her perfume. Now my heart aches, empty, missing you, the days like decades as time passes so slowly, an eternity bridging our stolen moments together. How long will it be until you hold me again, your lips on mine, your hands gently touching me, teasing, making me want you even more as each delicious minute passes? I ache for your body, firm and chiselled, responding to my caresses, and your moist lips – I love when you nibble my ears and neck, taunting me before leaving a moist trail to my breasts. My heart is racing, my face flush, just thinking about our time together.

I may be able to go to Italy if you can't come to London. I told John that my dear friend Penelope had been admitted to a sanitarium in the Italian Alps and I simply must visit her. After all, she is my closest friend and confidante. Please tell me, darling, which you prefer – your return to London or my coming to Italy. I can probably manage at least ten days in Como if you can find somewhere to hide me, some quaint hotel on the lake, perhaps – away from prying eyes and ears so I can lie in your arms, *smothered by your love. Send a telegram upon your arrival in Como and tell me what I should do.*

All my love,

Mary.'

Falcone handed the letter to Minelli and gave him a moment to read it.

"If Mary Westcott has a husband, and I suspect that's who John is, we may have our first suspect," Minelli said.

"And a very strong suspect," Falcone agreed as he put the letter in his pocket.

They found nothing else in the parlour, only a book, a magazine and a dirty glass. They moved to the alcove that contained the desk – the last place left to search – and found a rifle tucked between it and the wall – a Carcano bolt action carbine, a popular model used during the war. Several En-blocs were stacked on top of the desk.

Falcone lifted the rifle and sniffed the barrel, his nose twitching. "It's been fired recently," he said. "I smell powder."

"We can have it tested," Minelli suggested, "especially since we have the bullet that killed him. Do you really think he was murdered with his own rifle?"

"I wouldn't rule anything out," Falcone said.

He turned his attention to the desk and started to rummage through it. The first drawer was filled with supplies: envelopes, paper, pens, and a folded document. Falcone took it out of the drawer and opened it.

"What do you have?" Minelli asked.

Falcone was quiet for a moment, his attention on the paper. "It's a life insurance policy," he replied, "very recent, dated March 1, 1921."

"Who's it for?"

"Penelope Jones Cavendish in the amount of fifteen thousand pounds."

"That isn't unusual," Minelli remarked, "even if it is recent. Who's the beneficiary?"

"That's what's confusing," Falcone informed him. "It's a man named William Flynn, of London, England."

Minelli shrugged. "A relative, perhaps?" he wondered aloud.

"I don't know," Falcone responded, "but it's something we need to investigate." He opened the second drawer and found a single sheet of paper covered with writing, clear and defined, neatly printed.

"What is it?" Minelli asked.

Falcone continued reading, studying the information, until he reached the bottom of the page. "It's a list of names," he replied, "and much, much more."

Chapter 45

Wellington Jones sat with William Cain on the veranda of his rented villa, occasionally glancing at the cottages and hotels sprawled along the shoreline.

"How much did the inspector know?" Cain asked. He sipped an Amaretto, enjoying the breeze that blew off the lake.

"Nothing," Jones said, "but the investigation just started."

"Has he questioned you yet?"

Jones shook his head. "No, not yet. But it was difficult to appear grieved when he told me Cavendish was dead. I felt like dancing an Irish jig."

Cain laughed. "I'm sure that would get the inspector's attention," he remarked. "Should I leave Como before he finds me?"

Jones thought for a moment before replying. "No, that would look suspicious."

"How would he even know I was here?"

"Penelope might say something and I don't want to take the risk that she won't."

Cain was confused. "What risk? I'm your business associate. I was here for a few days and then I left. There's nothing wrong with that. It happens all the time."

"Until the newspapers find out."

"Why would they care?" Cain asked.

"They'll find out about Cavendish – the women, the gambling, all his debts. And they'll assume I had something to do with his death. It'll look worse if you were in Como and then left just after he was murdered."

Cain shrugged. "I'll stay as long as you like."

Jones was pensive for a moment. "Don't underestimate the inspector," he warned. "He's crafty, cunning, and very intelligent. It may *appear* that he doesn't grasp the intricacies of an investigation, but he does."

"I don't think you have anything to worry about," Cain assured him. "Just play the role of grieving father-in-law, console your daughter. And don't forget – perception is reality. Ask any politician."

173

Jones paused, studying the mountains across the lake, the events of the last few days drifting through his mind. "Think about it," he said. "The press knows me, they're already hounding Penelope, and they know what type of work you do for me. If they smell a story, they'll find one."

"Even if it isn't true?" Cain asked, laughing.

"Why expend the effort, and the cost, to prove it isn't." Jones was quiet for a moment, reflective. He then said, "There is one problem we didn't consider."

"What's that?"

"Cavendish's debts. How much does he owe Billy Flynn?"

"At least fifteen thousand pounds. I'm not sure of the interest."

"What if he comes to Penelope to collect?"

Cain was quiet, considering options. "Do you want me to do something about it?"

"Like what? You can't kill him. The trail would lead right back to me."

"We could always make a deal?"

"Such as?" Jones asked.

"I can offer five thousand pounds. See if he takes it."

Jones sighed, wondering how he ever let Cavendish into his family. He had made many mistakes in his life, but none as bad as that. "Let me think about it," he told Cain. "The business has some liquidity problems right now, issues with real estate in Bombay."

"Anything I can fix?" Cain asked.

"Not unless you have a lot of money," Jones said. He sipped his Amaretto. "I made an offer to our creditors and I'm waiting to see if they accept. But either way, I'm still short of cash. It'll either be a little or a lot, nothing in between. I'll know in a few days."

"That sounds serious," Cain said warily.

"Typical problems in a global business," Jones replied. "It's just the timing. It couldn't have been worse."

"Maybe we should see if Flynn approaches us first," Cain suggested. "Then your financial situation may resolve itself. In the meantime, we'll pretend we know nothing about it."

"But then the police may find out and it'll be all over the newspapers."

"At least we have a few days to think about it. What other Cavendish messes do we have to clean up?"

"The woman he paid off just before the wedding," Cain said, "and her son. She was paid ten thousand pounds. But I don't know if it's an annual payment or not."

"Didn't Jackson Cavendish pay?"

"He gave Alexander the money, but only because he didn't have it."

"Then Jackson Cavendish can continue to pay," Jones said. "It might be a bit embarrassing if it comes out, but we have no obligation to the woman or the child."

"That leaves the affair. Mary Westcott."

Jones sighed and frowned. "That will sting," he said bitterly. "I've known Mary her entire life; she and Penelope are very close. And John Westcott is a friend of mine."

"Then we need to do everything we can to keep it quiet."

"As long as that damn fool Cavendish didn't leave any evidence behind."

Chapter 46

Rose Barnett got up from her desk and put her pen on a blank sheet of paper. "I can't concentrate," she said, unable to write. "I keep thinking about Cavendish."

"I try to stay distracted," Joseph said softly as he set his pyschology journal on the table beside his chair.

"I don't know how you do it."

"We can't let it consume us," he warned her, "especially with the police about to question us. It's better to not even think about it." He paused, seeming hesitant to continue, but did, speaking in a whisper. "He can't torment us ever again."

She sighed and briefly looked away. "It's so horrible, the impact he's had on our lives."

"He held us hostage – controlling us in some strange, demented way, keeping us anchored to the past while stealing our future."

"It's over now," she said, kissing him lightly on the lips.

"Yes, at last. We just have to survive the next few weeks."

"When will the police come?"

"In the next few days, I suppose. I saw them searching the cottage today."

She took his hand in hers and sat beside him. "It won't be long before they find the killer," she whispered.

"Or who they think the killer is," he added cryptically.

"Maybe we should leave Como when it's all over," she suggested. "It might be good for us, daring to dream, a new life with no links to the war."

He seemed surprised. "I didn't know you were unhappy here."

"I'm not" she replied. "I just think a change would be good for us."

"I never really thought about it," he said. "It's so serene here; it'll be difficult to duplicate."

"Como was good for healing, but maybe not for living, at least not for us."

He thought for a moment, apparently digesting her suggestion. "Where would you like to go?" he asked.

"Paris might be nice," she offered. "Some artists and writers are moving there."

"I suppose a change would be good," he said, deferring to his wife as he often did. "Especially now that part of our past died with Cavendish. If Paris would make you happy, then it's something we need to consider."

"It doesn't have to be Paris," she said. "I just want a new beginning. Maybe we can even risk going home."

He looked at her, pensive, as if considering a road that had always been detoured. "I suppose we could return to England," he said softly, "as long as we're sure it's safe."

"We'll know in a few weeks."

"Where would I practice?" he asked.

"Wherever you want to," she replied. "You could see patients privately or practice at another sanitarium. Maybe you can even help suffering war survivors."

He sighed, his expression showing nightmares that never waned. "It might make me worse," he said, "discussing it every day."

"Or it might help you," she pointed out. "You would have patients with the same afflictions. You'd realise you're not alone; many others suffer, too."

He was quiet for a moment. "I think I would like helping those who survived," he said finally. "And you would enjoy Paris, especially mingling with writers and artists."

"It's just an idea," she said, knowing change would be good for both of them. "We can go wherever you want."

"I'll do whatever you think is best," he said. "As I always have."

****

It was almost 2 a.m. Joseph Barnett lay thrashing in bed, moaning, kicking his legs, his arms flailing.

... A sick smile consumed Cavendish and his eyes blazed with evil as he pushed his pistol in the face of the first soldier, a boy with hardly a whisker, and forced him up the rickety ladder to the top of the trench and then the enemy fired and bullets shredded the boy's face and he fell back, grotesquely mangled and spouting blood. Cavendish pointed his pistol at the second man and he climbed from the bottom of the trench to the top and the enemy fired and he also fell back, his face torn and bloodied, parts of it missing, and then Cavendish pointed the pistol at the third boy and motioned him to climb the steps. I watched horrified, mesmerised, and

walked behind Cavendish and picked up a rifle and aimed it at his head and fired again and again and ...

"Joseph, wake up," Rose said as she held him tightly. "It's just a nightmare."

His eyes fluttered open, his breathing rapid and irregular.

"It's all right, darling," she said.

"No, it's not all right," he said frantically, consumed like a caged animal. "They didn't want to die."

"It's a dream, Joseph," she said softly, holding him, protecting him. "It's not real. It's not what happened."

His body relaxed, his breathing slowed, and he eased back against the pillows. "It seemed like I was there," he whispered. "In the trenches."

"I know, darling. But you weren't. You were sleeping."

"It was Cavendish," he mumbled. "He made them die."

"It's all right, Joseph. He didn't make them die."

"Except for Jimmy Spangler."

"Yes, except for Jimmy Spangler. But we can't bring him back. We can't change what happened, no matter how often we talk about it. It happened, there was nothing you could do about it, and we have to let it go."

He was quiet for a moment as his breathing slowed to a regular rate. "I'm glad Cavendish is dead," he whispered.

"I know you are," she said. "And in the end, everything will be all right."

"I have to control myself," he said, closing his eyes, willing away the unwanted images. "I have to make it stop. If I don't, they'll come for me."

"No-one will come for you," she promised. "I won't let them."

Chapter 47

Penelope Jones sat on the balcony of her suite, watching dusk shadow the day. The sun was fading behind the mountains on the far side of the lake and she watched intently as the minutes passed, streaks of orange and yellow and pink crossing the clouds as the horizon swallowed the sun.

She knew that Alexander would still be alive if he had stayed with her father instead of living in the cottage she had rented. Regardless of how or why he died, the cottage had been critical to the crime. He was dead the day she rented it, but she doubted anyone would ever realise that.

She didn't feel like a widow. But then, she had barely been married long enough to feel like a bride. Death stalked her, lurking in the shadows and then stealing happiness wherever it sprouted. Death took her mother, it took Oxford, and it surfaced again while the entire continent tried to find the future, forgetting a past that was haunted by the ghosts of an entire generation.

The whole world was collapsing, the global financial crisis filling the vacuum created when the world war ended, threatening to destroy the family business, eroding both its liquidity and reputation. Penelope wondered how her father did it – balancing business and family, right and wrong, risk and riches. She wanted to help, to offer the support he needed, become the confidant he wanted, the advisor he valued – because he had no-one else he could truly trust. But even without her, he would think of some way to survive; he always did. And he would emerge stronger, although guarded and scarred.

A knock on the door interrupted her, and a second later Adele entered. "I have tea and chocolates for you, Miss Penelope," she announced.

"Thank you, bring them in," Penelope called from the balcony, watching as Adele set a tray with cup and saucer and Swiss chocolates on the table and then turned to go.

"Wait just a minute," Penelope requested.

"Is there something else you would like?"

"No, this is fine."

"Are you feeling all right?"

"I am," Penelope said, not knowing how to proceed. She looked at the nurse, a woman not much older than her, who had given years of service to the sanitarium before, during and after the war. "Please, sit down for a moment."

Adele looked at her strangely but came closer, sitting tentatively across from her. She had had little social contact with her patient, it was more care-giver or servant, whatever Penelope's mood demanded.

Penelope hesitated, the words hard to find. After an awkward moment, she spoke. "I want to apologise for attacking you. I know you weren't trying to kill me."

Adele seemed surprised. She had probably expected a scolding, as was often the case, but had instead received an apology. "Miss Penelope," she said, apparently moved. "Thank you so much. I hope you realise I want nothing except for you to get well. I would never hurt you."

"I know that now. Hopefully you'll forgive me."

"I do, Miss Penelope. You are sick and that was the problem."

"Yes," Penelope said, looking away. "I am sick, very sick, I suppose. But sometimes the light pierces darkness and the truth becomes clear."

"I was never offended," Adele assured her. "I knew you didn't understand."

"I suppose I couldn't. But I do now."

Adele rose, bowing slightly, smiling. "Can I get you anything else?" she asked.

"No, this is fine. Thank you."

"Maybe no-one is trying to kill you after all," Adele speculated.

"That might be true," Penelope admitted, "or killer and victim were wrong."

Adele looked at her, perplexed. "I don't understand," she said.

Penelope looked at her with a vacant stare. "It was Alexander," she mumbled. "It was always Alexander."

"They were trying to kill your husband?" Adele asked.

"Yes, it was Alexander."

Adele studied her a moment more and then walked to the door. "At least you're safe now," she said.

"No-one realises," Penelope muttered. "It was always Alexander."

Adele left the suite and wrote down everything that Penelope said and gave it to Dr Barnett.

Chapter 48

The Como police station was on the southern side of a cobblestone square, an ochre building with green shutters that also served as the city municipal building. In the rear of the first floor, a few cells sat against the brick wall, rarely used in a village as quiet as Como. A larger room with four desks occupied most of the space near the entrance. A small office was located to the right, where a sign labelled 'Inspector Falcone' was posted on the wall beside the door.

Wellington Jones and William Cain entered the station and were greeted by a police detective sitting at the first desk.

"May I help you?" he asked.

"We're here to see Inspector Falcone," Jones said.

"And you are?"

"Wellington Jones and my personal assistant, Mr William Cain."

"Just a minute."

The detective went into the office and emerged a moment later. "Come this way," he directed.

They entered the office and were greeted by Falcone. "Please, sit down," he said, "I wasn't expecting you."

"I felt compelled to come," Jones informed him. "My associate, Mr Cain, and I have discovered some significant information about my son-in-law, as difficult as it is for me to discuss. I wanted to tell you as soon as possible."

Falcone called the detective into his office. "This is Captain Minelli," he told them. "He's helping me with this investigation."

Minelli nodded and sat in an empty chair against the wall and removed a pen and notebook from his pocket. He motioned for Falcone to begin.

"I appreciate you being so forthright," Falcone continued. "Please, tell us what information you found."

Jones looked at Cain and then to Minelli and Falcone. "I guess I'll come right to the point," he said. "With Mr Cain's assistance, I've learned that Alexander Cavendish had a serious gambling problem. He owed a sizeable amount of money to a shady London bookmaker named Billy Flynn, who happens to be in Como with his bodyguard." He looked at Cain, pausing dramatically. "Or at least he was in Como."

Falcone glanced at Minelli, trying to hide his surprise. Flynn was the beneficiary on Penelope Jones's life insurance policy, certainly unknown to her. Now they knew why.

Minelli nodded, scribbling in his notebook. When he had correctly captured the information, he looked up to meet Falcone's gaze.

"How do you know that Mr Cavendish owed money to Mr Flynn?" Falcone asked.

Cain cleared his throat. "I overheard them in London, sir," he said, "where Flynn and his henchman, a thug named Jocko Jakes, confronted Mr Cavendish and demanded money owed. When Cavendish didn't have it, they roughed him up a bit. He was still bruised and beaten when he returned to Como."

"You witnessed this?" Falcone inquired.

"Yes, sir, I did."

"But you took no action?" Falcone asked. "Why is that?"

Cain shifted uncomfortably in his chair. "I did, sir," he informed them. "I summoned a policeman but Flynn and Jakes fled when he arrived."

"Did you give their identities to the policeman?" Falcone asked.

"No, sir, I didn't," Cain mumbled.

"Did Mr Cavendish?" Minelli asked.

"No, sir," Cain replied.

"Why did neither you nor Mr Cavendish tell the authorities what had happened?" Falcone questioned. "Especially with Mr Cavendish's life in jeopardy?"

"I thought it best not to intervene," Cain said. "I can't speak for Mr Cavendish."

"Did Mr Cavendish know that you witnessed the encounter?" Falcone asked.

"No, sir, he didn't."

"You never mentioned it to him, even after you saw Flynn and Jakes in Como?"

"I thought it none of my business," Cain replied.

Falcone paused, studying the man that sat before him. "I find that interesting," he said. "Mr Cavendish's life was in danger, but you thought it best not to intervene."

"Did you dislike Mr Cavendish?" Minelli asked brusquely.

Cain shrugged. "I didn't know him that well," he countered.

"I assume you do as Mr Jones directs," Falcone said, his voice a measured monotone. "And you would only tell Mr Cavendish what you knew if Mr Jones directed you to."

Cain shrugged. "Perhaps," he said. "But it's not like Cavendish didn't know that Flynn and Jocko Jakes were after him."

Falcone's eyes moved from Cain to Jones. "When did you first see them in Como?" he asked.

"About a week ago," Cain said.

"Cavendish wasn't hard to find," Jones pointed out. "Not with my daughter in the sanitarium for treatment. Especially with the news coverage she gets."

"Do you know where they are?" Falcone asked.

"No, but they're easy to identify," Cain replied. "Jocko is a massive hulk of a monster, while Billy Flynn is a slight man, impeccably dressed with a penchant for spats."

"Excuse me a moment," Minelli said. He left the office and summoned a policeman. They spoke briefly and then he returned, taking his former seat. "We'll check the local hotels and the passenger lists at the railway."

"How much money did Mr Cavendish owe Mr Flynn?" Falcone asked.

"Fifteen thousand pounds," Cain answered.

Falcone and Minelli shared a glance. "That's a tremendous amount of money," Falcone said, knowing it equalled the insurance policy on Penelope.

"Enough to die for, I would assume," Jones added quietly.

Falcone was silent for a moment, but then spoke. "Billy Flynn is probably gone by now."

"I don't think so," Cain said.

"Why not?"

"He hasn't collected his debt," Cain said.

"Do you think he'll try to get the money from Penelope?" Falcone probed.

"Either money or revenge," Jones said solemnly.

"Revenge?" Falcone asked.

"Yes, her life is in danger," Jones declared. "And it probably has been for months."

Chapter 49

The tavern sat in the centre of the city by Cattedrale di Como just off Via Maestri Comacini. Wrought iron tables were scattered around the outside entrance, a few patrons drinking espresso, others a glass of wine, while some had mugs of beer. It was a warm afternoon, only a few cottony clouds marring a sapphire sky, and a gentle breeze blew down from the mountains, bathing the residents of Como with the faint scent of lilacs.

It was dark inside the establishment, some sunlight filtering through glass blocks that formed the windows that flanked the front entrance, and a dim overheard light splashing shadows on tables in the centre of the room. A bar occupied one wall, a few older men sitting on stools, drinking, and at a table in the darkest corner of the room. Billy Flynn sat against the tavern wall, a half empty mug of beer before him. He rubbed his chin thoughtfully, considering the proposal just offered.

"That's very kind of you, Mr Cain," he said. "It's comforting to know that the Jones family recognises Mr Cavendish's debt."

"Mr Jones wants the matter resolved," Cain said, "although he thinks that Cavendish's family should honour the debt."

"Perhaps," Billy Flynn replied evasively, "but it's not likely. After Cavendish came to Como, I tried to persuade his father to pay." He leaned back and shrugged. "After all, why should I incur the expense of coming to Italy?"

Cain sipped his beer. "What was the outcome, Mr Flynn?"

"Jackson Cavendish refused."

"He might be more inclined to cooperate now that his son is deceased," Cain suggested.

"Perhaps," Billy Flynn said, lighting a cigarette. "Or maybe he'll reconsider the matter once his broken leg has healed."

"Broken leg?" Cain asked. "Was Mr Cavendish in an accident?"

Flynn shrugged and replied, "I'm not familiar with the nature of his injury."

"Let's hope he has a speedy recovery," Cain said, raising his glass.

"By all means," Flynn agreed, mimicking Cain.

They were silent for a moment, establishing the foundation for the next phase of the discussion, and then Cain continued. "Mr Jones agrees you have the right to collect, but insists responsibility for the debt rests with the Cavendish family."

"Some would argue that Miss Penelope is responsible for the debt," Billy Flynn countered, "especially considering what she'll inherit."

Cain knew the situation was tenuous. He suspected inheritance of Cavendish's trust was unlikely. The family would have legally protected the estate, ensuring it remained with them, excepting any children of the marriage. But then, Flynn may have researched the issue. He certainly had a vested interest in the outcome.

"Mr Jones has authorised me to provide payment of five thousand pounds, in the interest of maintaining good relations, even though he doesn't accept any responsibility," Cain offered, carefully phrasing the commitment.

"That's much appreciated," Flynn said, "very much appreciated. But I'm afraid it's only a fraction of the monies owed."

Cain showed shock, pretending not to know the full amount. "We were under the impression a debt of ten thousand pounds had been incurred," he said. "And as an act of good faith, we're willing to pay fifty percent of monies owed."

"And that's an accurate amount," Flynn explained, "but for a prior debt."

"A prior debt?" Cain asked, feigning ignorance.

"Yes, I'm afraid Mr Cavendish incurred a debt of ten thousand pounds a few months ago. Miss Penelope made that payment."

"I didn't know that," Cain mumbled, appearing confused. "What is the amount of the current debt?"

"It's fifteen thousand pounds," Billy Flynn informed him. "But with interest and the expense of coming to Italy, we're now owed twenty-two thousand pounds."

Cain was quiet, knowing Jones would never pay it, nor would he let Penelope. "As I said, Mr Flynn," he stated, "I'm authorised to pay only five thousand pounds."

Flynn was quiet, glancing at Jocko by the door, then around the room at the half dozen patrons at the bar and surrounding tables. After a few minutes had passed, his attention returned to Cain. "I don't want it said that Billy Flynn is an unreasonable man," Flynn informed him. "I will accept a payment of ten thousand pounds and, as a good faith gesture, reduce the debt by two thousand pounds."

"But that still leaves the debt at ten thousand pounds," Cain pointed out.

"Yes, it does. After all, Mr Cain, I have expenses, too."

"Then I assume the Cavendish family will pay the remainder of the debt?"

"I don't think I would make any assumptions, Mr Cain."

"Then who will pay? I'm currently in Italy," he pointed out, "and since Miss Penelope will likely inherit the Cavendish trust, she certainly has the means to satisfy the debt. I think legally, if such matters were ever settled in a court of law, even though we both understand they never will be, the debt is Miss Penelope's responsibility.

"Mr Flynn, I can categorically state, for your ears only, that Miss Penelope does not have the means to satisfy the debt. Inheritance of the Cavendish trust, if she's even entitled to it, and at this point we don't know that she is, will take time. In the interim, all her available funds are devoted to her medical care."

"I assume Mr Jones will help his daughter."

Cain was quiet, acting as if he wondered whether to reveal a secret. "Again, for your ears only, Mr Flynn," he whispered, "but Mr Jones will need approval from other family members for that type of expenditure. Any monies under his control, other than his usual expenses, are not liquid assets. He can't access funds immediately; it would take time."

"I wasn't aware of that, Mr Cain," Flynn admitted. "That's unfortunate."

"Given the circumstances, and our initial agreement for payment of five thousand pounds with an additional consideration of five thousand pounds more, can we at least agree to freeze the remaining debt and consider payment at a later time?"

"I suppose I could consider that," Flynn said, "if I was so inclined." He paused, rubbing his chin, pretending to contemplate. "Of course, I still suggest that, as wife to Alexander Cavendish, the ultimate responsibility for the debt rests with Miss Penelope."

"And as I just proposed, it's my opinion that Mr Jones has been very generous in his offer of five thousand pounds, with a potential consideration for five thousand more."

Flynn studied his beer for a moment and then raised his eyes to meet Cain's. "Here's my proposition, Mr Cain," he stated firmly. "I will contact

Mr Cavendish and ask him to reconsider payment of his son's debt. If he declines, I will accept Mr Jones's offer of ten thousand pounds."

Cain looked at him quizzically. "What about the balance," he asked, "the remaining ten thousand pounds, assuming you freeze the debt?"

"I will collect the balance from Miss Penelope."

Cain was confused. "Mr Flynn," he said, "I thought I made Miss Penelope's financial position quite clear."

"You did," Flynn replied evasively. "But Miss Penelope has another option for providing payment."

"Mr Flynn, as I stated, Miss Penelope's liquid assets are accounted for."

The corner of Flynn's lips turned slightly, and he said, "She won't need liquid assets for the option I'm considering."

Chapter 50

The coroner released the body of Alexander Cavendish for burial even though the post-mortem report had yet to be issued. Everyone knew he had been murdered, the cause of death apparent, and with a grieving family in London waiting to bury a loved one and a nation anxious to honour and mourn a war hero, it seemed the only thing to do.

A simple funeral was held at Duomo di Como, a beautiful Gothic cathedral built of stone, graceful arches, a majestic cupola and a rose window flanked by statues of Pliny the Elder and Pliny the Younger, originally residents of Como. Built with a central nave and two side aisles separated by pillars, the large church was almost empty, the steps of visitors echoing across the black and white marble tiles, the casket perched near the altar with floral arrangements of carnations and lilies on either side.

Dr Barnett and Adele brought Penelope to the service and then sat in the pew behind her with Rose Barnett. Wellington was at Penelope's side, gently holding her hand, wrapping his arm protectively around her. William Cain sat alone in a rear pew, as if he didn't belong, and a sprinkling of residents came to pay their respect – the fisherman who found the body, the man who worked at the gun range, a barmaid from a local tavern who mysteriously wept as much as the family did, as well as the mayor and two policemen. Antonio Falcone stood respectfully by the door, Captain Minelli beside him. They watched those in attendance, who in turn respectfully viewed the coffin.

The casket was simple, constructed more for the journey to London than beauty or a celebration of the life of the deceased. After several minutes of silence, when assured no-one else would be attending, a priest appeared, serious and solemn, making his way to a podium beside the altar. He opened the Bible, leafing through the pages until he found the verse he wanted, and proceeded to quote the scriptures, using the word of God to somehow celebrate the passing of a man who was both hero and husband and much too young to die, although some believed he had not died soon enough. The eulogy was humble, discussing the accomplishments of the deceased, dissecting the heavens and hells that comprised his life. When the service ended, the priest consoled the mourning family and the attending residents of Como.

Penelope went to the open casket wearing a modest black dress and veil, and spent a few moments kneeling before it. She said a prayer, whispering, the words inaudible to those in the church, holding the hand of her beloved. She stood when finished, wiped tears from her eyes, and used her hand to gently brush the hair from her husband's forehead. She lifted the veil that covered her face and kissed him, her lips delicately placed on his. She then returned to the pew, crying softly.

Wellington Jones followed, his expression sombre, his eyes glazed. He knelt before the casket, appeared to mouth a short prayer and then stood, emotions masked and thoughts unknown, looking at the man who lay before him. He spent several moments in apparent reflection and then returned to his pew and sat beside Penelope, kissing her lightly on the cheek.

Joseph Barnett walked to the casket but did not kneel. He stood motionless and with eyes vacant looked at the deceased. Perhaps he mourned the men who served under Cavendish or those who crossed his path and now lived in shadows, the light too bright. After a few minutes elapsed, he turned, a hint of anger flickering across his face, and sat behind Wellington and Penelope.

Rose Barnett remained in the pew with Adele, as did William Cain. A few of the residents bade their farewells, kneeling before the casket, making the sign of the cross and mumbling a prayer. When finished, they gave their condolences to Penelope Jones.

"Barnett seems angry," Falcone observed, "instead of being upset."

"There's something suspicious about him," Minelli remarked. "Remember what his receptionist said."

"Which we have no evidence to support," Falcone reminded him. "We only have a witness who may not have seen what she thinks she saw."

"What she saw is the tip of an iceberg," Minelli countered. "If you ask me, Miss Penelope isn't acting like a grieving widow."

"She's still in shock," Falcone argued. "She can't comprehend what happened."

"If she is in shock, it's because she's about to inherit a lot of money. Then she can run away with her lover, the doctor."

Falcone hid his scepticism. "The problem with that theory is that she doesn't need a lot of money."

Minelli ignored him, apparently unconvinced. "And Mr Jones seems quite pleased his son-in-law is dead."

"He is acting strangely," Falcone agreed. "We know Cavendish wasn't an angel. And I doubt there was any love between them."

"Which makes him a suspect, although not as strong as the doctor. Or do you think the gangster could have killed him?"

"He has motive," Falcone said, "non-payment of a substantial debt. But there are many other suspects – the doctor, Jones, and the doctor's wife among them."

Chapter 51

"The whole country bets on horses," Billy Flynn said as he sat in Antonio Falcone's office. "The majority collect their winnings and pay off their debts."

"Was Mr Cavendish one of the exceptions?" Falcone asked as he studied Flynn closely.

"Mr Cavendish usually paid," Flynn said. "He did, however, amass a sizeable debt recently."

"What tactics are used to collect debts?" Captain Minelli interjected. "I imagine you have to get rough sometimes."

Flynn looked confused. "I'm not sure I understand the question," he said. "It's a fairly simple process – 'Pay what's owed by the date due. If payment is not received, my associate and I will attempt to collect.' If not successful, especially over an extended period of time, family members are informed of the obligation and given the opportunity to reconcile."

"How much did Mr Cavendish owe?" Falcone asked.

"Twenty-two thousand pounds, including interest and expenses," Flynn informed them. "The original debt was fifteen thousand pounds."

Falcone glanced at Minelli. It was a tremendous sum to two police officers in northern Italy – or to most on the planet.

"Did Mr Cavendish ever incur debt before?" Minelli asked.

"Yes, he did," Flynn replied, "quite often, actually."

"What was the sum of his last debt," Minelli probed, "prior to what's currently outstanding?"

"Ten thousand pounds."

"And that debt was satisfied?" Minelli continued.

"Yes, a few months ago. Actually, Miss Penelope paid it."

"Does she know about the current debt?" Minelli asked.

"I don't know," Flynn admitted. "But she does have the means to pay."

"How do you know that?" Falcone asked.

"Because she's wealthy," Flynn replied, "and she'll also inherit Mr Cavendish's trust fund, which by all accounts is a sizeable fortune."

191

"You assume she'll inherit the trust fund," Falcone stated, correcting him. "We don't know how it's structured legally. The assets could revert to the family in the event of death, rather than the wife."

Flynn shrugged. "I doubt it," he countered, "but I suppose it's possible."

"Does Mr Jones know about the debt?" Minelli asked.

"I don't know," Flynn replied. "You'll have to ask him."

"Where were you on the evening of May the third?" Falcone asked.

"I had dinner in Milan with my associate Jocko Jenks and an Italian friend of mine," Flynn answered.

"What is your friend's name?" Minelli asked.

"Pasquale Ruggeri."

"Hardly a credible alibi," Minelli smirked. "Ruggeri is a known crook."

"I don't believe Mr Ruggeri has ever been convicted of a crime," Flynn said with a sly smile. "And neither have I."

"What restaurant were you at?" Falcone asked.

"I don't remember the name, but it's a café with outdoor tables next to the opera house."

Falcone was quiet for a moment, reflective. "How long were you there?"

"Several hours," Flynn replied. "We returned to our hotel around midnight."

"Did you take the train to Milan?" Minelli asked.

"Yes, we did."

"Do you still have the ticket?"

"No, why would I?" Flynn replied sarcastically.

"Did you leave the hotel after you returned?" Falcone asked.

"No, I didn't."

"Do you know where Cavendish was staying?"

"Yes, at the cottage next to the asylum."

"Have you ever been there?"

"Yes, I have. I paid a visit when I arrived in Como."

"How did Mr Cavendish intend to pay?" Falcone asked. He was curious to see if Flynn mentioned the life insurance policy.

"He had several options, as I recall," Flynn said. "He could wait until next year, when he received annual payment from his trust, even though the interest would accumulate. Or he could get money from his father-in-law or Miss Penelope. I think he was also going to ask his father to lend him the money."

"But hadn't he already had money from Penelope," Falcone asked, "to pay the ten thousand pounds?"

"Yes, he had. And he hinted she wouldn't give him anymore."

"Did he have any other options?" Falcone asked.

"He also had a friend from the war who lives in Como," Flynn said. "Cavendish was confident she would give him the money."

Falcone studied Flynn closely. "Who was that?" he asked.

"A woman named Rose Barnett."

Chapter 52

Penelope was sombre after the ceremony. Her life had drastically changed. She sat passively in her suite at the sanitarium, looking beyond the balcony to the lake and the boats that serenely sailed upon it. Her face was pale, her hands trembling ever so slightly, her eyes glassy from the sedatives the hospital staff had given her. Occasionally, a tear trailed down her olive cheeks, which she dabbed with a silk handkerchief.

"Dr Barnett said you're doing well," Wellington Jones said softly. "If you continue to progress as you have been, you can probably return to London in a few months."

"As a widow," she said. "The press will love that. The spoiled princess haunted by death: her mother, her brother, her husband."

"Honour the dead, rejoice with the living," Jones remarked. "The phrase fit the war and it applies now."

"It makes no sense," she said bitterly. "The war was horrific. There's nothing to rejoice about."

"Honour the dead and the life they lived," Wellington explained, "but move forward. Life is precious and it goes on. Enjoy what time you have left."

"I'm a widow locked in a lunatic asylum and someone is trying to kill me. What exactly am I supposed to enjoy?"

Wellington wrapped his arm around her. "It's only temporary," he assured her. "You'll be well again in no time."

"Not likely," she said. "Whoever killed Alexander will probably kill me."

"Alexander had shortcomings, Penelope. Bad habits that were hard to break. They probably led to his death."

"I know more than you think," she said. "I gave him ten thousand pounds to pay off his bookie."

Jones frowned. "There was more owed than that."

She was quiet, reflective. "He asked me for more money," she said quietly, "but I wouldn't give it to him. I told him to talk to you."

"It was another gambling debt."

"No, it was to pay for damages from his motor vehicle accident."

"There was no motor vehicle accident," Wellington told her. "It was just a story Alexander concocted so you would feel sorry for him."

"What about his injuries?"

Jones shrugged. "Maybe his bookmaker demanded payment," he said cryptically, "and Alexander didn't have the money."

"What kind of man did I marry? I suppose I never really knew him," she admitted. "I just thought I did."

"None of us knew him," Wellington agreed. "But maybe it's better we didn't."

"I made a horrible mistake."

"We all make mistakes," he said. "But when you fall down, you pick yourself up and you go forward."

"Easier said than done," she said, looking away. "Especially when you're crazy."

"You're being too hard on yourself," Wellington said. "You've had a setback, a condition you couldn't control. Dr Barnett will ensure you're well again."

"It's not that easy," she said. "What if someone asks me where I was in 1921? Do I tell them I was in a lunatic asylum?"

"Stop it," Wellington said. "What difference does it make what anyone else thinks? The only person you have to satisfy is Penelope Jones."

She was quiet, barely listening, her thoughts again wandering to the man she had married. "He claimed he owed fifteen thousand pounds," she said. "How does that happen?"

"Picking the wrong ponies."

"But where did he get that much money to gamble?"

"From his trust fund."

She paused, reminiscing. "Alexander wasn't very good with money," she said. "His allowance was normally gone by March. He couldn't wait for his thirtieth birthday, when he would have received the full trust."

"And squandered it, I'm sure."

"I suppose we'll never know," she said.

"Penelope, do you realise you'll likely inherit his estate?" he asked delicately. "And without the stipulation of an annual allowance. The lump sum will pass to you."

She was quiet, still staring at the lake. "I haven't really thought about it," she said.

"You're about to become a wealthy woman. Not that you aren't already."

She looked at her father and the wrinkles that stress had worn in his face. He had spent his entire life making sure she wanted for nothing, not living his life to ensure she lived hers. "You can have all the money," she offered. "I don't need it. I have enough."

His face lightened, as if a tremendous burden had been washed away. "Penelope, that's very generous," he said, a sense of relief in his voice. "That money could be critical for the business. If the world only knew how close to bankruptcy we actually are."

"You've done a good job of hiding it," she told him. "This sanitarium alone must cost a small fortune. Let alone the upkeep on the estate in England and the apartment in Paris."

"I've managed the last few months by shuffling payments between accounts, borrowing on assets, selling what I could as discretely as I could to stay one step ahead of creditors. But that can't go on much longer."

"When will our finances improve?"

"If the banks in Bombay don't approve new credit terms, or if the global recession doesn't end quickly, I will need a tremendous amount of money to salvage our business empire. It's a complicated mess that ties up any and all liquid assets we have and probably will for several more months. But with your inheritance, it doesn't matter. We can pay our creditors and the business will survive, stronger than it ever was."

"We still have to find out who's trying to kill me."

He smiled weakly, gently caressing the back of her shoulder. "Penelope, I don't think anyone is trying to kill you," he assured her. "Isn't that why we brought you here, to help you understand that?"

"No, it isn't. I came here for protection. Dr Barnett is helping me with that."

"Yes, Dr Barnett is helping you. But I'm afraid it might take a little while longer."

Chapter 53

Inspector Falcone sat behind his desk, gazing at a family photograph – his wife, daughter and son – in happier times before the war. He thought of his daughter living in Philadelphia. It might be nice to go and see her. Maybe after he finished with Cavendish's murder. She was all he had left.

He looked at a chalkboard on the wall of his office. Equipped with a curtain that covered it when he had visitors, the details of Alexander Cavendish's murder were now scribbled upon it. Captain Minelli stood beside the board, a piece of chalk in his hand.

"I feel like we're missing something," Falcone said.

"I'm sure we are," Minelli agreed. "But we still have interviews to conduct."

They each looked at the board, studying the information scribed. Across the top were headers: name, motive, gun, alibi. On the left side of the board were four names: Billy Flynn or Jocko, Wellington Jones or Cain, Joseph Barnett, and Rose Barnett.

"Four suspects, or sets of suspects," Minelli summarised. "Some stronger than others."

"Let's discuss their motives," Falcone suggested.

Next to Billy Flynn's name, under motive, Minelli wrote 'money', then a question mark under gun, and the word 'weak' under alibi. "Can you think of anything else?" he asked Falcone.

The Inspector slowly shook his head. "Just the life insurance policy, which also falls under money, as a motive."

"But Flynn may not have known it existed," Minelli countered. "That could have been Cavendish."

"Which makes Penelope's claims that someone was trying to kill her more believable," Falcone said. "It could have been her husband."

Minelli turned his attention back to the board. "We can probably assume that either Flynn or Jocko is capable of making the shot that killed Cavendish," he offered. "Flynn said he was military."

"We can assume so, but we should address it with further questioning."

Minelli erased the question mark under gun and put 'probable'. "Let's move on to Jones." Under motive he wrote a question mark, scribbled 'yes' under gun and 'weak' under alibi.

"The man at the shooting range said Jones was the best shot he ever saw," Falcone commented.

"But many men are good shots," Minelli countered.

"Some women are, too," Falcone offered.

"On to Barnett," Minelli said. He put 'yes' under motive and then question marks across the board. "We know that he was having an affair with Penelope. There's no stronger motive than that."

"There's the possibility he could be having an affair with Penelope," Falcone said in a fatherly tone. "But we only know what the receptionist witnessed, no validation."

"I'm convinced it's true," Minelli insisted. "And I think he has the strongest motive."

"For now, we'll assume it's true," Falcone cautioned. "Let's move on to Rose. I suspect she was being blackmailed by Cavendish about the five names on his list, considering his note that they were murdered by Rose Barnett."

"But we have no proof that Rose actually murdered anyone," Minelli said.

"There still seems to be a connection between the two, and both Rose and the doctor admitted they knew Cavendish from the war," Falcone said as he stared at the chalkboard and slowly shook his head. "I just find it hard to believe that Rose is capable of killing anyone."

"The best murderers are rarely suspected," Minelli said. He stepped back and glanced at the board. "Have we captured all the suspects?"

"I'm not sure," Falcone said, eyeing the board. "Add another, to be determined."

"Who do we question next?"

"I think we'll have the most to learn from Rose Barnett."

There was a knock on the office door. Falcone eyed Minelli and he lowered the curtain over the chalkboard.

"Come in," Falcone said.

It was one of the policemen. "I have the ballistic report, sir," he said, handing some papers to Falcone.

"What did they determine?"

"Only that the weapon was a Carcano, 6.5mm, Model M91. Although they couldn't conclusively state that Cavendish was killed with his own rifle, the gun found in his cottage, it is possible."

"Thank you," Falcone said as the policeman made his exit and closed the door.

Falcone sighed, studying the report. "Is it really plausible," Falcone wondered aloud, "that the killer entered the cabin, presumably via the back door with the broken lock, took the rifle, climbed to a ledge a hundred metres away, fired the shot that killed Cavendish, climbed down from the ledge, returned the rifle, and then fled?"

"Yes, I suppose it's possible."

Falcone was quiet, lips pursed, still looking at the report. "Why do I find that so hard to believe?"

Chapter 54

"Good morning, Mrs Barnett," Falcone said cordially. "May we talk to you for a few minutes?"

She seemed flustered, but recovered quickly. "Yes, of course," she replied. "Please, come in."

"This is Captain Minelli and I'm Inspector Falcone. We met on the lakefront on the day of the tragedy."

She smiled. "Yes, I remember," she told them. "You mentioned my poetry."

Falcone nodded respectfully. "I have all your books. I enjoy them very much."

"Thank you," she said as she led them into the house. "I appreciate that."

They sat in the parlour, the policemen in the two leather chairs normally reserved for Rose and Joseph, while she sat on the sofa across from them. Minelli, removed a notebook and a pen from his pocket.

"May I get you anything?" she asked.

"No, we're fine," Falcone replied. "We just have a few questions. I promise not to take up much of your time."

"I understand."

"Mrs Barnett, have you ever fired a rifle?"

She smiled weakly and shrugged. "I received training before being sent to France," she responded. "I can load a weapon and fire it, and do it properly. I just don't think I can hit anything. At least not what I was aiming for. And I never hunt; I love animals too much."

"Can you tell us how you met Alexander Cavendish?" Minelli asked.

"Yes, of course. It was during the war, in France. Just after the Battle of the Somme. He came to Amiens Hospital with others who were wounded."

"Where was he injured and how long was he a patient?" Falcone asked.

"He was wounded in the abdomen, shrapnel from bombing and a single bullet, as I recall. Surgery was performed upon his arrival and he was probably a patient for several months."

"Was your husband a patient at that time also?" Minelli asked.

"Yes, he was. Joseph was severely injured, as I'm sure you're aware. He came to the hospital before Cavendish and left well after."

"That seems to be a long stay in a hospital," Falcone said.

"By hospital I mean convalescing as well. The wing of the facility in which I was employed dealt primarily with the patients' recovery."

"Did your husband know Cavendish was in the same hospital?" Minelli asked.

"No, not at the time. Joseph was rarely conscious while Cavendish was a patient. They served together on the battlefield, different regiments whose paths often crossed. And they met again when Miss Penelope arrived as Joseph's patient."

"Was Mr Cavendish a popular patient?" Falcone asked.

She hesitated a moment and then replied. "No, he wasn't. To be perfectly honest, he was despised."

"Why?" Falcone asked. "Was it because of his behaviour – on the battlefield or in the hospital?"

"I don't think patients, nurses, or doctors knew him on the battlefield."

"Then can you explain his unpopularity?" Minelli prodded.

She paused, as if wondering how to phrase the reply. "He was arrogant and very rude," she answered, "obnoxious and belittling to patients and staff."

Falcone had been observing her closely, the inflection in her voice, her body motion. "Mrs Barnett, I don't mean to offend you," he said, "but I feel as if you're hiding something. Would you be more comfortable with an attorney?"

She studied him for a moment, no doubt wondering where the conversation would lead, but ignoring his suggestion. "Mr Cavendish assaulted several of the nurses," she replied firmly, "including me."

Falcone shared a guarded glance with Minelli. It wasn't the reply he expected. But it did offer another motive for murder. "I'm so sorry you endured that nightmare," he offered sincerely.

"Thank you," she said, her eyes looking away. "I don't ever talk about it."

"Were the authorities notified?" Falcone asked.

"No," she said, "not by me. And I don't believe anyone else notified them either."

"Why not?" Minelli queried.

"Who would ever believe us?" she asked. "He was Britain's hero of the Somme."

"Does your husband know?" Falcone questioned.

"No," she said curtly. "And I prefer to keep it that way."

"Why did you not tell anyone?" Minelli probed.

"It was one more tragedy in a time of tragedies. I prefer to leave it buried with the dead."

Falcone's mind drifted, memories of his own hell returning. "The world has many memories that would be best forgotten," he said. "If only they could be."

"I wish we could turn back the clock," she said, apparently seeing the pain in his eyes. "I'm sure it all would be done much differently."

"I suspect you weren't happy to see Cavendish in Como," Falcone said.

"No, I wasn't," she said, disgust marring her face. "I despise the man, as you can understand. And one of the reasons Joseph and I came to Como was to escape the war. Neither of us needed, or wanted, that reminder."

Falcone paused, collecting his thoughts. "Mrs Barnett," he said, "I would like to continue with your tenure at the hospital."

She seemed uneasy, but nodded.

"Did you know Captain Clark Hollingsworth?"

Her eyes misted, her face twisted in agony. She looked at the two policemen as if her entire world was about to collapse. "Yes, I did," she replied quietly.

"What happened to Captain Hollingsworth?"

"He succumbed to his injuries."

"How about Private William Digby?"

"Yes, I knew him," she said as she started to sob.

"What happened to Private Digby?" Falcone continued.

"He succumbed to his injuries."

"How about Private Thomas Custer?"

"Yes, I remember Private Custer," she whispered hoarsely.

"What happened to Private Custer?" Falcone asked.

"He succumbed to his injuries."

"Do you remember Lieutenant Jacob O'Hara?" Falcone asked.

"Yes, I do," she said quietly.

"What happened to Lieutenant O'Hara?"

"He succumbed to his injuries."

"How about Corporal Michael Willingham?"

"Yes, I knew him," she replied. A single tear dripped from her eye.

"What happened to Corporal Willingham?"

"He succumbed to his injuries."

"Mrs Barnett, was Alexander Cavendish blackmailing you?"

She started crying, unable to control a string of tears that trickled down her face, connecting the freckles that dotted her cheeks. "He tried to," she admitted. "But I refused."

"What did he know, that we do not?"

She paled, wiping away tears, even though they were quickly replaced. She tried to control herself, but couldn't. It took a minute for her to regain her composure.

Falcone watched, suspecting the answer he was about to receive. "Would you like to wait for an attorney?" he asked.

"No," she said softly. "I don't need an attorney."

"Can you please explain why Cavendish was trying to blackmail you?" Falcone repeated.

"He knew that I killed those men," she admitted.

Minelli gasped, but kept scribbling in his notebook. His gaze moved from Falcone to Rose and back again.

"Why did you kill them?" Falcone asked.

She cried harder, sobbing into her handkerchief. After a few seconds, she stopped, seemed to accept her fate, and wiped the tears from her cheeks.

Falcone leaned forward, lightly caressed her arm. "It's all right, Mrs Barnett. You can tell us what happened."

She took a moment to calm herself and then continued. "They were horribly wounded," she responded, speaking softly, a vacant look in her eyes. "And in such tremendous pain."

"Was there any hope of recovery?" Minelli asked.

"No, none at all," she explained. "They had burns over their entire bodies or head and facial injuries that were so severe they were more mannequins than men. They had no future, only the hellish present. And it would never get better for any of them. Some begged me to kill them, pleading, praying to die."

They stared at her impassively, not passing judgement, but not quite understanding.

She raised her eyes and looked at them. "I know it was wrong," she admitted, "but I played the role of God. I held a pillow over their faces to end their misery, although I had no right to do so. I know it was a crime.

But I couldn't watch them suffer any longer. Cavendish saw me do it, pretending to be asleep."

Falcone looked at her, a courageous woman who committed a crime, but a woman whose heart was as pure as the saints he prayed to. "I think that's all the questions we have for you," he said softly.

"That's why we never returned to Britain," she explained. "Joseph was afraid I would be arrested. He thought Italy would be safe."

Falcone nodded and rose from his chair, motioned to Minelli, and started towards the door.

"Can we stop at the sanitarium so I can tell Joseph?" she asked. "He depends on me. He can't manage alone."

"There's no need to stop at the sanitarium," Falcone assured her.

"I know you have to arrest me," she said, accepting her fate. "I realise I was wrong. But I'm not sorry I did it. I only ask that you let me see my husband before you take me away."

Falcone feigned confusion. "Mrs Barnett, I am investigating the murder of Alexander Cavendish," he informed her. "Nothing more." He nodded, smiling faintly as he opened the door. "Thank you for your cooperation. Have a nice day."

Chapter 55

"You're coping with Alexander's death quite well, Penelope," Dr Barnett said as he sat behind her during their session. "Especially considering the circumstances."

"I can't tell if it's real," she said, sounding drowsy and defeated. "It seems like a nightmare. How do I know he's really dead?"

"We attended the funeral," he reminded her. "Don't you remember? We celebrated Alexander's life and then said goodbye to him. His casket was taken to England for burial."

"That was a dream," she said. "Alexander isn't dead. He went to London to see his father."

"That was several weeks ago," Barnett informed her, "just after your arrival at the sanitarium. He was gone for a week but then returned. He stayed in the cottage next to the hospital. And tragically, someone killed him last week."

"Someone is trying to kill me," she said, not seeming to grasp what he said. "I think it's Alexander."

"Why would Alexander try to kill you?"

"He wants my money," she informed him. "He has debts to pay."

"Penelope, Alexander never tried to kill you. He loved you."

"What if he loves someone else?"

Barnett hesitated, not sure how to reply. Did Penelope know something he didn't? "Penelope, that's not true," he assured her. "Alexander loved you dearly."

"He thinks I have a lot of money," she continued, "that's why he's trying to kill me."

"Penelope, you're one of the wealthiest women in England."

"I use to be," she said, correcting him, "but then the Queen took it."

"Queen who? King George the Fifth is our ruler."

"No, Queen Victoria. My father told me it's something in India."

Barnett had read that the Jones family was overextended in India due to the global recession. He suspected it was temporary and wasn't interested in discussing it. As for Queen Victoria, Penelope mentioned her often, as if they were close friends.

"Why does your husband want your money? He's a very wealthy man."

She shrugged. "You'll have to ask him," she suggested. "Or maybe it's someone else – maybe he paid someone to kill me."

Barnett paused, seeking an effective way to counter her flawed logic. "Penelope, do you remember when you thought Adele tried to kill you?"

"Yes, I do," she admitted, "but now I know it wasn't her." She paused and glanced around the room, as if ensuring no-one could hear. "It was Alexander."

"Maybe it was a nightmare," he suggested. "Maybe you just dreamed someone was trying to kill you." He was pleased with her partial recognition of the truth, but disturbed she changed the narrative to fit her altered reality. It was a symptom of the disease, the relentless insistence that the delusion was true.

"No, I don't think so," she argued. "The intruder came in through the window. I fought with him. My fingertips were bloody."

"Yes, your fingertips were bloody," Barnett said, emphasising the only truth he knew. "And there were traces of blood on the window. Maybe you tore your fingertips wrestling with the window. Maybe it was stuck. Maybe as you forced it open, you scraped your fingers."

She was pensive, considering his argument. "I suppose that could have happened," she agreed, "but I don't remember the window being stuck."

He had cast doubt, hoping she would discern fact from fiction. He decided to discuss other supposed attempts on her life, to subtly discount them, and then maybe she would eventually recognise that they never occurred.

"Penelope, was it windy on the night you fell from the balcony?"

"I didn't fall from the balcony," she insisted. "Someone pushed me."

"I wonder who could have pushed you?" he asked. "Adele was on the fourth floor at the time. And no other nurses or orderlies were near your room."

"The intruder must have come in the window," she said.

"A tree branch comes close to the balcony," he said. "Did you reach for something on the tree, an injured bird, perhaps? Or maybe you thought you could climb the tree, but lost your balance."

She turned and looked at him strangely. "I had no reason to climb the tree, but I could have lost my balance leaning over the balcony. I do remember it was a very clear night and the stars were bright and beautiful."

"Then it's quite possible you fell over the railing," he suggested.

She was quiet, apparently reluctant to agree. "Perhaps," she muttered.

"We'll discuss it again, after you've had time to think about it. Are you sure about the other attempt on your life?"

"Yes, in Monte Carlo. Someone forced me to take too much medicine."

"How could they force you without you realising it?"

"I drank much more than I should have."

"Here's an interesting theory," Barnett offered. "Maybe you had been drinking and you accidentally took too much medicine."

"I suppose that could have happened," she said. "But I don't think it did."

He paused, allowing her thoughts to wander, to digest the solutions he had offered. "Now that we've examined each of these incidents, do you still think they represent attempts on your life?"

She turned in the chair and her eyes met his, clear and determined. "Yes, I do," she insisted. "Alexander is trying to kill me."

Chapter 56

"My sources in London claim there are several stipulations contained in the Cavendish trust," William Cain said as he sipped Amaretto in the library of Wellington Jones's rented villa.

Jones frowned. He had suspected complications. "What type of stipulations?"

"It's all conjecture," Cain informed him. "No-one has actually seen the document. But my sources talked to solicitors involved in its preparation, in whole or in part."

"Tell me what you've heard," Jones requested, "and we can at least be prepared."

"One clause addresses accidental death," Cain explained.

"That's standard," Jones commented. "But this wasn't an accidental death."

"I understand that, sir. Provisions in the accidental death clause include murder. I think it states sudden death not due to medical conditions or something to that effect."

"What happens to the trust in that event?"

"I haven't been able to determine," Cain said, lighting a cigarette, "at least not yet. There's also an age provision. For example, if Cavendish dies before the trust was transferred to him."

Jones was thoughtful for a moment. "That's actually a logical stipulation," he mused aloud. "Cavendish never actually inherited the trust, since he didn't reach the age of thirty, so the trust can't be included in his estate."

Cain shrugged. "I don't know, sir," he admitted, "but that certainly makes sense. There's also a clause for children, not relevant in this situation, and a required term of marriage."

"The clause for children is common," Jones acknowledged. "And term of marriage normally addresses weeks or months versus years."

"I think in this case the trust is inherited in percentages, based on years of marriage."

Jones was wary. "What does this mean for Penelope?"

"I think the best she can hope for, given the provisions as explained to me, is to inherit half the value of the trust."

"And I assume the rest remains in the family?"

"Correct."

He sighed, pensive. "That's actually a reasonable agreement," he said, "given the marriage produced no children. What's the worst we can expect?"

"Miss Penelope inherits the annual allowance that Mr Cavendish was receiving at the time of his death."

"Which is very limited," Jones said, frowning. "Maybe thirty thousand pounds?"

"At the most," Cain replied. "And she would only receive that for a brief period of time, probably until the age of thirty."

"Which were the same conditions Cavendish was subject to."

"Exactly. My sources claim that is the most likely scenario."

Jones envisioned his global real estate empire unravelling. If what Cain said was true, Penelope's inheritance wouldn't help him.

"There's one other clause you should probably know about," Cain said.

"What is it?" Jones asked, frowning. "It can't get much worse."

"I'm afraid it can, sir," Cain informed him. "There's also a debt clause."

Jones looked at him strangely. "What does it specify?"

"Apparently, it was a very late addition to the trust," Cain said, "added only a few weeks ago."

"Prompted by Cavendish's recent debt," Jones surmised.

"Or Billy Flynn's visit to Jackson Cavendish. It seems the debt clause was added shortly after that."

"I'm not sure that I blame Jackson Cavendish," Jones admitted. "I probably would have done the same if our roles were reversed. How specific is the clause?"

"My sources claim that if Cavendish dies before the age of thirty—"

"Which he did."

Cain nodded and continued, "And he has unpaid debts that surpass a specified amount, then the debts will be paid by the trust."

"If we come to terms with Flynn, do we get credit for partial payment, should we choose to make it?" Jones asked. "Does that negate the clause?"

"I don't think so," Cain answered. "My sources say the trust pays the debt and Miss Penelope's inheritance is null and void."

"Damn that man," Jones said angrily. "He was worth nothing alive and even less now that he's dead."

****

Wellington Jones was sitting on the veranda having breakfast when the cable arrived. The servant laid a silver tray at the edge of the table, an envelope centred on it. Jones looked at it after the man departed, knowing the future of his empire could be contained within the correspondence.

He sipped his latte and finished his biscottate and glanced at the lake, watching a boat skim across the water before stopping, apparently finding a good location to fish. He looked at the mountains sprawling behind the water, immersed in tranquility, and then glanced into the house, the villa luxurious and comfortable, one he had rented many times over the course of his lifetime, and he knew it could all be gone, depending on what the correspondence contained. He drank the rest of his latte and reached for the envelope, gently tearing it open.

It was from his office in Bombay, referencing the half dozen banks that controlled the liens on his Indian real estate. The cable stated that the consortium had reached a decision regarding the decreased value of his Indian real estate holdings and their need to minimise risk associated with assets of declining value. Jones frowned, skimming through the legal jargon that prefaced the agreement and moved to the last paragraph, which contained the banks' offer. All liens would be restructured with existing terms, the amount of each mortgage to be adjusted ten percent below the existing fair market value.

Jones sighed with relief. The banks had agreed in part. They weren't demanding payment in full, but required a cash infusion for each property. It was a good compromise. Now he needed to find the money.

Chapter 57

Rose Barnett watched her husband work in his garden, fussing with his flowers. She knew how much pleasure he got from his plants, creating a kaleidoscope of beautiful colours from edelweiss, roses, carnations and lilies. She smiled as he worked, pruning stalks, pulling weeds, brushing a small hand rake across the soil. She scribbled words on paper, turning them into poems, saving fragments and phrases, molding them together in a dreamy world of rhymes and alliterations. She nurtured words; he nurtured plants.

She knew how badly he suffered, the horrific memories never fading. Sometimes he seemed to improve, but then an atrocious nightmare would overwhelm him, and he would scream in the middle of the night, trembling, dripping with sweat, and the battle waged within his mind began again, ending where it had started. All she could do was support him, care for him, and hope that the demons would someday disappear and let him live in peace.

When he finished his gardening, he wiped his hands with a rag and came to sit beside her. "I enjoy that so much," he told her.

"You should do it more often," she said.

"Yes, I should. It's very relaxing."

She paused, sipping a glass of wine. "Inspector Falcone came to see me today."

"What did he want?" he asked, alarmed.

"He asked me about Cavendish."

"What did you tell him?"

"I told him the truth."

He looked at her, panicked. "Even about the men at the hospital?"

"Yes, Cavendish kept records of their names. Falcone found them and realised he was trying to blackmail me."

He grasped her hand, holding it tightly. "Did you tell him how they died?"

"Yes, I did," she said. "I admitted everything."

"Is he going to arrest you?"

211

"I thought he was, but he didn't. He said he was investigating Cavendish's death and nothing more."

"Why would he not do anything? It doesn't make sense."

"I think he understood," she said. "He knew it was hell, especially in a hospital filled with battered bodies and men who lived but wished they didn't. It seemed like he had been through it."

"Then we don't have to be afraid anymore."

"I'm not so sure," she said cautiously, eyeing him closely.

"Your secret is safe," he continued. "Cavendish was the only one that knew."

"He may have told the police in London. And if they find me, they'll arrest me."

"They would have tried to find you already. And they never did."

"Then we can go back to England," she said. "I can see my family."

"Do you think they'll understand what we've been through?"

"Of course, they will," she replied. "They've suffered just as we have. And we don't have to go to Clovelly. We could live in London."

He thought for a moment, seeming to consider the alternatives, and then asked, "Is Paris safe, since the hospital was in France? Do you think anyone there knows what happened?"

"No, I don't think so," she replied. "We can live in Paris if we want. We're safe anywhere now that Cavendish is dead."

"He deserved to die," he said, bitter and angry.

She squeezed his hand, feeling his anger. "It's over now," she assured him.

"But we can't do anything for those he killed."

"Joseph," she said, her voice calm and soothing. "Falcone will be coming to the sanitarium tomorrow."

"Penelope still can't comprehend what happened," he said. "I prefer that he wait a few more days."

"Joseph," she said firmly, "he's not coming for Penelope. He's coming for you."

He seemed surprised, as if he should be beyond suspicion. Or maybe he just hoped he would be. "What does he want me for?" he asked. "I already talked to him."

"He wants to make sure you didn't kill Cavendish. You must be careful what you tell him. He's a very intelligent man."

"Anyone could have killed Cavendish. He had no friends, only enemies. He was an evil, nasty man."

"Then that's what you should tell Falcone," she said. "And nothing more."

Chapter 58

"It's a disgrace," Barnett complained bitterly. "How could the king give Cavendish a state funeral with military honours. He wasn't a hero. I saw him kill a boy named Jimmy Spangler. Maybe Cavendish didn't pull the trigger, but he came as close as you can to murder without actually committing the crime."

"I understand," Falcone assured him as he and Minelli sat in Barnett's office, listening to the psychiatrist rant. "Sometimes we get what we don't deserve, good or bad."

"Did you feel any compassion when Cavendish was murdered?" Minelli asked, his notebook open, his pen poised.

"Absolutely not," Barnett said tersely. "I did feel badly for Penelope, although I'm sure she'll be better for it. But I didn't grieve and I wasn't upset. I was relieved, overwhelmed that a merciful God ensured justice was served."

"It may seem acceptable to commend whoever killed him," Falcone said, gently correcting him, "or to accept that he deserved it. But justice wasn't served, was it? We're a civilised society, Doctor. Cavendish should have been tried in a military court during the war. Don't you think that would have been more appropriate?"

... Soldiers scaled ladders to the top of the trench or scrambled up the planks that contained its earthen walls while Cavendish stood behind them and aimed his pistol and forced them to attack. Bullets riddled man after man and they fell backwards screaming as their blood spilled into the mud and stained it crimson.

The human wave continued climbing over the top and dashing across the scarred landscape blotted with acrid smoke that partially hid the broken trees, their branches blown away and their leaves long gone, standing like tombstones sticking from the grassless soil, little more than gruesome, disfigured trunks with the advancing army swarming like ants around them.

Cavendish waved his weapon and ordered the attack to continue even though men fell as fast as they could climb over the top until only Jimmy

Spangler remained, surrounded by dead and dying, begging Cavendish to spare him. The revolver was cocked, pointed in the boy's face and then ...

"Don't you think so?" Falcone repeated. "Doctor?

"I'm sorry," Barnett stammered. "Yes, of course I do. But it was different in the trenches. No-one considered civilised societies."

"There must have been witnesses other than you," Minelli suggested.

Barnett shrugged. "I don't recall," he admitted. "It's all a blur now, a fog, marred by the smoke on the battlefield."

Falcone watched Barnett closely, searching for signs he had seen before, images of a man who tried to do the right thing, but found the extreme justifiable, the verdict his to render. But Barnett seemed undisturbed and merely looked at him, his stare a bit vacant.

"I noticed a rifle above the fireplace mantle in the hallway," Falcone said carefully. "Why would a man who hates war as much as you let a rifle be displayed outside his office?"

"The rifle has been there since my arrival," Barnett responded. "But it's meant as a symbol; nothing justifies its use. The rifle is unloaded, a symbol of neutralisation. It's only an object. It can harm no-one. But the person who holds it can. It's meant to remind us of what men can do to each other."

"It's a Carcano, is it not?" Minelli asked.

"Yes, I believe so.

"Did you have a Carcano during the war?" Falcone asked.

"No, of course not," Barnett replied. "I was in the British Army. The Carcano is an Italian weapon."

"Why would a hospital have a rifle?" Falcone asked.

"They had several," Barnett informed them, "but only one remains. The weapons were used to guard wounded Austrian prisoners of war. The rifle over the mantel has been untouched for years; I'm not even sure it's functional."

"Do you have any bullets?" Minelli asked.

Barnett thought for a moment, apparently trying to visualise where bullets might be stored. "Not that I know of," he finally said with a shrug.

"Do you own a Carcano?" Falcone asked.

Barnett hesitated, his eyes quickly moving from Falcone to Minelli and back. "Yes, I do," he admitted. "I bought one for protection when I arrived in Como. It's never been needed."

"What protection would you need in Como?" Minelli prodded curiously.

"I didn't know," Barnett said. "I wasn't sure what to expect."

"Have you ever fired it?"

"Not for over a year," Barnett replied. "And even then it was target shooting, only to become proficient. I could never shoot a person or an animal."

"Do you have bullets at home?" Minelli asked, his demeaner harsher than Falcone's.

Barnett shifted in his chair, understanding the implications. "Yes, I do," he replied quietly.

Falcone glanced at Minelli, motioning towards the door with his eyes. "Thank you, Dr Barnett. We have no more questions at this time."

Barnett rose and walked them to the exit.

"How's Miss Penelope doing," Falcone asked.

"As well as can be expected, given the circumstances."

"How long have you known her?" Minelli probed. "Since before the war?"

Barnett seemed confused. "No," he replied, "I first met her when she was admitted to the sanitarium."

"I assumed you knew her in London," Minelli continued.

"No, I'm afraid not," Barnett replied. "I'm not sure why you thought that."

Minelli shrugged. "You seem very comfortable around her," he pointed out. "I thought you were friends."

"It's a different relationship," Barnett replied, "that of doctor and patient. It's difficult to describe."

"Yes, I suppose it is," Minelli said as he followed Falcone out of the office.

Chapter 59

"I received a cable from Jackson Cavendish," Billy Flynn said as he entered Antonio Falcone's office. He laid it on the desk.

Falcone picked it up, scanned the message and handed it to Minelli:

'MR FLYNN: I ACCEPT RESPONSIBILITY FOR £22,000 OF MY SON'S DEBT WITH PAYMENT DUE UPON YOUR RETURN TO LONDON.'

"Is Mr Jones aware of this arrangement?" Minelli asked.

"He is," Flynn replied. "And even though he offered to pay a portion of the debt, Mr Cavendish insisted on satisfying the entire amount." He leaned forward, as if sharing a secret. "I suppose he wanted to protect his son's reputation, so to speak."

Falcone was quiet for a moment and then asked, "Did Mr Cavendish specify any conditions?"

"He did," Flynn acknowledged. "It's a private agreement and neither party shall reveal the terms to any third party. I trust I have your discretion."

"Yes, of course," Falcone replied warily. "Was he concerned about the amount?"

"No, he didn't seem to be," Flynn remarked. "He almost seemed relieved,"

"Congratulations," Minelli said sarcastically. "You successfully collected your debt."

"It's a business situation," Flynn responded with a shrug. "I make a living same as you, mate."

"That's a unique way of looking at it, Mr Flynn," Minelli pointed out, "but I make a living ensuring people obey the law and that they're penalised if they don't. I'm not sure there's a comparison."

"I take offence to that," Flynn replied testily. "The message proves I run a legitimate business."

"The message proves you were owed money and payment has been promised," Falcone said. "But that's all it proves."

Flynn seemed tired of the discussion. "I came here voluntarily to provide information," he reminded them.

Falcone realised a confrontation would lead nowhere and continued the questioning. "Other than protecting his son's reputation, did Jackson Cavendish give any other reason for repaying the debt?"

"No, he didn't."

"How did he know you were in Como?" Falcone asked.

"I recently contacted him to inquire about the debt."

"Was that your first communication with him since you arrived in Como?"

"Yes, it was."

"It seems strange that he suddenly promised payment for a debt that's several months old," Falcone remarked skeptically. "And a debt that, arguably, he isn't responsible for."

"I don't know what his motivation was," Flynn admitted. "But I'm glad we came to an agreement."

"Did you know that Alexander Cavendish purchased a life insurance policy on his wife Penelope?" Minelli asked.

"No, I didn't."

"You were named as beneficiary," Minelli said. "Do you find that unusual?"

Flynn crossed his arms, sitting smugly in the chair. "Perhaps," he admitted. "But Cavendish could do whatever he wanted."

"It suggests that Miss Penelope's life might be in danger," Minelli said.

Flynn shrugged. "It's a shame you can't ask Cavendish. He purchased the policy."

"Did you know that Miss Penelope claims someone tried to kill her on three separate occasions?" Minelli asked.

"News to me," Flynn said. "Like I said, it's a shame you can't ask Cavendish."

Falcone looked at Minelli and leaned back in his chair. "You're right," he said, "it is a shame we can't ask Cavendish. We would ask him the nature of his debt, accumulated interested, attempts made to collect, why he obtained the insurance policy, and if he felt his life was in danger, perhaps because of the debt."

"I had nothing to do with Cavendish getting killed. I told you, I was having dinner in Milan."

"Can you actually prove that?" Minelli asked.

"I guess you're going to have to take my word for it. Or ask Mr Jakes, my associate, or my Italian friend, Pasquale Ruggeri. I'm sure he'll vouch for me."

"We already asked him," Minelli replied, "and he claimed he had dinner with you."

"Then it's settled."

"Not quite," Minelli said. "I told you the last time you were here that Mr Ruggeri has about as much credibility in Milan as you do in London."

"I'm not sure who you think you are, Captain, but I don't take kindly to insults."

"Just as I don't like having people murdered in Como," Minelli replied.

"That has nothing to do with me," Flynn assured him. "I was in Milan when Cavendish got killed."

"The problem is," Falcone interjected, "we never said what time he got killed. If you returned from dinner at midnight, you still could have committed the crime."

"Not likely," Flynn said, "because I returned to my hotel and went to bed."

Falcone studied the man before him, a criminal in every sense of the word, a murderer, perhaps, but someone certainly capable of it. He took a different tack.

"Let's assume that you do have an alibi," Falcone suggested. "Was Jocko, your associate, with you the entire time?"

Flynn pointed to Jocko Jakes, standing by the front door of the station. "Just like he is now," he said, "never more than ten metres away."

Chapter 60

"I've been told you're an excellent shot," Inspector Falcone said.

"Most men of my status and generation are," Wellington Jones replied. "My whole family shoots well." His eyes become vacant, a bit misty. "My son Oxford was the best. No-one came close."

"Are you familiar with the Carcano rifle?" Captain Minelli asked.

"Of course," Jones said. "It's a good weapon."

"Have you fired one recently?" Falcone asked.

"Yes, I have. Shortly after my arrival in Como, I went skeet shooting with Alexander."

"What was your score?" Minelli asked.

"It was perfect. Fifty out of fifty."

"Is that your usual score?" Minelli questioned.

"Usually, yes."

"How about your son-in-law?" Falcone asked. "What was his score?"

Jones thought for a moment and then said, "I believe he got forty-eight out of fifty."

"Still very good," Minelli remarked.

"Yes, I suppose."

"Did you have a close relationship with Alexander Cavendish?" Falcone asked.

"No, I didn't."

"You didn't have a close relationship or you didn't like him?" Minelli prodded.

Jones looked at Minelli, apparently agitated. "To say I didn't like him isn't entirely accurate," he said. "I actually despised him. But I think you already know that."

"Were you upset when he was murdered?" Falcone asked.

Jones shrugged. "No, not really," he admitted. "I'm sorry Penelope had to go through that, but I think she'll be much better for it."

"Were you surprised?" Minelli asked.

"No, I wasn't."

"Why not?" Falcone questioned.

"Alexander was deeply in debt. He had issues with gambling and women. Both vices are expensive and either one can get you killed. They're also unacceptable, especially where my daughter is concerned."

"When did you first learn of his gambling debts?" Minelli asked.

"A few weeks ago, when Mr Cain informed me."

"Didn't he receive payments from a trust fund?" Falcone queried.

"Yes, he did. But it was structured to provide an annual allowance until he reached the age of thirty. Cavendish was broke and in debt by March of this year."

"What was his latest debt?" Falcone asked.

"He owed a London gangster named Billy Flynn twenty-two thousand pounds."

"Flynn claims that Jackson Cavendish paid off the debt," Falcone said.

"Yes, that's correct."

"He also said that you initially offered to pay part of it," Minelli said.

"That's also correct," Jones replied. "I didn't want any problems for Penelope."

"Were you surprised when Jackson Cavendish promised to pay the debt in full?" Minelli asked.

"Yes, I was," Jones answered. "But I'm sure he has a motive for doing so. Eventually we'll know what it is."

"Did you know Cavendish had a life insurance policy on Penelope, payable to Billy Flynn upon her death?" Minelli asked.

Jones looked surprised. "No, I didn't."

"Penelope claims that several attempts have been made on her life," Minelli said. "Do you think she's telling the truth?"

"Yes, I do," he said angrily. "I've had suspicions, and I even shared them with Dr Barnett. Do you think she's in danger?"

"We have no actual evidence that she is," Minelli said. "But we did assign a policeman to the sanitarium to assist with security."

"Do you think Billy Flynn tried to kill Penelope?" Falcone asked.

"I don't know," Jones replied testily. "You're the Inspector. Shouldn't you be telling me?"

"Do you think Flynn killed Cavendish?" Falcone asked, ignoring his question.

Jones was quiet, thoughtful for a moment. "The easy and most obvious answer is yes," he replied. "He certainly has motive, which is money. But if Flynn killed Cavendish, it would be harder to collect the debt. Unless he frightened Jackson Cavendish into paying through the murder of his son."

Falcone looked at some notes in front of him and then shared a glance with Minelli. "Tell me about the women."

Jones frowned. "This is a very distasteful conversation."

"But it's necessary," Falcone insisted, "regardless of how unpleasant."

Jones hesitated, as if determining the most respectful way to continue. "Cavendish was involved with another woman while he was engaged to Penelope," he said. "She announced her pregnancy just before the wedding."

"How was that situation reconciled?" Falcone questioned.

"Cavendish paid her off."

"A one-time sum or recurring payments?" Minelli asked.

"I don't know."

"Are there other women?" Falcone asked.

Jones hesitated, but then spoke. "He was having an affair with a family friend named Mary Westcott. Her husband is a Member of Parliament."

"Define 'family friend'," Minelli said.

"Mary Westcott is Penelope's closest friend and always has been."

"How much of this did Penelope know?" Falcone asked.

"She knew about the gambling, but thought the latest debt was related to a motor vehicle accident. I don't think she knows about the woman with the child."

"How about Mary Westcott?" Minelli questioned.

Jones was quiet for a moment, thinking of prior conversations. "I would say she didn't," he explained, "except for a statement she made when Cavendish was in London."

"What did she say?" Minelli asked.

"It was almost as if she made the comment without thinking," he told them. "She said she should have told Alexander to tell Mary she was asking for her."

"Why is that such a suspicious statement?" Minelli asked.

"Mary Westcott isn't in London too often," Jones said. "So how did Penelope know Cavendish would see her?"

Falcone studied the man before him, judging his sincerity. He had questioned many suspects. Some lied; others offered relevant information. He still hadn't determined how involved Wellington Jones might be in his son-in-law's murder. "Mr Jones, did you kill Alexander Cavendish?" he asked abruptly.

Jones raised his eyes to meet Falcone's and said, "I only wish I did."

Chapter 61

Penelope sat on the balcony, enjoying the spring sun. Her life had changed dramatically since her arrival in Como. Her husband had been murdered. It was all very confusing, a road that started in Monte Carlo, took her to Como, but seemed to lead nowhere.

She didn't grieve for her husband like she thought she would. It wasn't like they spent every minute of their courtship and marriage together; they hadn't. He was often travelling and she was often alone.

The door to her suite opened and a man entered that she hadn't seen before. He carried a silver tray, plates and glasses on it.

"Would you like your lunch on the balcony, Miss Penelope?" the man asked.

"Who are you?"

"I'm Giacomo," he replied. "I work in the kitchen."

"I never saw you before," she said.

"I don't normally serve the patients, but the staff is occupied." He laid the tray down on the table, filled one glass with water and another with red wine. He removed a cover from the dish. "Pasta," he said.

She crinkled her nose. "Again?"

"It's very good," he assured her. "The sauce is from the best restaurant in Como. You'll enjoy it. And then we have some fish and a salad."

She sat at the table. "It does look good," she admitted.

"Enjoy," he said with a bow and left the suite.

Penelope sipped the wine and then swirled some spaghetti on her fork. She put it in her mouth, chewing thoughtfully as she watched a bird glide over the lake. It was good. She thought about what the cook had said: *The sauce is from the best restaurant in Como.*

She spat out what was in her mouth and screamed. "Help me! Giacomo tried to poison me."

Minutes later a nurse came into her room, followed by Giacomo. Penelope picked up a knife and stood beside the table, pointing it at the chef.

"You tried to poison me," she accused him.

"No, Miss Penelope, I would never do such a thing," he said, surprised. "Here, let me show you." He rolled some spaghetti on the fork and put it in his mouth. "See, it's fine."

She watched him warily, waiting to see if he had any reaction to the food.

"It's all right, Miss Penelope," the nurse said. "No-one is trying to hurt you."

Giacomo left to get a plate of different pasta and more utensils as the nurse calmed Penelope. Eventually they convinced her she was safe, nothing was wrong with the food, and she ate her lunch. The nurse remained until she was finished.

****

Wellington Jones arrived an hour later. Penelope was still on the balcony, reading Shakespeare's *Hamlet* as she sipped a glass of wine.

He walked over and kissed her on the forehead, and then sat beside her. "How are you feeling?"

She glanced to her left and right, as if someone might be hiding, eavesdropping, and then spoke softly. "They tried to poison me."

He looked at her, his expression anxious. "Penelope, I don't think they tried to poison you," he assured her. "They take very good care of you."

"It wasn't the staff," she said, wondering why he couldn't understand. "They got my lunch from a restaurant in Como, at least the spaghetti sauce."

"And you think the sauce was poisoned?"

She nodded. "It was pretty obvious. I spat it out as soon as I tasted it."

"What did the staff do?"

"The cook ate some, to prove it was all right, but they got me something different for lunch."

"Is the cook ill?"

"I don't know," she said. "I didn't ask."

"Penelope, why would someone want to kill you?"

She looked at him strangely. "I think it's obvious, don't you?"

Chapter 62

Antonio Falcone leaned back in his chair and studied the chalkboard on the far wall. "I think we've almost solved the crime," he said to Captain Minelli.

"Excuse me, sir?" Minelli asked, bewildered.

"The killer," Falcone replied. "We're getting closer."

"*You* may know who it is," Minelli said. "But I don't."

Falcone looked at him thoughtfully. "Let's talk through it," he suggested. "It may become clearer."

Minelli looked at the board and pointed to the first name. "Rose Barnett. She had secrets that had to stay hidden, especially since she's a public figure."

"And she was being blackmailed," Falcone added.

"She also committed murder five times," Minelli continued. "She might be persuaded to do it again."

"A question that remains to be answered," Falcone said. "Cavendish also accosted her, so revenge could be a factor. She's the strongest suspect, the only one with multiple motives."

"Agreed," Minelli said. "Blackmail, revenge, someone who has killed before, regardless of the reason – all implicate her."

"Except for one weakness that destroys our theory."

"She has little knowledge of firearms," Minelli concluded.

"Which makes murder by such a difficult shot unlikely."

"She may have lied about rifles," Minelli said, unwavering. "There is a Carcano in their cottage. And she has killed before."

Falcone was quiet for a moment. "We both served in the war," he said softly. "We know the hell she lived." He raised his eyes and looked at his companion. "Maybe we would have done the same thing."

Minelli shrugged and moved on. "Joseph Barnett," he continued. "He has two motives – his alleged affair with Miss Penelope and revenge. He has a horrid history with Cavendish, blames him for the murder of many men, and he might suspect what Cavendish did to his wife. He served as a medic during the war and has some knowledge of firearms."

"But can he make the shot," Falcone wondered aloud. "A hundred metres at night, on an incline, with only a lantern and a moonlit lake to serve as backdrop."

"I checked the accuracy of the Carcano," Minelli informed him. "At one hundred metres, the bullet would be twenty-eight centimetres high. You would have to aim at the lower back to hit the heart."

"Which was missed," Falcone reminded him. "The bullet was high by at least five centimetres. There was a slight breeze, which also would have been a factor, plus firing down an incline."

"The wind drift would be three to five centimetres."

"The bullet missed the heart, high and to the left."

"But still killed him," Minelli insisted.

Falcone was quiet, pensive. "The question becomes," he offered, "could a medical officer make that shot? How much weapons training did he have?"

"He also has a bad leg," Minelli added. "Even the climb to the killer's location would be difficult for him. Especially if not done routinely."

"His ability to make the shot is questionable," Falcone pointed out, "regardless of how strong his motives are."

Minelli turned to the board, moving to the next suspect. "Wellington Jones," he continued.

"Jones knew what a scoundrel Cavendish was," Falcone said. "And if Penelope discovered the affair with Mary Westcott, it may have triggered her breakdown. Jones might know that, whether he admitted it or not."

"Jones also knew that Cavendish had gambling debts and bore a child out of wedlock," Minelli added.

"And Jones admitted he despised Cavendish," Falcone reminded him. "He's also an excellent shot, proven with a Carcano and verified by the skeet shooter."

"I rate him as a strong suspect," Minelli said, "perhaps stronger than both of the Barnetts. We just need to tie some things together, put him at the scene, find the weapon, assuming it isn't the rifle in the Cavendish's cottage."

"So maybe not so strong," Falcone said, studying the board and folding his arms. "At least not yet."

"Perhaps," Minelli agreed. "But worthy of further consideration."

Falcone nodded. "What about Billy Flynn?"

"He certainly has motive, since he was owed a sizeable debt." Minelli said, looking at the notes scribbled on the board. "His alibi is weak, even though we verified he was in Milan."

"He could have taken the train back, driven to the spot on the road where we found the cigarette butts, climbed down to the perch, and waited for Cavendish to leave his cottage."

"Or he could have fired from the vehicle," Minelli said. "Although the shot is almost impossible. And if it wasn't him, it could have been Jocko."

"Something bothers me about this scenario, though," Falcone said.

"What is that?"

"It assumes Flynn knew Cavendish was at the cottage and that he would walk down to the lakefront," Falcone said. "How would he know that? And how would any of the others know that?"

"There's also the theory offered by Wellington Jones," Minelli reminded him. "If Cavendish is dead, it's harder for Flynn to collect. Although he still had the life insurance policy on Penelope."

"Which I find intriguing," Falcone said. "If Penelope was found dead, and Flynn collected on the policy, he would be the most likely suspect."

"Or Cavendish, who could have killed her to pay the debt."

"Penelope claims attempts were made on her life," Falcone said. "What if that's true?"

"If it is true, and it wasn't Cavendish, then her life is still in danger. But why?"

"It would have to be for the life insurance," Falcone said. "Unless she has information that's damaging to one of the other suspects."

Minelli looked at the board and sighed. "Four suspects," he said. "Two strong, two even stronger, and we still have someone listed as 'to be determined'. Who do you think the killer is?"

Falcone paused for a moment, his eyes vacant. A thousand images rolled through his mind before he finally spoke. "The war is the killer," he said softly. "It left a continent of ghosts and shadows, shattered lives forever broken. Look at us. You lost a brother, I lost a son and a wife that died of grief, a daughter that ran away to America, unable to live in the footprints of her family."

"I understand," Minelli said quietly. "We all mourn, but life goes on."

"Yes, it does, but in a twisted, tormented variation of the truth. Like Rose Barnett, who witnessed suffering so severe she took God's place, killing those whose lives she knew could never be lived. Her torment is painted in poems with horrific images, grief so painfully described it tears your heart and soul from your body. And her husband, a gifted psychiatrist that's horribly maimed, physically and mentally. How great would he be if he hadn't served in the trenches? I think a part of him will always be there, watching seventeen-year-old boys die."

"We all suffer," Minelli countered. "We just cope differently."

"Yes, we do. The world suffers. The Joneses suffer. Wellington, a man broken by his son's death, tries to form the foundation for what's left of his family. Penelope was pushed to the brink of madness, betrayed by her husband, a stranger when he returned from the battlefield."

"We live in tragic times," Minelli said simply, "but it still doesn't justify murder. Which leads us back to the board. Six survivors of the war, one corpse and one killer."

Falcone rose from behind his desk. "I think we need to talk to all the suspects again," he recommended, "and ask the questions we've withheld until we gathered more evidence. Then we can probably eliminate some."

"We should also have the post-mortem results soon," Minelli said.

Falcone paused, rubbing his chin. "Which could change the course of the entire investigation," he said, deep in thought, studying the chalkboard.

Minelli watched him curiously and then turned to the notes scribbled on the board. "What is it?" he asked, knowing Falcone saw something with different eyes.

Falcone didn't speak, but looked from the board to Minelli and back to the board. "Erase 'to be determined'," he said. "And in its place put 'Penelope Jones'."

Chapter 63

Antonio Falcone manoeuvered his motor car up to the Lakeside Sanitarium, pulling into the circular drive and parking off to the side, away from the entrance. He got out of the car and eyed the landscape rolling gently from the mountains to the lake, sprinkled with flowers and dotted with large sprawling juniper trees. He paused and studied one tree on the north side that was among the largest.

Dr Barnett walked out of the front entrance to greet him, glancing at his watch as he did so. "Good morning, Inspector," he said.

Falcone nodded a greeting. "Hello, Doctor. Where's Penelope?"

"She's finishing breakfast, after which Adele has some therapeutic exercises for her. She'll be occupied for at least an hour, as you requested."

"Thank you for accommodating me."

"Of course," he said, "although it's a most unusual request. But understandable given the investigation."

They walked to the side of the sanitarium and stood before the sprawling tree, the branches thick and gnarled, twisting in a dozen different directions. It was beautiful, broad, sweeping, hundreds of years old, offering a peaceful wisdom not found in most living things.

Falcone removed his hat and jacket and placed them on the grass. He looked at the tree, as if studying an adversary. "I thought this would be a daunting task for a man of my age," he admitted, "but it may be easier than I thought."

"Please be careful, Inspector," Barnett advised, "and don't get hurt."

"I don't intend to," Falcone replied with a weak smile.

He walked up to the tree, lifted his right leg and stepped into a natural cleft between two trunks united at the base. He pulled himself higher, stepping from limb to limb, climbing from branch to branch. The limbs were stout, easily supporting his weight and offering numerous locations for use as steps, and within minutes he was at the railing that bordered Penelope's bedroom window. The last branch sprawled less than a metre away from the balcony, robust enough to support him. He sat on the limb, shimmied forward, reached the railing, and easily stepped over it.

The balcony to the bedroom was smaller than the main balcony off the sitting room. It was barely a metre wide, not quite two metres long, with two wrought iron chairs flanking a tiny oval table. Falcone stepped past them to the window, which was partially open. He examined the sill, pushed open the vertical halves of the window which moved easily, before returning them to their original position and studying the moulding. He spent several minutes on the balcony, looking at the table and chairs, the tiled floor, the balusters. Then he climbed over the railing onto the tree branch, taking an alternate route down the tree. Minutes later, he was back on the ground.

"It's easier to gain access than I thought," Barnett said in apparent amazement once Falcone stood beside him.

"It is," Falcone replied, winded. "There are actually several paths up and down that work nicely."

"Maybe Penelope wasn't delusional when she said someone tried to kill her," Barnett said warily, "especially after watching you access her suite so easily."

"Perhaps," Falcone said, studying the doctor closely, "but do you really think that's a possibility? We've assumed to this point that she suffered from a mental breakdown."

Barnett frowned, apparently considering his patient's symptoms. "Quite frankly," he said, "I think Penelope does have problems. I never found the alleged attempts on her life plausible."

Falcone nodded. He respected the man's expert opinion, even though he was also a suspect. "There's no question that her suite is accessible," he said, "regardless of her mental condition."

"I should have demanded that she change rooms after the first incident," Barnett said. "But both Wellington and Penelope insisted that she stay."

"That's interesting," Falcone replied, "especially if her life was potentially in danger. Why would they demand she remain?"

Barnett shrugged and said, "We weren't convinced, given her delusions, that it was really a problem. And she has the only suite in the sanitarium that offers such luxurious accommodations; they seemed to like that. But we did increase security and staff observations to provide additional protection."

"I would value safety over luxury, wouldn't you, Doctor?"

"Yes, I would," Barnett agreed, "assuming she really was threatened." He paused, as if reaching a conclusion. "But I suppose she's safe now, regardless."

"Why is that?" Falcone asked, curious.

"Cavendish is dead," Barnett said casually. "If the attempts on her life were real, he's the one who would have tried to kill her."

Chapter 64

Antonio Falcone and Captain Minelli walked into Milan General Hospital, went to the desk by the entrance, and politely asked the young woman seated behind it how to get to the mortuary. After verifying their credentials, she directed them to a set of stairs that led to the basement.

The office of Dr Giuseppe Rizzo was at the opposite end of the hall from the stairwell. They walked down the corridor, the floor tiled, the walls white, smudged a bit near the baseboard as if objects had rubbed against it, probably the wheels of trolleys carrying corpses. There was an aura of death – the temperature lower than the rest of the building, no windows, chairs or chapels, just a stark hallway with a few scattered doors, all closed.

"Here it is," Minelli said, stopping at the doctor's door. He rapped lightly.

A voice from within told them to enter and they walked into the office to find an older man behind a cluttered desk, round wire-rim spectacles perched on his nose. He was looking down at some papers.

"Thank you for meeting with us, Dr Rizzo," Falcone said after introductions were made and they were seated.

"Of course," he replied. "It was very unusual, quite challenging actually. And not what I expected."

"Our investigation hinges on your results," Falcone informed him. "We're hoping the post-mortem answers some lingering questions."

"I realise you've been waiting patiently," Rizzo said, "and I apologise for the delay."

"The case is highly publicised, given the victim, as I'm sure you can imagine," Minelli offered.

"I realise that," Rizzo said, "so I wanted to be absolutely certain of the cause of death."

"Is your investigation completed?" Falcone asked.

Rizzo nodded. He handed a manila envelope to Falcone. "I've captured everything in detail."

"Can you summarise your conclusion?" Falcone asked, smiling weakly. "I'm afraid the report may focus on medical details we won't understand."

"Of course," Rizzo said. He paused as if collecting his thoughts. "I suppose the obvious cause of death, and original focus of the post-mortem, was the gunshot wound to the left upper back."

"Can you determine when the shot was fired?" Falcone asked.

"Not exactly," Rizzo said, frowning. "But I estimate that death occurred near midnight, maybe a bit after."

"We've done ballistics testing, found where the killer was when he fired the shot, and believe we know the gun that was used," Minelli told him.

"All of which is important in your investigation, I'm sure," Dr Rizzo replied.

"You seem doubtful," Falcone observed, noting the scepticism in the doctor's voice.

"Yes, I am," Rizzo admitted. "Although the bullet wound appeared to be the most likely cause of death, it wasn't what killed the victim."

Falcone and Minelli looked at each other, shocked and surprised.

"The bullet entered the back but missed the heart," Rizzo continued. "Not by much, but it was high enough that the wound wasn't fatal."

"Did he drown?" Minelli asked. "He was lying face down in seven or eight centimetres of water. I know that isn't very deep, but his face was covered."

"No, he didn't drown," Rizzo said. "That was actually my second conclusion, given the photographs I saw of the body."

"Was the victim put in the water after he died?" Falcone asked.

"I don't think so," Rizzo replied.

Minelli looked at Falcone and then to the doctor. "I'm confused."

Rizzo removed a photograph of the crime scene from a desk drawer. "Do you see how disturbed the soil along the shore is?"

Minelli and Falcone studied the image. The dirt was marred, as if the body had been dragged forward three or four metres so the face was submerged in the water.

"This photograph suggests that the body was moved," Falcone said, "to give the appearance that it fell face first in the water after the shot was fired."

"Yes, it does," Rizzo agreed. "And it was my initial assumption, also. It appears that the victim was shot and fell to the ground, probably motionless. I assumed the killer then came to examine the body, realised

234

the wound wasn't fatal, and dragged him forward, so that his face lay in the water, ensuring death."

"What changed your mind?" Falcone asked.

"The toxicology report," Dr Rizzo answered. "Although this type of testing is still in its infancy, it does prove the cause of death beyond any doubt."

"Cavendish was poisoned?" Minelli asked.

"Not quite," Rizzo said, glancing at the photograph and then looking up to face the policemen. "Alexander Cavendish died of a barbitone overdose."

"Barbitone?" Minelli asked, shocked at the turn the investigation had taken.

"I think he dragged himself forward after the gunshot wound and tried to signal for help," Rizzo said. "Maybe he saw a boat on the lake or heard voices nearby. But it was the drug that actually killed him."

"You're absolutely certain?" Minelli said.

"Yes, I'm afraid so," Rizzo said firmly. "Even though the victim was shot, and someone tried to kill him, he very well could have killed himself."

"Or he was still murdered," Falcone suggested, "but not by whom we thought."

Chapter 65

Wellington Jones sat on the veranda of his villa and stared at the full moon. It was so serene, the sky cloudless, the stars twinkling. There was a reason he continually returned to Como for holiday. It was the only place where he truly relaxed.

His visit with Penelope had been disturbing. Her continued belief that her life was in danger made him wonder if she would ever get well. Sometimes her explanation seemed so real, her descriptions so vivid, that he believed it. He had actually been convinced that Cavendish was trying to kill her. But now Cavendish was dead, and if alleged attempts were being made on her life, the villain existed only in her imagination. Billy Flynn was the only other person with a motive to kill her, which was fifteen thousand pounds in insurance money. But with Cavendish's debt paid off, and the insurance policy known to everyone, it was unlikely Flynn would make an attempt on her life.

He had to admit that Penelope's claims seemed credible. A barbitone overdose, an intruder trying to smother her, someone throwing her off the balcony, a fisherman coordinating with hospital staff, a mysterious man chasing her through the asylum, a cook trying to poison her. She was either very sick or very much in danger.

Wellington looked at the letter lying on the table. It had arrived earlier, from his solicitor in London. It detailed final disposition of Alexander Cavendish's trust fund. Jackson Cavendish was a shrewd man – far more cunning than his son. And after reading the report, Wellington realised just how good William Cain and his contacts were. He had described the various clauses contained in the legal document perfectly, missing only very minute details. His sources were very good.

Jackson Cavendish had exercised a number of the trust's individual clauses. First, the early death clause had minimised Penelope's inheritance to one-half the estate at a maximum. The debt clause, triggered by any outstanding debt greater than twenty thousand pounds, incurred after the marriage, bound the family to pay the debt, but relegated Penelope's share to what Cavendish received prior to death – an annual allowance of twenty-five thousand pounds until the age of thirty, the figure adjusted in the final year to allow for her May birthday. Jackson Cavendish and his lawyers had structured the trust to protect the family. Wellington didn't blame him. He would have done the same thing.

When he realised that Penelope's inheritance couldn't provide the capital needed to save his global real estate empire, Wellington Jones had been forced to offer another compromise to his Indian creditors. He obtained a list of his real estate assets in Asia, the purchase price and amount owed, and after studying the balance sheets the answer became obvious. And he was convinced the banks would accept it.

He had been so focused on the debt associated with his newer purchases that he failed to recognise the equity in his older properties – those liens that he had methodically paid down with his tenants' rents. The net value of these properties, even after declining during the global collapse, was still far more than what was owed. His final offer to his Indian creditors was quite simple. In exchange for carrying the liens on those properties whose debt exceeded the value, he would offer a percentage of the asset on those properties worth more than the debt.

It was ingenious really. By transferring assets he needed no cash, had no liquidity issues, no looming financial crisis. He knew the banks would accept the deal because his properties were highly desirable, architecturally significant, and well maintained in good locations. And the banks knew as well as he did that the real estate market would correct and prices would increase. They always had and they always would.

He had sent his newest proposal to his Bombay office that morning. He expected papers to be drawn and the asset transfer to be fully executed by the end of the month. Once again, he had walked a tightrope, his global empire balanced on his shoulders, and he had survived.

With the financial collapse of his real estate conglomerate less of a concern, a strange thought occurred to him. Penelope was to receive twenty-five thousand pounds a year. Cavendish's final debt was twenty-two thousand pounds, adding interest and expenses to the original debt of fifteen thousand pounds. The life insurance policy on Penelope was for fifteen thousand pounds. Jackson Cavendish paid his son's debt in its entirety – even though Jones had offered to contribute – to trigger a clause that specified the trust would remain in his family. An inheritance agreement littered with exceptions and clauses, yet William Cain knew them all, as well as every amount offered or owed. How could he?

Chapter 66

"There's just one problem with Dr Rizzo's hypothesis," Falcone said as they drove from Milan, in route to the sanitarium.

"There was no barbitone in Cavendish's cottage," Minelli replied.

"No bottles, pills or capsules, not even in the rubbish."

"He may have ingested the pills elsewhere," Minelli offered. "Then he came home, had some whisky, and walked out to the lake to say goodbye to the world."

"Or someone came in his unlocked back door and put the barbitone in his whisky," Falcone theorised.

They drove into the sanitarium parking area, arriving later than planned, and brought the motor car to a stop. As they got out and walked towards the entrance, Falcone paused and looked at the sprawling tree on the north side of the building, the branches stretching to Penelope's balcony.

"What's the matter?" Minelli asked, watching his partner curiously.

"Nothing," Falcone muttered as he stared at the tree. "Nothing at all."

They walked into the sanitarium, across the tiled floor of the lobby, and up the sweeping staircase. They continued down the hallway, greeting a nurse and an orderly, and then reached Dr Barnett's office. His receptionist led them in.

"I'm sorry we're late," Falcone said as they entered, finding Barnett and Penelope sitting near the French doors. "We were detained in Milan."

"Please, sit down," Barnett offered. "Penelope has been waiting for you."

"Do you know who's been trying to kill me?" she asked anxiously.

Falcone glanced at Minelli and then at Barnett. "Not yet," he told her, "although we have several clues."

"It has to be someone capable of climbing the tree by my suite," she told them. "Whoever it is gained acccss twice."

"Have there been any attempts on your life since your husband passed?" Minelli asked delicately.

Penelope was quiet, reflective. After a moment, she responded. "Yes, someone tried to poison me the other day."

"Is that true, Doctor Barnett?" Falcone asked, surprised.

Barnett looked at Penelope and then seemed to phrase his reply carefully. "Penelope thought she was served poisoned spaghetti sauce," he informed them. "The cook sampled the sauce and later became ill."

"Where's the sauce now?" Minelli asked.

"The cook discarded it," Barnett replied. "He thought it may have been spoiled because it was sent from Como. It wasn't prepared here."

"You should have called us," Falcone said, frowning. "We could have had the sauce tested."

"It didn't occur to me or the staff," Barnett admitted delicately, "given the circumstance."

"Other than the sauce, have there been any attempts on Miss Penelope's life since her husband's death?" Minelli asked.

"No, the other three attempts occurred while her husband was still alive," Barnett said.

"Could that be more than coincidence?" Minelli queried.

It didn't seem like Barnett liked the question. "I believe we've already discussed this," he replied. "Several times."

"Did you know, Miss Penelope, that your husband had a life insurance policy on you?" Minelli asked abruptly.

She looked at him strangely. "No, I didn't."

"Did you know your husband had significant debts?" Falcone asked.

"Yes, my father told me." She hesitated, and then asked, "Do you think he planned to pay his debts with the insurance policy?"

Falcone watched her closely, his face firm, before continuing. "The insurance policy was purchased on or about the time you arrived at the sanitarium."

"Which doesn't necessarily mean it was tied to the gambling debt," Dr Barnett interjected. "It could very well have been a precaution, based on what we all viewed as a decline in Penelope's condition."

"Perhaps," Falcone responded carefully, "except for the beneficiary."

Penelope looked at him strangely. "Who's the beneficiary?"

"A London bookmaker named Billy Flynn," Falcone replied. "As it turns out, your husband owed him over twenty thousand pounds."

Penelope's eyes widened, as if it took a moment to grasp the implications. "Then that means … my husband was trying to kill me?"

"It's a possibility," Minelli clarified.

"Is it plausible or probable?" Barnett asked, as if his expertise as a psychiatrist had been challenged.

"As Captain Minelli said," Falcone replied slowly, "it's just a possibility. We have no proof."

"The theory offers a strong motive for murder," Barnett suggested stiffly. "Perhaps I should reconsider Penelope's diagnosis."

"It's purely conjecture," Falcone emphasised, "made by policemen, not psychiatrists."

"We have much more to investigate," Minelli added. "But we're closer to solving the crime."

"This revelation changes everything," Barnett said. "Or at least has the potential to."

"We still have the first attempt on Penelope's life to consider," Falcone reminded them.

Barnett looked at Penelope, as if asking for permission to continue, before he spoke. "Penelope experienced an overdose of barbitone, which occurred in Monte Carlo. She was admitted to the sanitarium shortly thereafter."

"Everyone thought I took too much medicine," Penelope explained, "but I didn't. Alexander and I were drinking and someone forced me to swallow pills."

"Why were you taking barbitone?" Minelli asked.

"For sleeping disorders," Barnett answered for her. "It's very commonly prescribed."

Falcone feigned ignorance. "I don't understand the dosage," he admitted. "How could someone be given enough pills to kill them?"

"It wouldn't be difficult," Barnett explained. "Penelope is given one capsule when she has difficulty sleeping. A capsule contains about a gram of barbitone."

"What is a lethal dose?" Falcone asked.

"For a woman Penelope's size, four capsules would be deadly."

"Does the capsule contain a powder?" Minelli asked.

"Yes, it does," Barnett said.

"Does the sanitarium have supplies of barbitone here at the facility?" Falcone asked.

"Yes, of course," Barnett said. "It's very widely prescribed, by me and the other psychiatrists at the hospital."

"Did you provide any barbitone to Alexander Cavendish?" Falcone probed.

Barnett's eyes narrowed, apparently suspicious of the question. "No, of course not," he replied. "Cavendish wasn't my patient. Besides, the attempt made on Penelope's life was in Monte Carlo."

"But he could get the medicine from any doctor or pharmacy?"

"Yes, of course," Barnett said. "As I said, it's a very popular sleeping aid."

Chapter 67

"Do you have problems sleeping, Mr Flynn," Falcone asked, his elbows on his desk, his chin in his hands.

Captain Minelli sat in a chair against the wall, notepad and pen in hand, while Billy Flynn and Jocko Jakes sat before them.

"I sleep like a baby," Flynn said with a sly grin. "No reason not to."

"How about you, Mr Jakes," Minelli asked.

The big man shrugged. "I sleep fine."

"Neither of you take any medication?" Falcone asked.

The two gangsters looked at each other. "Don't have a need to," Flynn replied.

"Did you see much action during the war?" Minelli asked, changing focus.

"Enough to not want to talk about it," Flynn said.

"Same here," Jakes echoed.

"But you're both decent marksmen?" Falcone probed.

"Come on, Inspector," Flynn said with disgust. "How many times are you going to ask the same question? Can't you finish your investigation and let us go back to London? We're in Como voluntarily, as a courtesy to you. We can leave at any time."

Falcone ignored him. "Were you ever in Mr Cavendish's cottage?"

Flynn looked at Jakes. "Yes, once," he said. "When we first arrived in Como. I told you before, we went to collect our debt."

"Was Cavendish home?" Minelli asked.

"No, we went inside and waited for him," Flynn said.

"Which door did you enter?" Falcone asked.

"Inspector, you sound like you belong in the sanitarium with Cavendish's loony wife," Flynn complained.

"Answer the question," Minelli said forcefully.

Flynn slowly shook his head. "We went in the front door."

"Wasn't it locked?" Minelli asked.

"No," Flynn replied.

"Did you know the lock on the back door didn't function?" Minelli asked.

Flynn shrugged. "I don't remember. Maybe we went in the back door."

"Which was it, Mr Flynn, the front door or the back door?" Falcone probed.

"I suppose we went in the back."

"How did you exit?" Falcone queried.

"Through the front door," Flynn responded.

Falcone paused, studying both men before him. He sighed, reflective, his eyes moving to Minelli and then back to Flynn. "I want to discuss the night of the murder."

Flynn rolled his eyes. "I told you," he said. "We took the train to Milan. I had dinner with my friend Pasquale Ruggeri. We left for Como around midnight."

"We told you Ruggeri is not a valid alibi," Minelli interjected. "And with all due respect, neither is Mr Jakes. Especially since you both had an interest in the deceased."

"My interest was in keeping Cavendish alive," Flynn argued. "I wanted to collect what was owed me."

"The tavern where you had dinner is next to the Opera House?" Falcone asked.

Flynn looked at Jocko Jakes and then turned to Falcone. "Yes, I already told you that," he said sarcastically. "Is the Boar's Tavern the name of the establishment?" Falcone asked.

"Yes, it is," Flynn replied. "I remember now. The sign had a wild boar on it."

"It's the symbol for the city of Milan," Minelli added.

"Do you always wear spats, Mr Flynn?" Falcone asked.

Flynn showed surprise. He straightened his suit jacket, a bit indignant. "Yes, I do, Inspector. I like to dress nicely."

Falcone looked at him grimly, shuffled some papers on his desk, and then cleared his throat. "Mr Flynn, Mr Jakes," he said, "You're both free to go. You may return to London, if you wish."

Flynn and Jakes looked at each other, stunned. "Did I hear you right, Inspector?" Flynn asked.

Falcone rose and extended his hand. "Yes, you did," he replied. "Thank you for your cooperation."

Flynn and Jakes rose, laughing lightly, shook hands with Falcone and then Minelli. "Let's go, Jocko, before they change their minds," Flynn said.

They exited the office, closing the door behind them. There was silence for a moment, Falcone and Minelli waiting until the London gangsters left the station.

"I have no idea what just happened," Minelli admitted.

Falcone sat back down. "We know Cavendish was shot near midnight," he said. "The barbitone was probably put in his whisky bottle sometime prior. It could even have been days before, although that's unlikely given Cavendish's penchant for alcohol."

"And because Jakes and Flynn don't use medication, they couldn't have put barbitone in Cavendish's whisky?"

Falcone shrugged. "They were too confused by the question," he explained. "And they were only in the cottage once, when they first arrived. That was too early to put anything in Cavendish's whisky without him drinking it sooner."

"But they knew there was no lock on the back door," Minelli countered. "They could have returned at any time."

"It's possible, I suppose, but not likely. I don't think Flynn would even think to use barbitone as a murder weapon. He's a physical man, someone accustomed to violence."

"They still could have shot Cavendish," Minelli said. "They might be guilty of attempted murder."

Falcone shook his head. "No, they have an irrefutable alibi for the night of the murder."

"I wouldn't call Pasquale Ruggeri or the Boar's Tavern a good alibi."

Falcone sighed. "The tavern is next to the Opera House," he said. "I know that shortly after 11 p.m. on the night of the murder, Jocko Jakes, Billy Flynn, and Pasquale Ruggeri were seated at an outdoor table in the Boar's Tavern."

"How do you know that?"

"Because I saw them," Falcone said. "I attended the opera that evening. *Madame Butterfly* by Puccini – it was spectacular. I left the opera house around 11.30 p.m. to catch the train to Como. I walked past the tavern. When I did, something caught my attention."

Minelli was still confused. "What was that?"

"Billy Flynn's spats."

Chapter 68

Rose Barnett sat by the lake, watching cottony clouds drift across the horizon, hiding the mountains and briefly blocking the sun before serenely gliding past. She had a notepad in her lap and a pencil in her hand as she massaged metres and rhymes, working the words that would become another poem loved by thousands of her readers. She thought a moment more, changed a word or two, and then looked at what she had written:

'If you tell me not to love you
If you tell me not to care
I will turn and walk away
But I'll wonder what was there.'

She was so deep in thought that she didn't see the police boat approach. As it came closer, and the noise of the engine grew louder, she slowly raised her eyes from the page and watched the launch idle to the bulkhead twenty metres past the cottage. Her body tensed, the visit was unannounced and unexpected. She anxiously thought of the Amiens hospital and the lives she took, playing a role she had no right to play, a secret revealed that she hoped would stay hidden. They must be coming to get her. Or maybe their reason was different, but the result would be the same.

"Good morning, Mrs Barnett," Falcone said. "May we ask you a few more questions?"

She hesitated, not sure if her entire world was about to collapse. "Yes, of course," she said dully. "Would you like to come in?"

"If you would be more comfortable," Falcone said.

She led them to the house, suspicious, wary of what she might say, and showed them into the parlour. They sat in the leather chairs she and Joseph normally occupied; she sat on the edge of the sofa across from them.

"Mrs Barnett, rest assured that any discussion we have here today is limited to the murder of Alexander Cavendish," Falcone offered.

She settled back in the sofa, slightly relieved. "Thank you, Inspector," she said. She respected him, knew instinctively that he was a fair man. But he could also be dangerous; he was competent, intelligent and cunning. He could trick you into saying something you shouldn't be saying. But that's what he was supposed to do.

He nodded politely. "Can you tell me, Mrs Barnett, if you have any problems sleeping?"

She was confused, wondering why he asked the question, but knowing he had a reason for doing so. "No, I don't," she replied. "I mean, no more than anyone else."

"What do you consider normal, in regard to the inability to sleep?" Minelli asked, his pen scribbling in his notebook.

She shrugged. "I have a restless night occasionally," she admitted. "But not too often."

"What do you do when you can't sleep?" Minelli asked.

"Sometimes I get up and read," she responded. "If the weather is nice, I might sit outside and look at the lake."

"Do you ever take sedatives, like barbitone," Falcone asked.

"No, I don't," she said, guarded, wondering where the discussion was leading. "As I said, my inability to sleep is infrequent, not difficult to deal with. I have no need for medication."

"Is there any barbitone in the house?" Falcone asked.

She knew this was an important question. "Yes," she said softly. "Joseph has a difficult time sleeping." She eyed them each, searching for compassion and finding it. "The war," she added. "The nightmares are sometimes severe."

"I understand," Falcone said. He leaned forward, closing the gap between them. "I have them myself."

She fought not to cry, but felt a tear trail down her cheek. She wiped it away. "Thank you," she said softly, relieved that he understood, but knowing something horrible was happening, like a noose tightening around her neck.

Falcone was quiet for a moment, his expression pensive. A few seconds passed, an awkward tension mounting, before he asked, "Have you ever suspected your husband of being unfaithful?"

She was shocked. The thought never occurred to her and never would. She paused, wondering if they knew something she didn't, and felt her hands trembling, her heart racing. "No, I never have," she stammered. "He's very devoted. We love each other very much."

Falcone smiled, as if trying to put her at ease. "The love you share is obvious," he said, "even to a casual observer like me."

246

"Were you ever at Cavendish's cottage?" Minelli asked abruptly, not as compassionate as his superior.

"Yes," she said. "I was there once. I confronted him after I received his first request for money."

"Did he know you were coming?" Minelli queried.

"No, he didn't. I went to the cottage after running some errands in Como."

"Did you go inside?" Falcone asked.

"No, we sat beside the cottage, near the lake."

"How long were you there?" Falcone asked.

Rose sighed, remembering a day she wanted to forget. "About fifteen minutes."

"And at no time were you ever inside the cottage?" Minelli asked.

"No, I wasn't," she said firmly.

"Did you know that there was no lock on the back door?" Falcone asked.

She hesitated. "No, I didn't."

Falcone was quiet for a moment, as if collecting his thoughts, and then said, "Mrs Barnett, during our last visit we discussed Mr Cavendish's attempt to blackmail you. If you had agreed to his terms, how were you supposed to make payment?"

She paused, briefly reliving the horror that Cavendish created. "He said he would wait outside his cottage, by the lake, at midnight," she told them. "He would hold a lantern so I could find him."

Falcone and Minelli shared a guarded glance. "And did you ever go to meet him?" Falcone probed.

"No, I didn't."

"Is there anything else?" Falcone asked, looking to Minelli.

"The rifle," Minelli said, and then turned towards Rose. "Are any bullets missing?"

She thought for a moment, overwhelmed with the image of Joseph grabbing the gun, determined to kill Cavendish. She had stopped him; he didn't do it. At least he hadn't done it then.

"I don't know," she said, shrugging. "I never touch the rifle." She looked away, knowing her next statement was damning. "You would have to ask Joseph."

Chapter 69

"Please, sit down," Barnett offered as he led Falcone and Minelli into his office. "How can I help you?"

"We have a few questions to ask," Falcone said. "Do you have time?"

"Yes, of course," Barnett replied, glancing at his watch. He had another patient in twenty minutes – Lafite, the artist with one ear. Hopefully they wouldn't take too long.

Falcone glanced at Minelli, apparently waiting for him to withdraw his notebook and pen. He asked, "Dr Barnett, do you have problems sleeping?"

Barnett looked at them warily, wondering what type of web they were trying to weave. "Yes, I do," he admitted. "I suffer from nightmares, haunting memories of the war. The dreams often distort what really happened, which was bad enough, and make it even worse."

"Do you take a sedative, like barbitone," Falcone asked.

"Yes, I have no choice," Barnett replied. "I can't let the disorder affect my ability to treat patients. They rely on me. I can't let them down."

"I understand," Falcone said softly. "I think all who served suffer from the same affliction."

Barnett nodded and said quietly, "It's difficult." He appreciated that the Inspector shared the same experiences, or at least seemed to. They had both been to hell.

"Is the barbitone kept in your house?" Falcone asked.

"Yes, it is."

"As I would expect," Falcone said, "should you need to use it. Do you know if Cavendish used barbitone?"

Barnett shrugged. "No, I don't," he replied. "As I told you before, if he did, I certainly didn't prescribe it."

"On evenings that you can't sleep, do you ever walk out to the lake?" Falcone asked.

"Yes, sometimes," Barnett replied.

"Did you ever notice Cavendish by the lake, holding a lantern?" Minelli queried.

Barnett looked at him strangely. "No, I didn't," he said. "I don't think I can see his cottage at night."

"Were you ever at Cavendish's cottage?" Minelli questioned.

"No, I wasn't."

"Did you know that the back door had no lock?" Falcone asked.

Barnett thought for a moment. "Yes, I did," he replied, "I think Penelope mentioned it."

Falcone glanced at Minelli, who was jotting something in his notebook. Falcone nodded, as if directing Minelli to continue.

"How long have you owned your Carcano rifle?" Minelli asked.

"I thought we addressed this," Barnett said, starting to feel like a suspect for the first time.

"Yes, we did," Minelli said hastily. "I just need clarification."

"I purchased the rifle shortly after our arrival in Como," Barnet said, feeling his face get flush. "I have limited experience with it. I'm a respectable shot, but not great. I was in the Medical Corps so I received minimal military training."

"Are any of your bullets missing?" Falcone asked.

Barnett was surprised by the question. He was guarded, wondering what they knew that he didn't. "No, not that I noticed," he answered.

"How long did you say you've known Penelope Jones?" Minelli asked.

"Since her arrival at the sanitarium," Barnett replied. "A matter of weeks, I suppose."

"How would you describe your relationship?" Minelli asked.

Barnett hesitated, sensing something amiss. "I think we have a good relationship," he said. He noticed Falcone was probing, but kind and compassionate. Minelli was abrupt and confrontational.

"As doctor and patient or something more?" Minelli asked in an accusing tone.

Barnett was offended. "I don't know what you're trying to insinuate, Captain," he said angrily, "but our relationship is strictly professional."

"Your receptionist saw you and Miss Penelope locked in an embrace, kissing passionately," Minelli informed him.

Barnett frowned. He was quiet for a moment, formulating a response. "Penelope suffers from a variety of mental instabilities," he replied quietly, choosing his words carefully. "She experiences severe mood swings – from a frightened, anxious woman in fear of her life to someone extremely buoyant, telling jokes and laughing."

"That didn't answer my question," Minelli snapped.

Barnett glared at him. "During a session in which we made notable progress," he said testily, "Penelope hugged me and kissed me on the lips as our appointment ended. It was a gesture of gratitude, of trust, of optimism. It was hardly a passionate kiss. And it has never been repeated. Quite frankly, I'm insulted by the accusation."

"I'm not sure your receptionist interpreted it that way," Minelli continued.

"I think a more accurate statement would be that you incorrectly interpreted what my receptionist told you," Barnett declared. "I think you heard what you wanted to hear."

"Perhaps," Minelli said, noncommittal. "Or perhaps not."

"There are other factors in the equation," Barnett continued, subconsciously raising his voice. "I have a professional relationship with Penelope, not a personal one. She is my patient and a married woman. And I am married to the most wonderful woman in the world."

"Thank you for clarifying that point," Falcone said quickly, nodding to Minelli as if to signal an end to the confrontational questions. "It was just another issue that had to be addressed."

Barnett settled back in the chair, his indignation dissipating. "You're welcome, Inspector," he said, "but it was still distasteful just the same."

"I understand," Falcone assured him. He paused, as if collecting his thoughts. "Who do you think killed Alexander Cavendish?"

Barnett shrugged. "I'm not sure," he admitted. "But you may be making a mistake limiting your suspects to recent acquaintances."

Falcone looked at him curiously. "I don't understand."

"There were many people that hated him," Barnett told them, "fellow gamblers, jealous husbands, even former friends."

"Anyone else?" Minelli asked.

"Yes," Barnett said with no hesitation. "Every man who served with him in the trenches."

Chapter 70

Wellington Jones answered the door to his villa, waving away his servant.

"Good morning, Mr Jones," Inspector Falcone said as the door opened.

"Inspector and Captain Minelli," Jones replied. "To what do I owe this honour?"

"We have a few questions to ask," Falcone said, "if this is an opportune time."

Jones opened the door, wondering how many times they were going to question him. "As opportune as any, I suppose. Please come in."

"Is Mr Cain here?" Minelli asked.

"Yes, shall I get him?" Jones asked as he led them to the parlour.

"Not just yet," Falcone replied. "Maybe after we speak to you."

"As you wish," Jones said. He motioned to two stuffed chairs adjacent to an octagonal table. "Please, sit down," he said as he occupied the sofa across from them.

Falcone sat down, his hat in his hand. Minelli removed a notebook from his pocket and then a pen, and prepared to take notes.

Jones eyed them curiously, suspecting this interrogation was far more important than the last. He respected both men, they seemed competent in their profession, but he preferred not to be bothered. He realised his son-in-law had been killed, but they were all better off for it. The whole world was. "What questions did you have, Inspector?".

"Do you have any problems sleeping?" Falcone asked.

Jones was surprised by the question. He hesitated, suspecting a trap, but answered anyway. "Yes, I do," he replied. "I'm a horrendous insomniac and always have been."

"Caused by the pressure of running a global corporation?" Falcone suggested.

"Yes, I suppose," Jones replied. "It's also indicative of a continuous operation – a business not restricted by the clock. Much of my communication is with Asia. I get cables from Bombay, or Hong Kong, or Singapore while Europe is sleeping."

Falcone nodded, apparently in admiration. "It seems a tremendous amount of responsibility, so many priorities to balance."

"Yes, I suppose it is," Jones agreed, still wary. "But I enjoy it very much."

"How do you cope with your insomnia?" Minelli asked.

"Usually I get out of bed and work," Jones replied. "I always have reports to read, cables to dispatch, letters to write. Tasks that can be done at 3 a.m. as well as 3 p.m."

"Do you ever take a sedative, like barbitone," Minelli queried.

"I have some, but I rarely take it," Jones said. "Sometimes if I don't sleep well for several nights in a row, I'll take it. But not usually."

"If it helps you sleep, why wouldn't you take it?" Minelli asked.

"I don't like to take medications," Jones responded. "And I rarely do."

"Is there any barbitone in the house?" Minelli questioned.

"Yes, I'm sure there is," Jones replied, "probably in the bathroom. You're welcome to go and look if you like. Although I can't understand why you want to."

"No, that's quite all right," Falcone said. "But thank you."

"Do you ever have any nightmares?" Minelli asked.

Jones sighed, rubbing his eyes. He could feel them moisten, as if about to tear, but he willed it away. "I sometimes have nightmares about the war," he said softly. "But more often I have dreams about my son. I miss him terribly."

Falcone was quiet, watching a man who always seemed so cold suddenly seem tender. "I lost a son during the war, also," he said softly. "I'm afraid I'm plagued with similar dreams."

"It's difficult," Jones said, sympathising with Falcone. "I don't know how I failed him, how I could have done anything differently." His hand wiped the remnant of a tear from his eyes.

"I share the same thoughts," Falcone admitted. "As does an entire continent."

Jones sat up straight, summoning strength from his vast reserve. "Honour the dead and rejoice with the living," he mouthed. "That's what they say, anyway. We must go on."

"And we shall, Mr Jones," Falcone agreed. "But as shadows, not as men."

Jones stood up and paced the room, grief etched in every wrinkle in his face. He didn't know the inspector had also lost a son. He felt the same pain, the agony, the loss, the emptiness that would never be filled.

Falcone watched him for a moment. A few seconds passed before he spoke. "Were you ever at Cavendish's cottage?"

"No," he replied. "But I did drop him off there after target shooting."

"But you never entered?" Minelli asked.

"No, not that I recall."

"Did you know, prior to your arrival in Como, that Penelope had arranged to lease the cottage?" Falcone asked.

"No, I didn't. I was surprised her thoughts were organised enough to do so," Jones said. "I had assumed Cavendish would be staying with me."

"Do you know why he didn't?" Falcone asked.

"Yes, I do," Jones answered. "He preferred to live alone. He said he didn't want to impose. But with what I know about him now, I suspect he didn't want me aware of his wanderings, and ultimately, his indiscretions."

"Did you know that there was no lock on the back door?" Minelli asked.

Jones shrugged, not really caring. "No, I didn't."

Falcone paused, as if organising his thoughts. "Do you own a Carcano rifle?"

"No, I don't. But I have fired one, as I told you before."

Falcone studied him for a moment, and then asked, "Do you know who killed Alexander Cavendish?"

Jones frowned. "No, I don't," he admitted, "but I wish I did."

"Why is that?"

Jones's face tensed, his eyes hardened. "Because I would thank them," he stated curtly.

Falcone glanced at Minelli, who nodded as if they had pre-arranged who would ask what questions.

"What was the final distribution of Mr Cavendish's trust fund?" Minelli probed. "Does Miss Penelope inherit it? In her incapacitated state, would you manage the money for her?"

Jones was offended but hid his emotions. It seemed that the captain wanted him to be offended, to torment him, to force him to say something he would later regret. "The trust fund had a series of clauses and contingencies," he explained patiently.

"Which affect distribution?" Minelli questioned.

"Yes," Jones answered. "They involve length of marriage, age and manner of death, as well as debts incurred."

"And what exactly does that mean?" Minelli asked.

"Because of Cavendish's age and manner of death, the trust fund will be equally split between Penelope and the Cavendish family. By exercising the payment of debt clause, Penelope's share of the trust was voided. She receives the same terms that Cavendish had, an annual allowance of twenty-five thousand pounds until her thirtieth birthday, and then nothing."

Minelli shared a glance with Falcone. "Were you aware of that?"

"Mr Cain was able to obtain information on the trust and warned me about its structure," Jones answered.

"Which explains why Jackson Cavendish was so quick to pay his son's debt to Mr Flynn," Falcone offered.

"Yes, exactly," Jones replied. "Ethical, who knows? Legal, absolutely."

"It's still a large amount of money for Miss Penelope, especially given the short duration of the marriage," Minelli suggested.

"Yes, I suppose it is," Jones said, annoyed at the questioning. "Is there anything else?"

"Do you find any of these financial arrangements unusual?" Falcone asked.

Jones paused, reflecting. "The correlation between amounts of money is interesting," he offered.

"What do you mean?" Falcone asked.

"Fifteen thousand pounds for the gambling debt, before interest and expenses, and fifteen thousand pounds for Penelope's life insurance policy. I suppose for payment of the debt. But why wasn't the policy on Cavendish?"

"A problem that has plagued me since the beginning of the investigation," Falcone revealed. "Unless Flynn demanded that the policy be placed on what was most precious to Mr Cavendish."

"I doubt it," Jones said with distaste. "Apparently, Mrs Westcott was most precious to Cavendish."

"Do you suspect there's more to this investigation than Cavendish's murder?" Falcone asked.

Jones thought for a moment. "There is something that troubles me," he admitted, "but I haven't discussed it with anyone."

"And what is that?" Falcone asked.

"Mr Cain's knowledge of what was in the trust agreement," Jones informed them. "What if Cain and Jackson Cavendish have some sort of agreement? Or what if Jackson Cavendish is trying to kill Penelope to split the life insurance proceeds with Billy Flynn?"

Falcone thought for a moment, apparently wanting to carefully word his reply. "I assume you trust Mr Cain?" he asked quietly.

"Yes, I do," Jones replied with no hesitation. "And I always have."

"I think then, Mr Jones, that your theory is based more on emotion than logic," Falcone said softly. "Maybe you're trying to neatly tie everything together so it makes sense, because that's the way your mind works. But there may be no relation at all."

Jones was pensive, considering Falcone's statement. "Maybe Cain isn't involved," he agreed, "even if the links are suspicious."

Falcone studied him a moment and then asked a final question. "You know Jackson Cavendish," he said. "Do you really think he would arrange the murder of your daughter to split fifteen thousand pounds with a London gangster?"

Jones looked at both men as he digested the question, and realised Falcone was correct. Emotion had overridden logic, something he prided himself in always avoiding. "No, Inspector," he admitted, "I don't think he would. My suspicions are unfounded."

Chapter 71

Wellington Jones left the room, returning a few moments later with William Cain. "I'll leave you to your discussion," Jones said, exiting the room and closing the door.

"Please sit down, Mr Cain," Falcone offered. "We're finishing up our investigation and wanted to ask you a few questions."

Cain sat down and crossed his legs. "That's fine, Inspector," he said. "I have nothing to hide."

"Thank you," Falcone replied. "We appreciate your cooperation." He paused, collecting his thoughts. "I wanted to revisit your whereabouts on the night that Alexander Cavendish was murdered."

"I was here, Inspector, with Mr Jones. We sat on the veranda, smoked cigars and drank good whisky. The servants can attest to that."

Falcone listened intently, watching Minelli, waiting for his companion to finish writing. He then nodded to him, signalling him to continue the questioning.

"Do you have any problems sleeping?" Minelli asked.

Cain looked at his questioner strangely. "I don't see what that has to do with anything."

"It seems that it doesn't," Falcone informed him. "But it's actually a critical component of our investigation."

Cain stirred uncomfortably, maybe wondering if he was a suspect. "Not really," he replied. "I can sleep anywhere at any time. It's a habit I developed in the navy. We often worked odd shifts, eight hours on, eight hours off. I can close my eyes and be asleep minutes later."

"Do you have access to any drugs?" Minelli asked.

"What do you mean by drugs?" Cain asked.

"Sedatives, primarily," Minelli replied.

Cain shrugged. "They're as accessible to me as anyone else," he said. "You go to a doctor and, if they determine you need them, you get them."

"Can you tell me about your war service?" Falcone asked.

"Sure," Cain replied, "I was in the Royal Navy for twenty years. I was primarily an instructor."

"What did you teach?" Falcone queried.

"Boxing, hand-to-hand combat, bayonet usage."

"Did you receive ballistics training?" Minelli asked.

"I did," Cain said.

"How good of a shot are you?" Falcone asked.

"Very good," Cain replied smugly.

Falcone and Minelli shared a secretive glance before Falcone spoke. "Did you kill Alexander Cavendish?"

"No, sir, I didn't."

"You have motive, Mr Cain," Minelli said. "You despised Cavendish, were assigned to spy on him, and might take his life to protect your employer and his daughter."

"I don't deny a word you said," Cain admitted, folding his arms across his chest. "But there's a very good reason why I didn't kill Cavendish."

"And what is that?" Falcone asked.

Cain glared at him smugly. "Because nobody asked me to."

Falcone studied the man before him, wondering if he was as tough as he claimed. After a few seconds of consideration, he determined he probably was. "You would kill Cavendish, because of your loyalty to Mr Jones?"

"I am loyal to Mr Jones," he said, evading the question. "I've been in his employ for fifteen years."

"And what is it that you do?" Minelli questioned.

"Whatever he asks me to," Cain answered.

"Have you spent much of the last six months spying on Mr Cavendish?" Falcone asked.

"I would say some of the last six months," Cain replied, "not all."

"Were you in Monte Carlo?" Minelli asked.

"I was, but just for a few days."

"And you were in London?" Falcone probed.

"Yes, I shadowed Mr Cavendish when he went to London, shortly after Miss Penelope was admitted to the sanitarium."

"That's when he was beaten by Mr Flynn," Falcone surmised.

"It was actually Mr Flynn and Jocko Jenks," Cain corrected.

"What else did you observe?" Minelli asked.

"Mr Cavendish spent much of his time in London with his mistress."

"Mary Westcott?" Falcone asked.

"Yes."

"Do you know Jackson Cavendish?" Minelli asked.

"I know who he is," Cain said, "but I've never met him personally."

"Mr Jones informed us that you knew much of the details involving Alexander Cavendish's trust fund," Minelli said.

"Yes, I suppose I did."

"How are you privy to such information, if you don't know Jackson Cavendish?" Minelli asked.

Cain studied the men for a moment before replying. "I'll answer the question, but only if the reply is confidential."

Falcone glanced at Minelli and then nodded. "Agreed."

"An old navy mate of mine works for Cavendish's solicitor. He was able to see the document, not examine it thoroughly, he didn't have time for that, but he did scan the clauses."

"When did you come to Como?" Falcone asked, satisfied with the answer.

"Shortly after Cavendish's return."

Falcone looked to Minelli, signalling he had no further questions.

"Do you have anything to add?" Minelli asked.

"I do have a question," Cain asked. "If Cavendish died from a gunshot, why all the questions about sedatives."

Falcone decided to share information and watch Cain's reaction. "Apparently, he had been drugged shortly before being shot," he informed Cain. "The bullet didn't kill him: the overdose did."

Cain shook his head. "I would never have done it that way."

"Really, Mr Cain?" Minelli asked. "And what would you have done?"

"I would have beaten him to death. He deserved it."

Chapter 72

Falcone and Minelli sat in the Como police station, studying the chalkboard that referenced suspects and motives. The name of Billy Flynn and Jocko Jenks had a large 'X' next to their names, leaving Wellington Jones, William Cain, Rose Barnett, Joseph Barnett and Penelope Jones.

"Do you want to discuss pros and cons of each?" Minelli asked.

"If you care to," Falcone replied. "Do you have a strong suspect?"

"I do," Minelli said. "I think Dr Barnett is the killer."

Falcone showed no shock or surprise, neither agreement or disagreement. "What is your basis?" he asked.

"He has access to barbitone, has a Carcano rifle, and he despised Cavendish. Barnett had horrific war experiences and may be half crazy himself. Cavendish was blackmailing his wife. Cavendish assaulted his wife. Most importantly, although we can't prove it, I think he's having an affair with Penelope Jones."

"What about Wellington Jones?" Falcone asked. "Aren't his motives just as strong? He despised Cavendish and had his daughter to protect. Or maybe Cain did his dirty work."

"Not as strong as Barnett," Minelli insisted, his arms folded across his chest.

"Rose Barnett has a stronger motive," Falcone countered. "A public figure being blackmailed for committing five murders. Revenge for Cavendish assaulting her. And she alone knew Cavendish would be standing on the lakeside, lantern in hand, precisely at midnight."

"But she can't fire a rifle, at least not well enough for the shot."

"Are you certain?" Falcone asked. "All she really said was that she can't hit what she aims at. Under what conditions? Is that from one hundred metres or from ten metres?"

"Should we test her shooting skills?" Minelli suggested.

Falcone shrugged and didn't reply and instead studied the board. "Do we have two killers – one successful via barbitone, one almost successful via the rifle shot?" he wondered aloud.

"We've yet to determine that," Minelli replied.

"Then let's discuss them separately. Who could make the shot?"

Minelli thought for a moment. "Jones, Cain, and Joseph Barnett," he replied. "Potentially Rose, if we can prove it."

"Who had access to barbitone?"

"Dr Barnett and Rose, if she took it from her husband. Wellington Jones, maybe Cain. We're only talking about four pills."

"Who could do both?"

"Dr Barnett," Minelli said firmly.

"Which is why you're convinced he's the killer."

"Yes, there's no doubt in my mind."

"What about Wellington Jones?"

"I don't think it was him."

"Why not?" Falcone challenged.

Minelli shrugged. "I don't know," he replied. "Instinct, I suppose."

"Who knew that the back door to the Cavendish cottage had no lock?" Falcone asked.

Minelli studied the chalkboard. "Flynn, but no-one else," he answered.

"What about Penelope Jones?" Falcone suggested. "She can shoot, as her father implied, she has access to barbitone."

"And she's locked up in a lunatic asylum," Minelli interrupted. "She's the weakest of the suspects. Actually, I don't know why she's even on the board."

Falcone paused, reflective. He read the names, the motives, the strengths and weaknesses of the suspects, and then continued. "Who among them has been in the Cavendish cottage?"

"No-one," Minelli said. "At least none admitted it. Except for Penelope when she leased it."

"Where's the En-bloc, the cartridge, with one missing bullet?"

"Probably discarded."

Falcone sighed and then adopted the role of teacher. "I believe the same person who fired the shot also administered the barbitone," he told Minelli.

"Why do both?"

"I think they drugged Cavendish's whisky and watched, waiting for him to die. When it didn't happen, they grew impatient and resorted to the weapon."

Minelli studied the board, apparently unable to see what Falcone saw. He shrugged and shook his head. "I give up," he said finally. "Who is it?"

"Penelope Jones."

Chapter 73

Minelli looked at him strangely. "That makes no sense at all," he said. "We have no proof that Penelope Jones killed her husband."

Falcone sat back in the chair. "What proof do you need?"

"Even if she could get out of the asylum, she couldn't make the shot. I still think Dr Barnett is the killer."

"Based on what Wellington Jones said," Falcone countered, "Penelope could make the shot. He claimed everyone in his family was a great shot, but his son was the best."

"Although he didn't mention Penelope specifically."

Falcone shrugged. "He didn't have to," he said. "He implied it. Penelope also has access to barbitone and she knew the back door to the cottage didn't have a lock."

"But she had no means to get there," Minelli argued.

Falcone studied the board, arranging his thoughts. "Of the interviews we conducted, Dr Barnett provided the most interesting information."

"And what was that?"

"He described Penelope's nightmare – when she thought someone was trying to kill her. There was blood on her fingertips, as if she fought off an intruder."

"Supposedly, someone gained access via the tree outside her room," Minelli said, "even though she initially blamed the nurse."

"If she was certain someone was trying to kill her, then why didn't she move to another room?" Falcone asked.

"Especially when she claimed she was thrown off the balcony," Minelli conceded. "But it's easy to explain. Why change rooms when no-one believed her? I think the more likely conclusion is that Penelope isn't delusional. Someone was trying to kill her. And that someone was Cavendish."

Falcone was quiet for a moment, pensive. "Dr Barnett has an impeccable reputation," he said. "He's certain Penelope suffers delusions from a mental breakdown. If that premise is the foundation of Penelope's psychological profile, her motives are easy to explain."

"I'm sorry, Inspector, but I don't follow you."

"No-one gained access by climbing *up* the tree," Falcone explained, "but Penelope left the sanitarium by climbing *down* the tree. She probably bruised her fingers on the bark, presenting bloody fingertips as evidence she fought off an intruder."

"I hadn't thought of that," Minelli admitted, as if picturing the scene and reconsidering his opinion.

"Penelope could have left her room as many times as needed to commit the crime."

"That doesn't explain when she was allegedly thrown off the balcony," Minelli said.

"I think she was trying to climb down a different tree and fell. Maybe the tree outside her bedroom is difficult to access or the security guard may have been patrolling the area."

Minelli still seemed sceptical. "We don't even know if she can even climb a tree," he countered.

"Wellington said they hiked as a family and climbed mountains. I'm an old man and I was able to climb the tree."

"If we accept that she could leave the sanitarium at will, and assume that she could shoot, do you think the shot was planned or impulsive?"

"She probably found the lair, the shooting position, after observing Cavendish by the lake. The way the grass and shrubs were trampled, it appeared as if someone was there many times. When she was afraid the barbitone didn't work, she shot him."

"Do you think she took the gun and bullets from the cottage?"

"I'm convinced she got bullets there, but I'm more inclined to think she used the weapon in the hallway of the sanitarium."

"If we find the En-bloc, we'll know which weapon was fired," Minelli offered.

"I suspect the En-bloc is still in the rifle hanging above the mantel in the sanitarium hallway," Falcone theorised. "That's why we never found it."

"I'm still not convinced," Minelli said stubbornly. "What would her motive be?"

"It's difficult to assess, with a mind as broken as hers, but the whole scenario started with her suicide attempt," Falcone explained. "I think she suspected something in Monte Carlo – an affair between her husband and Mary Westcott."

"And she searched the cottage for evidence to try to prove it while Cavendish was in London," Minelli surmised.

"She probably found the life insurance policy and the love letter," Falcone continued. "She knew about Cavendish's debts and perhaps his illegitimate child, and then there's the potential inheritance of his trust fund – not that she needed any money."

"She could have planned the barbitone murder after the cottage search," Minelli mused aloud. "She knew how effective it was because of her suicide attempt."

"And when she got anxious it didn't work, she returned to the cabin and took an En-bloc, knowing there was a rifle at the sanitarium," Falcone said.

"Do you think she's having an affair with Barnett?"

"Absolutely not," Falcone replied.

"The receptionist saw them kissing," Minelli argued.

Falcone looked at Minelli. "Maybe that's what Penelope wanted her to see."

Chapter 74

Dr Barnett led Falcone and Minelli down the tiled corridor, stopping at the stone fireplace. "There it is," he said, pointing to the Carcano rifle mounted above the mantel.

Falcone removed the rifle from the wall. "Just as I suspected," he announced. "The En-bloc is still in it." He removed the magazine, finding one bullet missing.

Joseph Barnett paled. "I had no idea it was loaded," he assured them. "The rifle has hung above that mantle since my arrival, along with the sign – 'Never Again'."

"Do you ever check it?" Falcone questioned.

Barnett hesitated. "No, not personally," he replied. "I just assumed I was told the truth."

"Do you have any idea who loaded it?" Minelli asked.

"No, of course not," Barnett replied.

"Could it have been one of your patients?" Minelli asked.

"No, I don't think so," Barnett said. "Where would they get the bullets?"

"Are any of your patients acting differently?" Minelli queried.

"No, not that I noticed," Barnett stammered.

"How about Miss Penelope?" Falcone asked.

"She's been very quiet," Barnett said, "mourning the loss of her husband."

"May we speak to her alone?" Minelli requested.

"Yes, of course," Barnett replied. "You can use my office. My receptionist will summon her."

****

"My husband was trying to kill me," Penelope Jones said when faced by the two detectives. "I know that and so do you."

"Were you ever in your husband's cottage after you were admitted to the sanitarium," Minelli asked sharply.

"Yes, I was there with Alexander," she admitted. "But that was before I realised he was trying to kill me."

"Were you ever there alone?" Falcone questioned.

She was guarded, like a caged lioness. "Why would I go there alone," she asked, "especially with someone trying to kill me?"

"Were you aware of your husband's gambling debts?" Minelli queried.

"Yes, I was," she replied. "I paid one debt and my father told me about his latest obligation, which was paid by Jackson Cavendish."

"I have a delicate question," Falcone said, "and I hesitate to ask, but it's something we must discuss."

She looked at him warily. "Go on."

"Do you have any reason to believe that your husband may have been involved with another woman?" Falcone asked.

She closed her eyes, as if willing away the hurt. "Yes, I do," she replied. "That's one of the reasons he was trying to kill me." She leaned towards them, as if sharing a secret. "Now his mistress is trying to kill me."

Falcone shared a glance with Minelli. "Who is his mistress?" he asked.

"I don't know," she said. "But when you find the person she hired to kill me, he'll lead you to her. They recently poisoned my spaghetti sauce."

"What other reasons did your husband have to kill you," Minelli questioned, ignoring her allegation, "assuming there was more than one?"

"To pay off his debts," she answered. "That's what the life insurance policy was for."

"Did you see the life insurance policy?" Minelli probed.

"No, but you told me about it."

"You didn't know about it before then?" Minelli asked.

She shook her head. "No, I didn't."

"Or maybe you climbed down the tree beside your bedroom window, went to the cottage, and found the insurance policy," Falcone suggested. "And maybe you found a letter there, too."

"Is the letter from the person who's trying to kill me?" she asked.

"Have you ever fired a rifle?" Minelli queried, ignoring her question.

"Of course," she scoffed.

"Are you a good shot?"

She shrugged. "I'm not sure. I haven't fired a rifle in a long time."

"Do you have problems sleeping?" Minelli asked.

"Yes, every night."

"Do you take medication?" Minelli questioned.

"Yes, barbitone."

Falcone motioned for Minelli to proceed.

"Miss Jones, can you please stand?" Minelli asked.

She looked at him strangely, as if she didn't understand, but complied.

"We're placing you under arrest for the murder of Alexander Cavendish."

Chapter 75

The murder trial was held in Milan, both the nature of the crime and the global attention it received far too much for the village of Como to manage. Six judges were assigned to oversee the proceedings, the public barred from the courtroom, but a sprinkling of pre-selected news agencies, heavily weighted towards the Italian organisations, were allowed to attend. An army of reporters descended on the city from all corners of the globe: the BBC, the *New York Times,* European newspapers and, given Wellington Jones's presence in Asia, representatives from India, Singapore and Hong Kong.

The courthouse was a massive building constructed of Italian marble, Corinthian columns supporting an overhanging roof. Across from the building a public square contained a statute of Giuseppe Garibaldi, considered by most to be the father of modern Italy. Some of the reporters who were denied court room access occupied the square and adjacent pavements, while others preferred the shade of the courthouse steps. Wise to the financial opportunities offered by the trial, street vendors appeared on each corner, offering everything from food to books to leather goods. Policemen surrounded the courthouse, providing protection to those within from both criminals and curiosity-seekers.

The courtroom chosen for the proceedings was elegant but functional – beige marble floors, the walls smoothly plastered and painted white. Rows of chairs occupied the rear, many more than needed for normal trials conducted in the courtroom, and the bench where the judges were perched, elevated above the floor, was made of hand-carved chestnut. Two tables for the legal teams, the prosecution and the defence, were placed before the judges. Several interpreters were also present – one for the prosecution, one for the defence, and an official interpreter provided by the court.

Wellington Jones hired four barristers and support solicitors to represent Penelope, two specialised in justifying murder in self-defence and two were expert in representing the criminally insane. Jones sat behind the defence team, the lawyers and interpreter flanking their client. Penelope sat quietly, elegantly dressed, her eyes wide, her face marked with fright and apprehension. It was as if she knew something horrible was about to happen, but she didn't know what it was.

The lead solicitor for the prosecution, Alberto Bianco, was a stocky man both cautious and cunning, a well-known litigator employed by the government. He was a gifted prosecutor, having successfully tried murder cases and other serious crimes – armed robbery, kidnapping and blackmail. He had three assistants, all government servants, each with varying expertise, similar to the composition of the team assembled for the defence. As the judges gathered on the bench, and the reporters watched with notebooks ready, Mr Bianco began his opening statement:

"The prosecution, through the duration of this trial, will prove to the court that the defendant, Penelope Jones, murdered her husband, the war hero Alexander Cavendish. The calamity started when Miss Jones, a patient at the Lakeside Sanitarium, eluded her attendants and explored the nearby cottage rented by her husband.

"It was in this cottage that Miss Jones discovered two documents that provided her motive for murder. The first was a love letter that revealed her husband's affair with an unknown socialite – and it should be noted that all parties have agreed to keep the name of the alleged adulterer confidential. The second document was a life insurance policy on Penelope, payable to a London gangster named Billy Flynn, to whom Mr Cavendish owed significant gambling debts.

"The court shall hear further testimony, once motive is established, of Miss Jones's expertise with a rifle, as well as her access to sedatives. Ultimately, it was a bullet and barbitone that led to the death of Mr Cavendish, as the post-mortem will illustrate. When the prosecution finishes with all planned testimony, there will be no remaining doubt as to how and why Penelope Jones murdered her husband."

The lead barrister for the defence was the renowned Sir Richardson Cox, tall and thin with white hair and blue eyes. He was a skilled lawyer known for his successes in a variety of trials throughout the Empire, including his frequent appearances before His Majesty's High Court of Justice. Based in London, he had personally assembled the brilliant legal minds required to refute the case presented by the prosecution. Once Alberto Bianco had returned to his seat, Mr Cox rose and began his opening statement:

"The murder of Alexander Cavendish, a decorated war hero who served his country with unrivalled distinction, is a tragedy unmatched in recent memory by any criminal court in the global arena. It's easy to understand why anxious authorities have hurried to bring the alleged perpetrator of this crime to trial, given the public outcry demanding justice. However, in their zest to prove their case, in their haste to show that such a despicable deed will not go unpunished, even in a remote Alpine village, they have gathered supposed evidence that offers no proof at all, and when examined to the degree that the situation demands, will collapse when tested, showing that the actual perpetrator of the crime remains at large.

"Alexander Cavendish, for all his exemplary qualities, was a far from perfect man. The evidence and testimony soon to be provided will show a tortured soul, perhaps permanently scarred by the horrors of war, a man who led two lives: that of a devoted husband, known to one and all; and that of a more sinister man, run afoul, mired in gambling debts, impacted by excessive bouts with alcohol and, it pains me to relate, a man who conducted multiple extramarital affairs with women of ill-repute as well as those with impeccable reputations.

"The defence will show a cast of potential killers from all walks of society – loan sharks, jealous husbands, enemies from the Great War, those with secrets they don't want exposed, and others who simply wished that a good man who made the wrong decisions, perhaps too weakened by war to know any better, would be silenced forever. But for us, our purpose in this courtroom today, is not to prove who killed Alexander Cavendish. Our purpose is to show who did *not* kill Alexander Cavendish. And we will demonstrate beyond a reasonable doubt that Penelope Jones is innocent of any and all charges that have been brought against her."

The reporters scribbled furiously in their notebooks as the proceedings continued. Originally swayed by Alberto Bianco's remarks, they had been equally persuaded by the arguments offered by Sir Richardson Cox.

Antonio Falcone was the first witness Bianco called to testify. He described the tree next to Penelope's suite at the sanitarium, how easy it was to climb, and how she used it to leave the asylum. Further evidence was offered – the blood discovered on the windowsill – alleged to originate with Penelope, who bruised her fingertips during the climb. Falcone described the lair where the killer had waited, and the close distance it was to the asylum, as was the cottage, where the barbitone was put in the victim's whisky. He discussed Penelope's proven expertise with a rifle and offered ballistic testimony to indicate that, although the shot was difficult, it was quite possible for a marksman of Penelope's ability. He then emphasised that the bullet was the tool of an impatient killer – when the barbitone appeared to be unsuccessful.

Sir Richardson Cox offered an artful cross-examination of Falcone, defining various enemies the victim had, especially during the war, and multiple defects in Cavendish's character, which led to association with known criminals. He attempted to refute access to the sanitarium via the tree and the unknown source of the blood on the windowsill, claiming it was never tested and could have been left by an orderly injured during maintenance – or anyone else who may have been in the sanitarium. Hardly enough to sway the judges, Cox was successful in planting seeds of doubt that could potentially be nurtured, persuading the court of Penelope's innocence.

Captain Minelli was the next witness, and he was used largely by the prosecution to corroborate the testimony of Antonio Falcone. Once again, the cross-examination offered by Cox was successful only in presenting other possibilities, alternative answers, paths that potentially led to anyone but Penelope Jones.

Once the foundation of presumed guilt had been laid by the policeman, Alberto Bianco called Dr Joseph Barnett to the stand. He shuffled some papers at the lectern and then studied the doctor closely, as if he couldn't determine how to proceed. When he had collected his thoughts, he continued.

"Dr Barnett, we appreciate your attendance at the proceedings."

Barnett nodded and appeared conflicted, as if he wanted to do the right thing but also protect his patient – which might not be possible. "I am at your service," he said humbly.

"Is Penelope Jones a lunatic?" Bianco asked abruptly.

Barnett smiled. "No, not at all," he informed the court. "She suffers from a form of schizophrenia – a mental condition plagued by delusions."

"Delusions?" Bianco asked. "As if she imagines things?"

"Yes," Barnett replied.

"Can you please describe them."

"Penelope believes that her life is in danger. She thinks someone is trying to kill her."

"Do you believe someone is trying to kill her?"

"No, I do not."

"Has Penelope, while under your care, ever been violent."

Barnett hesitated, as if knowing his reply would be damning. "Yes, she has," he said softly.

"She displayed violent tendencies?" Bianco inquired loudly, showing surprise for the judges' sake. "Can you please describe her actions for the court?"

Barnett sighed reluctantly, but continued. "She attacked one of our nurses," he replied, "and tried to stab her with a nail file."

There were audible gasps from reporters who, in their haste to submit daily dispatches to their parent organisation, needed little information other than those few sentences to declare Penelope Jones guilty of murder.

"But she was defending herself," Barnett protested, speaking over the noise of the crowd. "She thought the nurse had tried to kill her, but it was only a nightmare."

The Chief Judge silenced the reporters, although it took several attempts to do so. "I expect quiet in the courtroom," he informed them, after the noise subsided. "Don't try my patience."

Bianco walked from behind the lectern, closing the distance to Barnett. "Would you say, Doctor, that Miss Jones is conscious of her actions?"

"Yes, she is," Barnett answered. "But those actions are sometimes affected by her delusions."

"Are you suggesting that her attack on the nurse was warranted?"

"To Penelope, her violent response was an act of self-defence. She was fighting for her survival."

"But you testified she was aware of her actions," Bianco countered. "Her life wasn't threatened when she attacked the nurse – so she wasn't defending herself." He paused dramatically and looked toward the judges. "I only wonder how many other acts of violence Miss Jones may have committed."

There were murmurs from the crowd, much quieter than the last outburst, but it seemed Bianco had made a valid point – even if he did twist Dr Barnett's words. The solicitor walked back behind the lectern and perused his notes. Finally, after a few minutes had passed, he resumed his questioning, focused on psychological details that few in the room could understand.

Barnett provided hours of testimony on schizophrenia and behaviour associated with delusional thought processes, referencing case studies and patients he had personally treated, and parallelling both to Penelope and her mental instabilities. And although he impressed all in attendance with both his credentials and unchallenged expertise on the human mind, the prosecution's case had been strongly built.

The defence team had little success in discrediting Dr Barnett and instead focused on his expert opinion that Penelope suffered from various mental instabilities. Although this tactic was successful, at least in demonstrating mental incapacity, they had little ammunition remaining to refute those who had testified for the prosecution.

Sir Richardson Cox realised that most of the evidence presented was circumstantial but, when woven with Barnett's testimony, it painted a portrait of guilt that would be difficult to erase. Cox planned to call witnesses from the sanitarium, to counter earlier claims made by the prosecution, but he knew he would have no alternative, after all testimony had been provided, than to call Penelope Jones to the stand.

Chapter 76

The legal team hired by Wellington Jones began their defence with a parade of sanitarium witnesses who provided testimony about perceived threats to Penelope's life: the nightmare when she thought someone tried to smother her, claims she had been thrown from the balcony; the stranger who followed her through the sanitarium; the two fishermen who supposedly watched her; the gardener who allegedly signalled an accomplice somewhere in the sanitarium; and the poisoned spaghetti sauce, culprit unknown. Detailed testimony was offered by Adele, the nurse Penelope once claimed tried to kill her, and various members of the hospital staff who witnessed Penelope's abnormal behaviour – usually associated with someone supposedly planning to take her life.

Three weeks after the trial had started, when all witnesses had offered testimony and been cross-examined, Penelope Jones took the stand. She looked pale, her face drawn, her shoulders slumped, almost cowering, obviously afraid. She sat in the witness booth wearing a plain beige blouse with a darker skirt, complimented by pearl earrings and a matching necklace. She glanced at those in attendance with confusion, as if wondering why her life suddenly seemed more important to them than their own. Sir Richardson Cox slowly rose from the table, a pair of half-glasses perched on the end of his nose, several pages of notes in his hand; she gave him her utmost attention.

"Penelope, have you ever felt that your life was in danger?" asked Richardson Cox.

"Yes, many times," she replied.

"When was the first attempt made on your life?"

"In Monte Carlo."

"Police reports indicate that the incident in Monte Carlo was a failed suicide attempt," Cox countered. "An accidental overdose of barbitone, perhaps after drinking. Maybe you were confused, disoriented."

She rolled her eyes. "What did you think the police would say?" she asked. "Of course, they tried to implicate me, rather than the real killer."

"And who is the real killer, Miss Penelope?"

She leaned forward, as if sharing a secret. "My husband."

"Why do you think your husband was trying to kill you?"

"Because he had a mistress," she replied. "And he preferred to be with her."

Sir Richardson Cox said, "May the panel of judges and the prosecution refer to the letter admitted as evidence for validation of the affair to which Miss Jones refers."

"Said evidence has been examined," the Chief Judge replied.

Sir Richardson Cox scanned the pages he had placed on the lectern. "When was the next attempt on your life?"

"At the sanitarium, just after I arrived. Someone tried to smother me."

"Who do you think the culprit was?"

"At first, I thought it was Adele, but Dr Barnett helped me understand it wasn't."

"Who do you now believe tried to kill you?"

"It was my husband," she said.

"And the next attempt on your life?"

"I was thrown from a third-floor balcony at the sanitarium," she informed him. "It was a miracle I survived."

"Who do you think pushed you from the balcony."

"My husband."

"Doesn't it seem unrealistic that your husband would try to kill you simply because he was having an affair?"

"May I remind you," she debated, "that my husband had significant gambling debts. In the event of my death, his loan shark would collect my life insurance policy, settling monies owed. And he would also be free to marry his mistress." She leaned forward, as if conducting a private discussion, and motioned to the table reserved for the prosecution. "You would think a child could understand that."

Her reply brought a series of chuckles from the reporters in attendance, but the panel of judges were not amused. "The witness will refrain from inflammatory comments," the Chief Judge ordered.

Cox paused a moment, out of respect for the court, and then continued. "How did you first find out about the life insurance?" he asked.

"Inspector Falcone told me."

"You never saw the policy?"

She looked at him, confused. "No, how could I?"

"The beneficiary was a London loan shark named Billy Flynn," Cox said, the life insurance policy already discussed at length during the trial. "Do you know who he is?"

"Yes, he's an evil man."

"Is it possible that Billy Flynn may have killed your husband for debts unpaid?"

"Of course," she responded, "but it also could have been someone else." She paused, reflective. "Or maybe Alexander took his own life. He was never the same after the war."

"Perhaps," Cox replied. "But that doesn't explain the bullet wound."

"He had many enemies," she countered. "You named some during the trial."

Cox shuffled through papers. "Hospital staff have noted that two fishermen were observed near the sanitarium," he continued.

"Yes, they were trying to kill me."

"Why would two fishermen try to kill you?"

"Because my husband wanted them to."

"They were in a boat, with fishing rods. Is that correct?"

"No," Penelope replied, correcting him. "They were in a boat with what appeared to be fishing rods, but they were really rifles. They were going to shoot me."

"Why didn't they?"

"I hid behind the drapes in my suite and they eventually went away."

"And they never returned?"

"No."

"Do you know why?"

"Yes, I think King George captured them."

The crowd of reporters sniggered, some shaking their heads with wide grins. "She's barmy!" someone exclaimed.

"Silence!" the Chief Justice ordered. "One more outburst and I will clear this court room."

The crowd quieted quickly, many reporters turning to their notebooks to hide grins or looks of disbelief. Penelope looked at them curiously, unable to understand the commotion. When the room was silent, she turned her attention to Cox.

"King George was in Italy?" Sir Richardson Cox asked, returning to his line of questioning.

"No," she replied, looking at him strangely. "King George is in London. But when Alexander went to London, he asked King George to help find whoever was trying to kill me."

"But I thought your husband was trying to kill you?"

"He was," she replied with a hint of agitation. "But he talked to King George before I knew that."

Cox studied her for a moment. "Did a gardener also make an attempt on your life?"

"He was going to."

"How would he do that?"

"The Spanish singer was telling him what to do."

"Why would the Spanish singer want to kill you?"

"Because the stranger told her to."

"The stranger is the man that, according to hospital staff, allegedly followed you through the sanitarium?"

"Yes," she replied. "He was trying to kill me."

"Why would he try to kill you?"

"Because my husband told him to."

"Were there any other attempts on your life?"

"Yes, someone tried to poison me."

"But that was after your husband had been killed. It couldn't have been him."

"It wasn't," she replied, eyeing Cox curiously. "How could a dead man try to kill me? It was the stranger. My husband's mistress told him to kill me."

"Why would your husband's mistress want you killed?"

"Because she didn't want anyone to know that she was my husband's mistress."

"Did you put barbitone in your husband's whisky?" Cox asked abruptly.

"Why would I do that?"

"To kill him before he killed you?"

"If I did kill him, I wouldn't do it with barbitone."

"How would you do it?"

"He can't swim."

"Would you drown him?"

"That would be easiest," she replied, "take him for a boat ride on the lake and push him overboard."

"Have you considered any other methods to kill your husband?"

She was pensive, reflective for a moment. "An elephant stampede?"

The courtroom erupted with laughter and even the judges suppressed a smile. Penelope maintained a serious expression and, as the laughter subsided, she studied those in the room curiously, as if wondering what was so funny. Most felt she simply played to the audience; others weren't so sure.

Cox waited for the crowd to quiet. "Did you shoot your husband?" he asked pointedly.

"How could I do that if I was locked up in a lunatic asylum?"

"You could escape the sanitarium by climbing down the tree."

"Someone climbed up the tree and tried to kill me. Why is that so difficult for everyone to understand?"

The defence rested their case and Sir Richardson Cox returned to his seat. Alberto Bianco rose to the lectern, prepared to cross-examine.

Chapter 77

"Miss Jones, why would the Monte Carlo police classify the attempt on your life as a suicide attempt?" Alberto Bianco probed.

"Isn't that obvious?" she asked. "They were part of it."

Bianco cast her a questioning look. "Do you honestly believe the police participated in a conspiracy to take your life?"

"It's a fact," she said confidently, "not an accusation. I was actually there; you weren't."

He frowned, as if annoyed by her response. "Who else was involved?"

"Shouldn't you be telling me?" she asked with just a hint of sarcasm.

"Miss Jones," the Chief Judge admonished. "You will cooperate with Mr Bianco."

She nodded, but offered no reply. She seemed confused, as if she didn't realise she was being uncooperative. Or maybe she did, but didn't understand it was wrong to do so.

"Miss Jones," Bianco continued, "you said that your husband went to London and asked King George to help find the person who was trying to kill you."

"Yes," she replied. "I asked him to."

"If your husband was trying to kill you, why would he ask King George for assistance?"

"Because then no-one would think he was the killer. That's very easy to explain."

"It doesn't seem like the actions an attempted murderer would take," Bianco said, more for the judges than Penelope.

"Maybe he never talked to King George," Penelope replied. "Maybe he only said he did."

"Perhaps," Bianco muttered, studying some notes he had laid on the lectern. He paused, turning pages, prepared for a different approach. "Have you ever fired a Carcano rifle?"

"Perhaps," she replied, mimicking the solicitor.

He glared at her, not appreciating her rudeness. "Did you, or didn't you?" he asked curtly.

"I've used many rifles," she explained. "I often went target shooting with my father."

"Did you ever fire the Carcano rifle at the sanitarium?"

"What Carcano rifle at the sanitarium?"

"The rifle that's displayed over the fireplace, just outside Dr Barnett's office."

"Why?" she asked. "Do you think that's the rifle the fishermen had when they were trying to kill me?"

"No, I think that's the rifle that was used to shoot your husband," Bianco replied. "I think you left the sanitarium, climbed down the tree, and went to your husband's cottage. You found his mistress's letter and the life insurance policy. You later returned, putting barbitone in his whisky. And when that didn't work, you went back to the cottage and took an En-bloc and loaded it into the rifle at the sanitarium. And when the opportunity arose, you shot your husband, not knowing he had already consumed a fatal dose of barbitone. Isn't that what happened, Miss Jones?"

"No, that makes no sense at all," she replied casually. "If anyone put an En-bloc into the rifle at the sanitarium, it would have been my husband."

"Why would he do that?" Bianco asked.

"In case he needed it to kill me."

"Miss Jones, in all the years that you knew your husband, did he ever hit you?"

"No."

"Did he ever, at any time, act violently toward you?"

"No."

"Then why would he suddenly make multiple attempts on your life?"

"Because he was in love with someone else and he had gambling debts he couldn't repay," she answered. "He had to kill me; he had no other choice."

Bianco paused, looking first at his notes and then at Penelope. "You claim that multiple attempts have been made on your life," he said. "But who is trying to kill you now – it isn't your husband, who is deceased. It can't be his mistress, who isn't here. And it isn't the Monte Carlo police."

"It's the stranger," Penelope said softly.

"The stranger who followed you in the sanitarium?"

"Yes."

"Have you ever seen this mysterious stranger again?"

"Yes."

"And where have you seen him?"

"In this courtroom," she said, as if afraid to continue.

There was a gasp from the crowd, and even the judges, Sir Richardson Cox, and Alberto Bianco seemed surprised.

"Can you identify the stranger?" Bianco asked, eyebrows arched.

"Yes," Penelope said. She was flush, frightened, hesitant to continue.

"We're waiting, Miss Jones," Bianco said, expressing his annoyance.

She glanced around nervously, eyeing the judges, the prosecution, the defence team, the Barnetts, her father, the reporters. Several seconds elapsed before she replied. "It's you," she said hoarsely, pointing to the prosecutor, Alberto Bianco.

The room was silent. No-one doubted her sincerity. She was truly convinced that Alberto Bianco was involved in a plot to kill her – along with her husband, her husband's mistress, and the Monte Carlo police. She had presented a tangled web of imaginary suspects that led nowhere and proved nothing, their only link that Penelope somehow saw them as a threat. All present, and even the most confrontational reporters, studied her with sympathetic stares. The judges looked on, unsuccessfully trying to hide their compassion, while Wellington Jones sat quietly, his eyes misty, consoled by William Cain. Rose Barnett comforted her husband – since all in the courtroom knew he had a daunting task ahead if he ever hoped to fix the broken mind of Penelope Jones.

****

After two days of deliberation, the six judges assigned to the case ruled five to one that no credible evidence existed to prove that Alexander Cavendish or anyone in his employ made any attempt on Penelope's life. They did, however, find unanimously that Penelope Jones was innocent by reason of insanity for the murder of Alexander Cavendish. Their opinion was swayed by the expert testimony of Dr Joseph Barnett and, to a lesser degree, the disturbed statements made by Penelope Jones. They ordered her to remain at the Lakeside Sanitarium, under supervision of three state-appointed psychiatrists, until such time she was deemed cured or not a threat to the general populace. Her portion of her husband's trust, in the form of an annual allowance, was forfeited.

Epilogue

Three weeks after the trial, Wellington Jones married Claudine Bonnet, the French author he had secretly been seeing, and went to Bombay, successfully righting his business empire. The global recession ended shortly after Cavendish's death and spawned one of the greatest decades for wealth creation in human history – the 'Roaring Twenties'. Unfortunately, the Depression waited, which taxed the abilities of even a business genius like Wellington Jones. Still he survived and prospered, again demonstrating an uncanny ability to weather financial calamities, somehow emerging wiser, stronger and richer than most could even imagine.

Billy Flynn and Jocko Jenks returned to London and expanded their business enterprises, their loan-sharking and gambling businesses continuing to prosper, operating on the fringes of respectability but never quite finding it. Although suspected of many different crimes, and questioned on multiple occasions, neither has ever been arrested or convicted.

Captain Minelli remained leader of the six-member Como police department. He employed many of the tools learned from his mentor, Inspector Falcone, which tempered personal shortcomings he found hard to control. He continued to serve the people of Como and the surrounding districts with unwavering devotion while winning awards for his home-made spaghetti sauce.

Antonio Falcone left the police department shortly after the trial, joining his daughter in Philadelphia. It was a new beginning for both, uniting the remaining fragments of their family and offering the pursuit of happiness, a dream that America promised, and always had, to any willing to embrace it. Falcone became a valued member of the Philadelphia police department, perfectly equipped to address the crime wave that was about to sweep the nation.

After transferring the care of Penelope to a team of psychiatrists at Lakeside Sanitarium, the Barnetts visited relatives in England, almost relocated to London, but eventually moved to Paris. Rose Barnett published *Love Poems* shortly after they arrived and it became the best-selling poetry book on the continent, its sales and literary acclaim exceeding those of all her prior books combined. They lived on the Left Bank, near the Sorbonne, and Rose was a regular at cafés and clubs frequented by the crowd of literary and artistic expatriates who found Paris so amenable and intriguing after the Great War.

Joseph Barnett became a psychiatrist at the Paris Institute for the Insane. He still treated Lafite, the artist with one ear, who was his patient in Como, as well as a sprinkling of socialites and working class. He volunteered much of his time to help those affected by the Great War, the haunting memories living on, both in his mind and theirs.

Some six months after Alexander Cavendish was murdered, Joseph Barnett opened the *Paris Soir* to find a picture of Penelope Jones on the front page. She had been released from Lakeside Sanitarium and returned to her father's estate where she quietly married Ian McKinley, her former lover, and her nanny Mrs Thistle served as chief bridesmaid. She also returned to Cambridge University to teach drama and Shakespearean literature.

Barnett smiled as he read the article, pleased his former patient was well. But then, as he reminisced about the days at Lakeside Sanitarium, the smile faded, his face growing pale. He reflected upon his sessions with Penelope and the titbits of personal information she had revealed. Ian McKinley had been the love of her life, and probably always had been, even though her father and the Cavendish family persuaded her to marry Alexander. It was interesting that almost four years later, McKinley and Penelope were wed.

His mind continued to wander, a sickening feeling coursing through his body. Penelope was extremely intelligent, with advanced degrees from Cambridge and Oxford. She had been examined by psychiatrists her entire life, knew their methods and processes, and was able to pretend she was hypnotised so convincingly that she once had fooled him completely. She had read Freud and Jung and other psychiatrists of note and was familiar with their theories and practices. Each alleged attempt on her life – from a supposed suicide attempt with an unlethal dose, to tainted spaghetti sauce, to intruders and observers – had all been witnessed by police or members of the hospital staff. He ran each event through his mind, like a kaleidoscope, and realised they were staged, like a play.

It was only then that he fully understood what had happened during those two months in Como. Penelope Jones was a Shakespearean expert –

arguably one of the world's foremost authorities on his plays and Elizabethan theatre. What better place to find revenge, plots, foiled murder attempts, maniacs and suicides, than Shakespeare himself? Could she possibly have created her own master plot, complete with a potential suicide, a feigned mental illness, and multiple murder attempts to manipulate her psychiatrist, her father, two expert policemen and a sympathetic panel of judges?

A smile turned the corner of Barnett's lips. It seemed he had been fooled, along with the rest of the world. Maybe nothing had ever been wrong with Penelope. Maybe she had only given an award-winning performance in a play she wrote and directed.

About the author

John Anthony Miller was born in Philadelphia, Pennsylvania to a father of English ancestry and a second-generation Italian mother.

Motivated by a life-long love of travel and history, John Anthony Miller's books are often set in exotic locations during eras of global conflict. Characters must cope and combat, overcoming their own weaknesses as well as the catastrophes spawned by tumultuous times. His four previous novels are: *To Parts Unknown; When Darkness Comes; In Satan's Shadow; All the King's Soldiers*. He lives in southern New Jersey with his family.